ELIETE:
A NORMAL LIFE

DULCE MARIA CARDOSO

ELIETE:
A NORMAL LIFE

Translated from the Portuguese by
Ángel Gurría-Quintana

MACLEHOSE PRESS
QUERCUS · LONDON

First published in the Portuguese language as *Eliete – A Vida Normal*
by Tinta da China, Lisbon, in 2018
First published in Great Britain in 2024 by

MacLehose Press
an imprint of Quercus
Carmelite House
50, Victoria Embankment
London EC4Y 0DZ

Funded by the DGLAB/Culture and the Camões, IP – Portugal

A CIP catalogue record for this book is available from the British Library.

ISBN (PB) 978 1 52941 881 1
ISBN (eBook) 978 1 52941 882 8

10 9 8 7 6 5 4 3 2 1

Designed and typeset in Sabon by Libanus Press Ltd
Printed and bound in Great Britain by Clays Ltd, Elcograf S.p.A.

Papers used by MacLehose Press are from well-managed forests and
other responsible sources.

And it knows not how to die or to live: And it knows
not that tomorrow is only a dead today.

DULCE MARÍA LOYNAZ

I am what I am and Salazar can go fuck himself. A dictator rules Portugal for almost half a century, almost another half century passes since his death, and then he shows up again. Suddenly it was as if he'd been here all along, running everything, I couldn't let that happen.

It was five months before the night of the big storm when the hospital called about Grandma, but I feel like that was the moment when Salazar started insinuating himself into my life.

At the hospital, Mother kept saying, My mother-in-law has always had her head screwed on, I don't know how this happened. It was no secret to anyone that Mother didn't like Grandma, Our saints don't get on, she would explain when she was in a good mood, at other times she would resort to cursing her, May a lightning bolt strike the old woman, let her die far away and see if I care. But, at the hospital, Mother's concern appeared sincere and it was surprising to see her struggling to accept that, at eighty-one years of age, Grandma could have gone off the rails like that. It can't be, my mother-in-law can't be perfectly well one moment and then like this the next, she pleaded with the doctor, as if displaying her disbelief might allow her to magically understand what was going on. Politely ignoring Mother, the doctor turned to me and asked, Have you noticed your grandmother behaving unusually before this episode? Episode, that was the word the doctor used to describe an event as unusual as Grandma leaving home in her nightgown and her Sunday shoes, and walking around Cascais, before falling and gashing her head open at the souvenir shop on Rua Direita, and then being all tearful when Mother and I arrived at the hospital. We found her on a hospital bed, her head wound already dressed with a white bandage. Restless and anxious, she insisted on going into Lisbon. What's wrong with her, she has always hated the city, Mother said with alarm. Do you think she drank something by mistake? I don't think that's what happened, the doctor replied. He was young, with a flat voice and an expensive aftershave. Mother smelled of the cheap scented water she bought by the half-litre at the pharmacy on Rua da Polícia, enough to fill twice the bottle of Bien Être that she kept on the chest of drawers in her bedroom. I would recognise that mix of synthetic lavender and lemon given off by Mother anywhere, her shaved armpits, the folds of her tummy, her fleshy thighs. I would recognise anywhere the smell of those evenings when I fell asleep on her lap while watching television.

God knows what else she'll do next, Mother fretted, which was unusual for her since, unlike Grandma, Mother never wanted anything to do with God. What misfortune awaits us now, she fretted, raising her eyebrows like the heroines in photo novels do at moments of concern or anxiety. If there was one thing Mother prized, it was her photo novels. She had them bound in sets of ten, with red and gold covers, and displayed them on the pine bookshelf that she had bought at the second-hand furniture store when we moved to Grandma's house. How does someone end up like that, Mother asked, clearly as troubled as I was. She was referring to the distress that had taken over Grandma, get me out of here, get me out of here, take me to Lisbon, she begged and shouted, trying to take off her hospital gown and rip out the needle that connected her to the drip.

She tore off the gown before we could stop her, revealing herself naked, unfettered by modesty, pink nipples cresting the trembling breasts, a perfect triangle of grey hair covering her pubis, very pale skin lined with the same wrinkles she had on her hands and neck, like an ancient piece of pottery gently worked over by time, a body in which everything seemed to be proportionate and casually delicate. I had never seen Grandma naked. Except for her face and hands, her body had always been hidden beneath layers of black, black skirt, black nightdress, black stockings and shoes. When I was a girl, I imagined she was like those mannequins from the bridal shop where Mother worked, a plastic body onto which someone had attached an old head and hands. At some point I became convinced that this was exactly what Grandma wanted us to believe, such were the lengths she went to in order to conceal her body. The mournfulness, the sombreness and the severity with which she always dressed and behaved hadn't hidden her beauty, but only now, seeing her undressed, did I realise that they had managed to conceal the alluring woman she had undoubtedly been. For Grandma, nudity was the devil's temptation, like almost everything else in life, the devil was tireless in his trickery, and Grandma needed to be even more tireless in her vigilance. Come here, Eliete, she called out to me one afternoon, a moment that remains whole and intact in my mind. I was passing by the kitchen, on my way to the garden to cool off under the hosepipe, wearing the swimsuit Mother had bought me at the market, a swimsuit with white stars on a blue background. Come here, Eliete, you're a young woman now, you mustn't be going around like that. Grandma was sitting on a dark wooden stool by the balcony door shelling broad beans, her hands still untroubled by the old age that would make them fragile and hesitant, Senhor Pereira on the other side of the house, locked away in his study as usual, and Mother at work, a late afternoon train-and-bus ride away. In my hand, the orange cotton towel that I would stretch out on the concrete slab, my rocky island in the middle of the garden.

The long holiday afternoons were so slow that they melded into each other, becoming a single never-ending afternoon. In my small world, changes always led, incessantly, to new beginnings, pomegranate flowers announced the end of summer, winter light gilded the persimmons, oranges ripened and were turned into the marmalade that Grandma kept in the cupboard in jars labelled "Bitter Orange", ants marched in single file, birds huddled in tree branches. In the morning the sun shone into Grandma's bedroom and in the afternoon it came to rest in my room and in Mother's, at night the moonlight shone wherever it wanted to.

Standing up, tightening every muscle in my little body, I would put the spout of the green hose pipe against my head, waiting for the cold water to leave the earth's bowels and run riot over my body. To release me from the spell of the interminable afternoon, my body would start moving of its own accord. *Feim aim gonnaliv forevar,* I would hear myself singing from within my swimsuit with its white stars, my feet muddy, *Feim aim gonnaliv forevar.* I knew no English, life was not yet able to offer anything other than the childhood I would never escape.

I would let the cold water run over my body, the skin on my hands wrinkling and my lips turning purple, just a little more, just a little more, the cold water streaming from the earth's bowels until I was unable to breathe. The longer I could withstand it, the greater the pleasure of lying down on the towel spread over the concrete slab, just a little more, I would say to myself, just a little more. The heat in the slab warmed my body, one pore at a time, and tamed it, made it once again submissive. I would open my eyes, notice the forming and unravelling of clouds, seeking out the animal shapes, a dolphin wrapping itself around a tiger's head before stretching into the form of a snake, a sky not yet crisscrossed by aeroplane trails, an endless and scattered world. Come here, Eliete.

The blue ceramic bowl almost filled with little green kidneys, Grandma not even raising her eyes, her fingers intent on bursting open the bean pods that piled up on newspaper sheets, and which we would chop up and throw into the chicken coop, made up of wire fencing and a corrugated tin roof between the garage and the wall at

11

the back of the garden. A decent girl cannot walk around the house like that, she can't be showing the world and his wife what belongs to her future husband. Grandma seemed to have no greater ambition than to tame my flesh and my soul. You don't want to be like the others, do you? The others, the sluts, the ones who had lost their way and were condemned to the hell of eternally grinding teeth and flames taller than mountains, the skanks, the ones I would soon be secretly envying. At that point, I no longer worried about the details of Grandma's stories, I no longer quizzed her about how God decided who to please if I prayed for sunshine but she prayed for rain, I knew her answer by heart, it's not you asking those questions, it's the devil himself. Grandma then explained that the devil made us doubt that God would, in time, reveal everything that needed to be revealed, and the proof that God wouldn't abandon us was in the stories of miracles told at Mass. Isaac, son of Abraham and Sarah, the manna from heaven as the chosen people crossed the desert, Elijah fed by ravens, the crumbling walls of Jericho, in due course God would supply all my needs. Apparently, the delay between the moment when I expressed a need and the moment it was satisfied was one of God's ways of testing my faith.

But that afternoon neither I nor the devil asked any questions. We both knew my body had changed and that it was dragging me helplessly along with it. The change had started quietly with the two fleshy bumps growing on my skinny chest, two fleshy bumps that I tried to smother against the mattress, always sleeping face-down, two fleshy bumps that ached close to my heart and that the boys made fun of, Stop the ball with your chest, Eliete, just don't puncture it, the boys played with their flat chests, dreaming of Maradona, Platini, Rummenigge and other names that took up all their conversations. I could have coped with the boys' laughter if the fleshy bumps hadn't been followed by the shame of dark hair between my legs and in my armpits, of my thighs filling out the denim trousers like legs of ham, of the smelly grown-up sweat that I covered with the deodorant Mother bought at the same pharmacy as her fake Bien Être, an aerosol that caused my armpits to itch.

Come here, Eliete. I knew nothing was the same in my body, that blood had started to seep out of me, thick and dark blood that forced me to use sanitary pads every month. Above all I was afraid of someone noticing I was using the pads, that the boys would start with their teasing. Benfica is playing in its red kit, or, Run away, there's a red tide today! The boys guffawing through crooked teeth that had yet to find their place, their faces nicked by shaving blades that seemed to cut through more pimples than hairs. The shame of them knowing that I used pads added to my fear of the disgusting blood staining my clothes, the new and humiliating habit of having to sneak into toilets to change the pad and the various precautions I was suddenly forced to take. To never, under any circumstance, leave the pack of pads in the toilet cabinet at home so that Senhor Pereira wouldn't have the unpleasant experience of finding it when he opened the cabinet to splash some Old Spice onto his face with loud slaps, Men don't want to know about such things, Mother or Grandma explained. The issue of menstruation was one of the few on which they agreed, men didn't like finding packs of sanitary pads or hearing about cramps and chocolate cravings, menstruation was a woman's business like embroidery, cooking and housework, it was discussed quietly and led to all sorts of prohibitions. On those days one shouldn't wash one's hair, walk around in bare feet, enter a cemetery, do any physical exercise nor go to the beach, since one's flower was open and blood might either rush to the head or flow non-stop. Even though they mostly agreed on the subject, Mother and Grandma disagreed on some of the details. According to Mother I could wash my hair as long as I didn't take too long, I could exercise as long as I didn't stand on my head, and I could go to the beach as long as I didn't sunbathe. To Mother's and Grandma's orders and counter-orders was added the conflicting advice from friends and classmates, from Milena who used tampons with no fear of losing her virginity, from Clara who knew of a home remedy to stop the belly from swelling, from Paulinha, who stopped the bleeding with cold showers, and so we grew together through pride in our common destiny as future procreators. We bled proudly every month, even if we were made uncomfortable by cramps, spotty faces and sanitary pads, because as long as we bled we could fulfil the destinies, given only to us, of bringing children into the world. The worst that could happen to a woman was to be unserviceable in that department, all we had to do was look at Dona Rosalinda, who lived a couple of houses away from Grandma and was forced to raise her husband's two little dark-skinned bastards, amid insults and thrashings. The poor woman cannot give him any children, Grandma explained, everyone knows that in such circumstances, the men will go and find them somewhere else. As everyone knew that this was how things were, Dona Rosalinda thanked God for having escaped the fate of unserviceable women, which was, as everyone knew, to be abandoned.

At the supermarket, when Senhor Pascoal stood in for his wife at the checkout counter, Mother took her time walking along the half dozen aisles as if she were visiting a museum. Men get ideas into their heads when they see certain things, Mother said to me once, enigmatically, as we killed time near the detergent shelves, the pack of sanitary pads hidden beneath the rest of our shopping. If there was no urgency, and if Senhor Pascoal's wife was taking too long to return to the checkout counter, Mother would give up on buying the pads. We'll get them next time, she'd say, as if some invisible superior force had made her stop. If there was some urgency, Mother would sigh as if resigned to face a volley of bullets and, discreetly, she would place the pack of pads on the checkout belt, not daring to meet eyes with Senhor Pascoal, who must have been getting into his head the ideas that men get into their heads when they see certain things.

Come here, Eliete. After that afternoon, there were no more hosepipe showers in the garden and the swimsuit was used only at the beach, where a certain lack of modesty was permitted for health reasons, because the sea was good for me, especially for the allergies that gave me breathing difficulties, and the spots that disfigured my face. The beach I liked most was Tamariz, but we always went to Rainha, Mother's favourite. We would arrive quite early, when the morning was still cool, the sun still low, to secure a good place near the large rock in the middle of the beach, around which other well-prepared beach goers would gather, and we would remain fully dressed until the sun was out. Every time, Mother would discuss with the other families the size of the waves, the level of the tide, the accuracy of the tidal forecasts, the inaccuracy of the weather forecasts, the haze that blocked her view of the cliffs, on top of which perched shops, restaurants and houses, their air conditioning units and aluminium awnings visible from the beach. Another thing that never changed was the spot she chose to keep the packed lunch we brought in a basket, egg sandwiches wrapped in rough paper towels, fresh oranges bought at the station bar. Here, in the rock's shade, she would always say, as if it were the first time, and I couldn't understand why it was so easy to predict tides and Mother's behaviour but so difficult to predict weather or visibility. When the sun emerged, the moment came for Mother to slather our shoulders, nose and cheeks with Nivea cream, taking care to always open the blue jar over the towel because of the sand. I must have looked like an ugly clown, if the state of Mother's face was anything to go by. After the daubing of the cream, Mother would lie belly-up and sleep with her mouth open as if she were at home. She even took a dip in the sea as if she were at home, bending over at the water's edge and using her cupped hands to gather the foam from the shallow waves to refresh her sun-burnt skin. She often asked for my help when she was bathing in the sea like this, but I avoided it when I could. I was even more embarrassed by Mother putting on that display than by me not knowing how to do the front crawl when I swam.

For years I dreamed of imitating the perfect movements of those girls who swam in the sea as naturally as if they were walking on dry land, but unlike walking, running and jumping, the mere passage of time wasn't enough for my body to learn how to swim properly, leaving me desperate to figure out how to coordinate my breathing, my strokes, my head rotations and all my other movements like those girls who swam with the boys all the way out to the boats moored in the distance. I could do breaststroke, and badly. One day I even made it as far as the rope with the orange floats a few metres before the boats, but I was never able to repeat the deed, I would get tired, swallow seawater, get cramps. I imagine I looked like I was being weighed down, like a stiff-necked turtle with frog legs and arms swinging in sad semicircles. Before falling asleep, in that brief interval between wakefulness and a slumber in which I was no longer properly myself, I pictured myself going into the water with a somersault or a pike jump and swimming front crawl out to the boats as fast as the heroines in Bond films, other holidaymakers would give me a standing ovation and I would walk out of the sea as if I were on a catwalk, no need to break the illusion by shaking my head to get water out of my ears or by shielding my eyes from the sun to find my towel. For a brief moment, I was the best and most elegant front crawl swimmer. If I was tired at bedtime, my dreams were less ambitious. I longed to have an even golden tan, to lose my fear of diving onto the ground as I reached for a ball during racquet sports, for

17

ten fewer centimetres of waistline and about as many more of leg length. Really, there was nothing wrong with me, it was just a question of redistributing those centimetres. On those beach days I also longed to find my role in that seaside theatre, that enormous theatre in which everyone knew what character they were playing, the tobacco-chewing lifeguard, the girl who took her time getting into the water and the other one who whispered and laughed, the pedalo rental attendant offering discounts to pretty girls, the embarrassing mother, the couple entwining hands and legs, the family playing cards or the other family eating breaded chicken and melon cubes, the boy playing with a ball or the other boy splashing the girls, the wafer biscuit seller, the people who walked at the water's edge, the ones who exercised, the ones who made an effort to get bronzed, the ones who read, everyone played their roles convincingly, except for me.

Now that you're a young woman, anything can happen, you don't have to look too far to know this. The first few times Grandma gave me this warning, I had no idea what she was talking about. It was the way she insisted that *you don't have to look too far* and the way she emphasised it when Mother was nearby that led me to think about Mother's past. I didn't want to be like Mother, I didn't want whatever had happened to her to happen to me, but it was too late to prevent Grandma's words from igniting something, her *anything can happen* foreshadowing a future of adventure that I intended to embrace with all my strength. *Anything can happen* resonated within me like an exquisite echo, as if I were a boy. Anything could happen to boys, they didn't need to feel fear or shame; fear and shame were always for the girls. Even if it was the boys trying to grope them or pulling them close to kiss them with tongues, the fault was always with the girls who had failed to avoid being harassed, the fault was always with the girls who had asked for it, the fault had always been with the girls since Eve gave Adam the apple, full-stop. Anything can happen, but within that anything, I would know how to become something different to Mother, to Mother and to Grandma, I would know how to be whoever I wanted to be.

Do something, doctor, please, do something, Mother begged, she seemed to be more upset about Grandma's distress and nudity than I was. While I tried to sort out Grandma, the man on the nearby hospital bed, a grumpy man who had driven off the road on a motor scooter, tugged once more at the doctor's coat to ask about the football score. I'm not interested in football, the doctor replied, a firm voice, a confident man. His lucky wife, I thought, she doesn't have to see her husband knocking back cans of beer while he watches a match, she doesn't have to listen to his ridiculous insults when he thinks someone has played badly or his throaty laugh when he reads what his friends are saying on Facebook, sneering at rival clubs. His lucky wife, she doesn't have to witness her husband's absurd anger at referees, how lucky not to be married to Jorge, how lucky not to be me.

There were no windows in the A&E room or in the corridor, where patient trolleys were lined up against the walls, and the strangely white light falling on us, especially the light falling on Grandma, was making me uncomfortable,

19

making me feel guilty for not having answered the doctor's question. Have you noticed your grandmother behaving unusually before this episode? I couldn't find a way to tell him that I knew almost nothing about my grandmother's day-to-day life, I was going to come across as the monstrous granddaughter who had abandoned her, but that's not what happened, even though I couldn't say what had happened. I wanted to escape and couldn't. The light falling on us, especially the light falling on the doctor, emphasised his body and the muscles rippling beneath the coat. He was a young doctor who didn't like football, and Mother wouldn't shut up, Do something, doctor, please, do something. Suddenly, I pictured myself naked, bent over one of the trolleys in the corridor as the doctor spanked me, asking repeatedly as he fucked me, Any unusual behaviour, have you noticed any unusual behaviour? while I pondered his use of the word "episode". Please doctor, I could still hear Mother's strident voice even as I imagined dragging the doctor to the Venus suite of the motel on the IC19 motorway that I sometimes passed on the way to viewings. I was a competent estate agent, diligent in securing properties, persuasive in selling them, good at establishing partnerships with the best clients and implementing strategies that delivered unbeatable results, even if I wasn't as eloquent as Natália, or had the photogenic looks that made her placards stop passers-by in their tracks wherever she put them up. Natália who had been named Platinum Agent many times before, and who is in a loving relationship with a caring husband, Natália upon whom I secretly wished small domestic accidents, small misfortunes that might chip away at her competence in managing life's hardships, that might ruin the confident air that buyers and sellers trusted, that might undermine the resilience she so often talked about. Instead of drowning out Mother's voice, my Venus suite reveries seemed to make her talk even louder. Eliete, look at how your grandmother's eyes are bulging out from their sockets. I had visited the Venus suite online, with its round bed, love seat and dance floor, a bathroom with a corner bath, jacuzzi, bidet and toilet, all lit by fake candles that allowed for romance without the risk of fire or the smell of a wake, Have mercy, Eliete.

The anxiety medication was finally having an effect, Grandma was no longer imploring to be taken to Lisbon and she let me hold her hand. Her arm stuck out at an angle like when she used to walk me to school, my hand in hers. Except that then we were side by side, not perpendicular to each other as we were now. Now I remained standing, but Grandma was lying down and weak. Grandma's smile when she walked me to school, shielding me from the cars that drove up to the Sintra Mountains and protecting me from the strangers at the campsite, was far from the mindless benzodiazepine smile she had now. Her hand, so strong then, was now a dead bird in mine. I wanted to embrace her like I did then, back when I tried to make my footsteps match hers, a time when Grandma's love rescued me from the solitude of that desolate set of houses between the sea, the mountains and the wind, I wanted to embrace her but I pulled my hand away as soon as I could.

The doctor asked again, Any unusual behaviour, differences in her personality, apathy, confusion, memory loss, have you noticed any of these? I noticed that as he spoke he twisted his gold wedding band around his finger. I had read in a book about body language that twisting a ring is a way of signalling willingness to betray the commitment the ring represents. I smiled at the doctor, and I fixed my hair pretending that the wandering of my hand and the gentle swaying of my body came naturally to me, while Mother responded evasively, At our age we are different from one day to the next. We must seize the day while we're young, I added. While we're young, the doctor repeated. I detected some irony in his voice as he no doubt tallied every one of my forty-two pitiful years and I admired his eyes not yet burdened by sagginess, his skin not yet wrinkled, his abundant hair. I then thought about Jorge's sunken eyes, his wrinkled skin, the horseshoe of hair around his bald spot. Age is unfair to us. Unstoppable, age would one day wear down the irony in the doctor's voice, and even sooner would wear down his body. Yes, what age does to us is unfair, but it's fair that it does it to everyone. The thought of this consoled me, time would be my great avenger.

As if we had agreed on it beforehand, neither I nor Mother told the doctor that we couldn't answer his question because, apart from a few festive dates, Christmases, Easters, birthdays, we rarely saw Grandma. Nor did I tell him that I suspected Grandma no longer had the strength to potter about in her garden or the eyesight to notice oil stains on her clothes, that she fell asleep with her head on the dining room table just to feel as though the girls from the television shopping channel were keeping her company. I suspected many other things, little things, but I never wanted to acknowledge them because I wouldn't know what to do with the confirmation that Grandma was vulnerable. Vulnerable and alone.

I heard myself saying, I'm the only granddaughter, even when it was obvious that the doctor, who was already putting out his hand to say goodbye, had no interest in that information. But I didn't waver, knowing that I was being ridiculous had never deterred me from doing anything, on the contrary, I stuck my chest out, composed my best smile, and shook his hand imagining a scenario where the doctor would regret not having found an excuse to give me his number and would go looking for mine in Grandma's records, a few days later he would invite me out for coffee, not everything was lost.

The doctor had left, Grandma had fallen asleep, Mother paced around, inspecting other patients lying about the place, and I didn't know what to do. I didn't like the idea of Grandma waking up in a strange place, surrounded by strangers, not seeing me nearby, she would be scared or confused. That lady has a foot on the other side, Mother said as she rejoined us, indicating a patient who had just been brought in on a trolley. The other side. As if death were some holding pen for dinosaurs and woolly mammoths, Ancient Greece and the Roman Empire, the giant Easter Island heads and, of course, Father. But Grandma wasn't dying, Grandma was strong, the way she had put up a fight just moments before proved it, she would stay in the hospital only to have tests that would conclude that the fall hadn't been serious. Your grandmother has been through so much, in spite of everything she doesn't deserve this.

In spite of everything was perhaps the most appropriate phrase to illustrate the relationship between Mother and Grandma and my relationship with each of them. In spite of everything the three of us were there and perhaps Mother wasn't deliberately making comments that seemed inappropriate in comparison with the professionals around us who acted like robots with their mechanical movements and short phrases, Your grandmother doesn't deserve it and we don't deserve it, and that air conditioner, the noise it makes is giving me a headache, I can't stand it. It had been a mistake to call Mother and ask her to come with me to the hospital. Grandma always said Mother was useless when Father died, I don't know what made me think she would be of any help.

Before leaving, Mother asked a nurse, lowering her voice as if she had suddenly remembered the hospital's code of conduct, How long will my mother-in-law stay here? Only as long as necessary, the nurse smiled, this hotel is always trying to send its guests away, we don't want people staying too long. I noticed her well-pressed uniform, the smooth leather of her shoes, the firm weave of her tights, anyone who puts so much care into her uniform will surely treat patients well, I thought to calm myself.

Out in the car park, I shielded myself from the June sunlight, concentrating on the weeds growing between the paving stones. Looking back at the enormous hospital building, Mother said proudly, It's a very dignified place, took them years to build it, but it's like the best hospitals abroad, much better than the ones in Lisbon. For Mother, abroad was still a faraway country where everything was better, and Lisbon, fewer than thirty kilometres away from Cascais, was the nearby rival, the decadent capital where nothing seemed right. But what Mother remembered most nostalgically was the old hospital, the hospital where I was born, in the centre of Cascais. I didn't have to check the tidal charts to know that a wave of memories would wash over us on the journey from the hospital to Mother's flat. The stories about my birth always arrived as if they were tied to a string pulled by an invisible hand. At the near end of that string was Father driving like a madman, hazard lights blinking, honking euphorically as he drove past his revolutionary friends huddled at the corner by the petrol station plotting the fate of the property left behind by the rich who had moved to Brazil. And at the hospital, after braking spectacularly, abandoning the car in the middle of the road and shouting, My wife is giving birth to my son. Mother enjoyed telling the rest of the story. You were born four months after the revolution, at the time revolutionaries were sprouting everywhere like mushrooms, you kicked over a stone and there was another one, of course your father had to become a revolutionary, your father could never let a fashion pass him by. How annoyed Senhor Pereira was, and your grandmother even more so, your father shouldn't have got involved with those people who went around painting hammers and sickles onto walls, jobless parasites, children of privilege, who are now business managers, heads of this, directors of that. Back then they coveted the houses belonging to rich fascists, now they covet everything from everyone and not even the poorest can escape their greed. Your father was already the head

25

of a family, he had responsibilities, he should have never got himself mixed up with that crowd. April 25 was your father's downfall, in that sense the old woman was right.

Because he was a man, Father was always allowed to do anything, and even if Grandma or Mother complained about this or that, anything could happen to him, he could make anything happen. When he met Mother, she was already a young woman, anything could happen to her too. And it did happen, Mother became pregnant with me when she was just sixteen. I didn't have to look very far to know that anything could happen to me. Come here, Eliete.

Mother was still talking, but I'd stopped paying attention, I was trying to work out what had happened to Grandma that day. As usual, she must have woken up that morning with the first rays of light to come through her window, then she'd got up and crossed herself in front of the little altar with saints she had in her bedroom, then put on her Sunday shoes, even though it wasn't a Sunday. That would have been the first slip-up, to mistake a Thursday for a Sunday. She then forgot to take off her nightgown, or perhaps she didn't forget, perhaps Grandma was tired of the dead that had kept her in mourning all her life. She hobbled to the bus stop. Sunday shoes are the prettiest, but wearing them is hell, she used to say. No neighbour would have stopped her, they didn't know her, the old neighbours had died or had been put into care homes by their children, the same children who had inherited their houses and sold them off at a good price. Or perhaps nobody had actually crossed paths with Grandma, the new neighbours rose early to go jogging wearing fluorescent clothes and earphones. God was a minimalist and repetitive composer when it came to that place, sea and wind, wind and sea, even the birdsong always sounded the same. Grandma walked with a handkerchief over her head to protect herself from the dust, forgetting that the road was now tarmacked and that the new houses had decking, bricks, lawns, paving stones, alleyways, the new houses had everything except soil, which was dirty and ugly, and cement floors didn't gather dust. The bus driver didn't recognise Grandma. Had it been Senhor Tadeu, who drove that route all his life and knew passengers' names and their family connections, everything would have been different. Senhor Tadeu would have persuaded Grandma to go back home, but Senhor Tadeu died many years ago and his successors were always changing jobs and didn't want to do small talk, they were paid a pittance to bus people from one place to another and they did it with varying degrees of punctuality, with varying amounts of bumps and jolts. From a distance or to the casual observer, Grandma's nightgown could pass for a daring dress that, along with her Sunday shoes, might be worn by a young woman. Between Grandma's house and the souvenir shop on Rua Direita, fifteen minutes by foot and a few more on the bus, the people whose paths crossed with Grandma would have seen her from a distance or would have been casual observers so nobody noticed she needed help, perhaps they thought she was an eccentric young woman, Grandma's body could be deceiving. Not even the souvenir shop manager, when he saw her come in wearing those clothes, recognised the old woman who had been there the day before. He remembered her well because she had wandered around in the shop until she found herself standing in front of the stand with the key rings. She had picked one up, and made her way to the door, without paying. When they stopped her, she apologised and said that she was distracted, lost in her thoughts. The manager was surprised to see her, the following day, dressed in that strange way and repeating an unusual name, perhaps a woman's. She was so distressed that she tripped over a wicker basket filled with toy sardines, and fell helplessly. The souvenir shop manager told this story to the first aiders who assisted Grandma, who told the story to the hospital nurses, who told it to the doctor I imagined taking to the Venus suite, who told Mother and me. Somewhere along the way the name Grandma was crying out got lost, possibly Eliete, my name, I guessed. The doctor couldn't confirm it, but didn't think it important to clarify this detail, explaining that in such cases socio-affective capabilities tend to deteriorate, because the patient remains trapped in her delusions. He seemed to be saying, in his medical jargon, that in such cases anything goes. What cases, I wanted to ask, but didn't have the courage, what did the doctor mean by *in such cases* if it was simply a fall? What sort of case might a fall be? People are always falling and Grandma fell too, we shouldn't make a big deal of it. Grandma hit her head on the souvenir shop floor, blood trickled out and stained her white hair. Your name and address, madam, and contact details for someone we can call?

I didn't mind driving Mother home, but I was bothered by her making such a fuss about my offer. You didn't have to bring me, I could have taken a bus, even though we both knew that the bus stop was far from her house and that the lift home wasn't just an excuse to spend time together. I always turned down her invitation to go up to her apartment. I can make you a coffee, she said, as if speaking to a visitor. At first I would make up urgent tasks, the girls, Jorge, work. Not even for five minutes? Everyone has five minutes. I would invent other even more absurd excuses and Mother would gladly assume the role of the wretched woman with an ungrateful daughter. How could I explain to Mother that the problem wasn't with her, but with the way time seemed to be warped in her flat? When I entered it time seemed to become a crude catapult, and I was at its mercy, a projectile against myself, pulled back in time and then shot out unprotected into the present, where all my mistakes and failures were on display. Mother's flat reminded me of everything I didn't want to be and which, ironically, I had become. You need to take better care of yourself, look at Dona Rosa's daughter, she is two years older than you but seems younger, Mother said to punish me for my rejection. Mother took no great pleasure in me coming upstairs, but insisted on inviting me so that my refusal would give her an excuse to hurt me. She would then delight in malicious insinuations, I lost track of the number of times my marriage was in crisis, the number of scrapes the girls got into, how often I was in danger of being fired, how much I needed to lose weight, change my hairstyle, remove my facial hair, learn to apply makeup, to dress properly, to behave. When I answered back, Mother said I was becoming bitter. I once made the mistake of

29

asking, Bitter in what way? The golden specks in her eyes flickered into life and she replied with no hesitation, Like an unhappy person. It was hardly surprising that she was so taken aback when, on the day of the hospital visit, I accepted her invitation to come upstairs, but she said nothing and hid her astonishment to avoid appearing weak. Never appear weak could have been Mother's motto.

My phone buzzed with an incoming message. It was Jorge asking about Grandma. Grandma is losing her mind, I wrote on the brightly lit screen, but immediately deleted it. I wrote, I miss being young in summer, not knowing where that sentiment had come from. I re-read the line. I deleted it. I liked phone screens, where words could be destroyed as easily as they could be created, leaving no trace. Luminous places, clean, with no marks or crossings-out or memory, where it's always possible to start again. I wrote, I'll call you when I leave Mother's flat, and sent the message. Two blue ticks confirmed that Jorge had read it. In return, I got an OK and a smiley face. I chose a heart to send back, but Mother distracted me with the marketing leaflets she had just pulled out of her postbox, I should buy myself one of these blood pressure monitors, and so the heart remained forgotten among my drafts.

Mother's flat always had the same smell. Spices and fried onions from the Goan family on the ground floor, worn carpets, tobacco smoke and old plumbing, green thick-leaved plants, plastic blinds warmed by the sun, all mixed up in the valley's stilled air. It wasn't a disagreeable smell, it evoked a kind of neglected domesticity, women with rollers in their hair, men washing the car in singlet vests, children rolling bus tyres along dirt roads, terraced houses bristling with television aerials, Sunday Mass and lunch, football commentators, girls dolled up in cheap jewellery, old men sitting on their balconies, soldiers on leave and bikers without their motorcycles, couples putting up with each other till death did them part.

For years, Mother's flat had only existed in dreams and in none of those dreams did it appear as it eventually materialised, third floor on the right in a council estate in Alvide, a flat previously occupied by returnees who left children's drawings on the wall, illegal electrical wiring and a jar of jindungo chillies in one of the kitchen cupboards. Even as the years passed, Mother never stopped believing that, one day, we would leave Grandma's house and have our own home. When she reached the end of her tether, Mother took me to the Sunday matinée at the Oxford cinema or at one of the cinemas in the Jumbo Shopping Centre. There was no shopping mall or McDonalds yet, no cinema sessions followed by a cheeseburger meal, where

I pretended to be in America, Mother hadn't yet developed the habit of asking for extra sachets of mayonnaise or ketchup to take home. They were happy days, the matinée Sundays, the films never disappointed, and, on the way home, Mother would once again dare to believe we would one day leave Grandma's house, it didn't matter whether the film had been about an Australian crocodile hunter or about a creature that lived in a spaceship, on the way home Mother once again believed in her dream, films were proof that life always bent to people's dreams, things would happen suddenly when we least expected them. Mother recognised and reaffirmed her faith in films, greater than her faith in Father Raul's sermons from the pulpit during Sunday Mass.

Almost thirty years later, Mother's neighbourhood remained as ugly and poorly kept as it had ever been, and it had lost its only advantage, the clean air from the valley's pine trees. I was already going out with Jorge when the fury of progress armed itself with chainsaws and concrete mixers to tear out the pine trees and replace them with buildings so forlorn that daylight refused to brighten their sad facades. The sewage, which trickled down from further up in the neighbourhood, now remained stagnant at the bottom of the valley, and of the former exuberance of tree trunks and branches only half a dozen pine trees remained, bordering the so-called new square, although there had never been an old one, half a dozen pine trees planted in small circles cut out of the pavement, withering away year by year, an agonising memorial to the development boom at the end of the second millennium and to the excesses of the period preceding the economic collapse, the great crisis.

As we entered her flat, Mother muttered, under her breath, Hell must be freezing over. I made small talk, pretending not to have heard her provocation, It's been so long since we've been alone together, we keep putting it off and off again, and then these things happen. I noticed the finger smudges on the glass tabletop, I knew that Mother would fetch a cloth to wipe them and for once I found her predictable behaviour comforting rather than irritating, Mother was doing what she had always done and that meant she was well, it meant she wasn't going to start begging me to take her back to Lisbon. What's happening with the girls, with Jorge, she asked, walking towards the kitchen and leaving me at the mercy of the enormous portrait of Father that hung from the living room wall.

I was five years old when Father died. I wouldn't have been quite six when Mother had the last photograph ever taken of my father enlarged, That way he'll always be with *us*, she said, satisfied, as if she had finally won him in a dispute with a lover. We were still living at Grandma's, I had stopped sleeping on the couch and had taken over Father's place in the double bed. Mother wanted a portrait that would take up our entire bedroom wall, but the quality of the negatives and the cost she was quoted checked her ambition and forced her to accept a print that was one metre twenty by eighty centimetres. To push back against the distance created by death, Mother hung the portrait very low, so that Father could watch over us as we lay in

33

bed. At that stage, when I stood next to the photograph, my height seemed right by comparison to Father's, he loomed above my head as it reached his waist, almost like other children and their fathers. But the passage of time meant that my head shot up, Father's portrait became a height chart, the following year the top of my head almost reached his chest, the next it touched his heart and the one after I could place it against his shoulder. When we moved out of Grandma's house and Mother had the portrait hung on our living room wall, Father's eyes were once again above mine even when I stood on tippytoes. Placed at the right height, Father's stature, life-size almost, made more obvious what he had become for me, a dwarf caught inside a wide aluminium frame.

I hardly remembered Father. I deceived myself into thinking that I had known the mischievous expression he had in the portrait, but I would have only ever seen it, long dead, on that piece of photographic paper. It was a studio portrait and Father stood in front of the backdrop of a rock face covered in moss and greenery, with a waterfall scattering into streams that flowed into a pool below. The right leg was slightly bent, and his left hand held the cigarette that he would have lit moments before the photographer pressed the camera's shutter. My memories of Father were jumbled, faded, uncertain, but all were suffused by the smell of tobacco, as if that smell were the glue binding the loose threads of memory that the passing of time made increasingly unreachable. It seemed unlikely that Father had actually been so steeped in the smell of tobacco, and I wondered whether I might have made that up because of the cigarette in the portrait and the conversations, over the years, in which I heard about Father's habit, I had almost certainly added it to my memories, as if it were a task of the present to shape the past. Nor could I be sure of those threads of memory in which Father carried me on his back, whistling, or plunging me into the waves, my memory or the memory I had access to was limited and disjointed, a couple of small islands surrounded by vague recollections, dozens, hundreds, thousands of submerged recollections, like bodies stirring underwater, until chance, a smell, the intonation with which a word was said, brought them mysteriously to the surface, before submerging them again. Only two clear and vivid recollections of Father were safe from oblivion. One night, Father arranging the sheets as he tucks me into bed, a loving father. One day, Father driving his brown Ford Taunus, with me in the passenger seat, an angry father. These two images for which I had no context, two images frozen in time with no before or after, were my only solid ground regarding memories of Father.

Mother was convinced that the landscape in the backdrop in front of which Father was posing was the same paradisal landscape from the film *The Blue Lagoon*, and she said that to my classmates whenever I took them home to do our homework together. Sure, *Blue Lagoon*, they repeated uninterested, brushing their Lady Di fringes out of their eyes, but Mother, pretending not to notice their lack of interest, continued the conversation that so embarrassed me. Perhaps Father already knew the silly things Mother would say about him when he posed for the portrait, which is why he had that mischievous smile. Or perhaps he smiled because he knew how ridiculous his full moustache would seem one day, with those sideburns that crawled across his cheeks like upturned commas.

I knew Father's portrait by heart. I knew how many squares there were on his chequered jacket, thirty-two, and I was able to recognise the electric blue of his pointy-collared shirt among a thousand shades of electric blue. I was impressed by Father's arm hair, strong and dark hair that made his death seem more unreal. I even tried to count the hairs, like I counted the squares on the jacket and the stripes on the socks, but my eyes ached from looking so hard and I gave up. What was I seeking so persistently in Father's portrait? Was it Father, was it Grandma, was it my grandfather the travelling performer, Senhor Pereira, Mother, myself, the certainty that Father loved his little girl?

Although Father's death underpinned almost all our conversations, we didn't talk openly about it. Our family was a complicated jigsaw with many missing pieces, pieces related to Father, whose absence left a gap in the middle of the puzzle. There was something close to reverence about our relationship with that absence, but no matter how hard I tried I couldn't find anything notable in Father's short life to justify the hushed tones of Grandma, of Senhor Pereira and even Mother. As they were unable to point to any heroism in Father being away from home for days at a time to paint revolutionary murals or to visit the rural districts in the throes of Agrarian Reform, or in Father racing down the wrong side of Avenida Marginal, or in Father having affairs, I was forced to conclude that it was his death that had turned him into a hero, that an untimely death can turn any common mortal into a hero.

As I grew up and understood more about life and death, I was increasingly unsettled by the silences surrounding Father's life and death, both of which became such mysterious spaces that I began to attribute excessive importance to insignificant triumphs, such as discovering the identity of the photographer who took Father's portrait on 30 November 1978. In my adolescence, the portrait became the only portal allowing access to what little remained of him. The photography studio, the name of which was printed below the date, on the portrait's lower right-hand corner, had closed years before I went there for the first time. I tried to get information from the owner of the business next door to the studio, a barbershop with countertops lined in light-blue Formica tiles with fine metallic edges that reminded me of films from the fifties. I remember being inside the barbershop, my cowboy boots on the black and white chequered floor, the camouflage coat I had bought second-hand from the flea market at the bullring, the dreadlocks that made my beautiful hair so unsightly. The patient barber took pity on the sad fourteen-year-old girl I was then, but had little to tell me, the studio owner had been an American, Christopher, he had come over to take photographs of the Revolution and had ended up staying, If it hadn't been for the floods he might still be around, he added, the floods ruined everything for him.

I was nine years old when merciless overnight rains and a rising sea joined forces to flood the town centre. The following morning Mother took me to see the buildings in the Baixa district, water still waist high, and I couldn't have known that the backdrop in front of which my father had posed and the negatives from his final photographs had been destroyed in the deluge. I remember a bar higher up with its doors open wide and its windows cracked, and the owner sweeping out the remaining water to the sound of a jazz band that had perhaps not stopped playing since the night before. According to the barber, the American rebuilt his studio, but with little enthusiasm, and one day, just like that, he bailed, leaving behind the photographs in his window display case, happy newlyweds, curly-haired babies, people looking serious for their ID photographs, all at the mercy of an unforgiving sun that made them fade until they had almost disappeared. I have his address, for some reason I never got rid of it, the barber said. I took down the address, even though I had no idea what I would do with it. I copied it into all my address books, year after year, hoping that one day I would find the right question to ask the photographer so I could feel closer to Father, the same hope that, only a few years later, would make me believe I would find the right words to finish the poems I started writing in my Hello Kitty notebooks. Even though I knew that nothing of Father remained in the studio, I always tried to walk past it when, on those days when she felt well disposed, Mother took me out for a light lunch at Bijou or for coffee on the terrace of Hotel Baía. I don't know why I did it, it filled me with dread to see the place where Father had posed for his portrait being destroyed by vermin, to imagine the inside of the studio decaying slowly and secretly like Father's body beneath the ground, at the Torre cemetery. The barber shut down before the big crisis. The hardware shop selling tools that glinted in the display cabinets beneath the sun also went bust shortly after, as did the draper's store with the floor-to-ceiling wooden cabinets. There was nothing in that block of shops that Father might have known, other than the sliver of sea that, from a certain angle, could be seen at the end of the road. Thirty-eight years after Father had his portrait taken, the letter he once had in his hands ended up in mine.

Everything is fine, I replied to Mother as she returned from the kitchen with peanuts, cold beer and two tall glasses, Márcia is still enjoying Italy, she's convinced that she belongs there, that she was Italian in some past life. Back in my days hardly anyone studied or travelled, Mother said, but those who could would study first and travel later, now people do everything at once and do none of it well. Mother had never forgiven Márcia for being so like Grandma. And Inês? she asked, with a smile. As fickle as ever, I replied, pretending not to notice the disapproval with which Mother talked about Márcia and the enthusiasm with which she asked about Inês. Now it looks like she wants to study theatre, with her we have to take it one day at a time, or rather, one idea at a time, luckily Jorge has the patience of a saint. Leave the girl alone, Mother said, when I look at her it's like I'm seeing you, she's just like you, like she was spat out of your mouth. I didn't like Mother's crude expressions, and I was particularly uncomfortable by how she said *spat out of your mouth* to emphasise my physical similarity to Inês. I'm so tired, I said, even though Mother hadn't asked how I was, there is so much work these days, it's either feast or famine, a couple of years ago houses were going for a song and nobody wanted them, now people are demanding a king's ransom for any old place, and buyers are happy to pay.

Mother poured the beer into the glasses and tipped some peanuts into a bowl, not paying much attention to what I had just said. She always liked peanuts. She shelled them by crushing them against the table, then she rolled them between her thumb and index finger to remove the skin, and once she had enough in her hand she popped them into her mouth in a quick and unseemly gesture. Mother's crudeness didn't just manifest itself in her expressions, if I looked closely enough I could confirm that everything about her was vulgar, the noisy chewing, the habit of sitting at the edge of a chair, the amulet she wore around her neck to protect her from other people's evil eye, the pride she took in exhibiting the emblems of the poverty she grew up with.

It was a good idea to take this week off work, she said, the white peanut mush visible on her tongue, if I had been at work I wouldn't have been able to go with you to the hospital, I have more work than I can shake a stick at, I don't know why brides bother with the dress these days, in a year's time they'll be getting a divorce, just look at the state of my hand. She put her hand out, showing me how the inflamed joints were making it crooked, Shaped like a bloody pair of scissors, she said, and I couldn't figure out whether her words were filled with grievance or with pride. The tip of her middle finger was deformed by the use of a thimble, the chipped nail varnish aged her hands, brown liver spots dotted her dry and neglected skin. I told her that a work colleague had some good results with acupuncture, but Mother looked at me with disdain, I was going to do something but I forgot, she said getting up to draw the curtain across the door that leads to the balcony because the sun was bothering her. It's rare for Mother to feel well, but it's also rare for her to feel poorly, almost nothing makes her well or poorly, but almost everything disturbs her, from the sun bouncing off the tabletop to the noise of the hospital air conditioner.

It was close to three o'clock. I regretted cancelling the house viewing at Monte Estoril, I would have had enough time to show the customers around. I thought about re-instating it, but then worried that changing the appointment twice in such a short time might make me seem disorganised and therefore less trustworthy in the eyes of the buyers. One of Natália's golden rules was never to cancel a viewing, to avoid upsetting the energy of a sale. Natália believed in energies, in sorceries, in karma, and I envied her more for that than for her Platinum Agent trophies, it was exhausting not to believe in anything.

With the curtains drawn, Mother sat down again and took more peanuts out of the plastic bag before proceeding to shell them by means of her noisy technique, I can't remember the last time you honoured me with a visit, maybe it was about a year ago, is that right? There must have been a time when Mother and I could talk to each other without irony saddening our words, when our words meant only what we were saying, but that would have been so long ago that it seemed to me it had never happened. Now, I could no longer identify the origins of many of the behaviours we had developed, which discussion had led to the creation of which new rule, which principles had been reconsidered to allow for a particular change, and even if I could identify them, I couldn't determine their importance in the jumble of feelings that joined me to, and detached me from Mother.

I replied, with no bitterness, trying to make Mother's question less loaded, I think it was when you asked me to help you sign up to Facebook, I came to teach you how to work the computer, you said you wanted to stay in touch with your friends. Mother looked at the side table by the television, on top of which lay a laptop covered with a flannel rag, and buried beneath a pile of leaflets, bills and bank statements. On the other two side tables that took up the fewer than fifteen square metres in the living room not a single square centimetre remained uncluttered by frames, vases, unlit candles or bowls of pot-pourri. My friends tell me I have to use it for days and days to get my head around it, she complained, but you only came over for a few minutes, how was I supposed to learn? I'm no genius, I never touched it again. I pretended we were only talking about the computer, that Mother wasn't reproaching me for the lack of help I provided, You can use the computer on your own, it won't break, and if you have any problems you can just call me. I didn't pay much attention to the smirk with which Mother discredited my words, and when she turned her attention back to the peanuts, to peanut shells and the white peanut mush in her mouth, I heard myself say, When Grandma is discharged from hospital, do you think she could stay here in my old room for a few days?

Mother couldn't have turned her head towards me so

fiercely if I had whipped her. She screwed up her eyes as if that gesture were indispensable to understanding what I had just said. Squinting, a handful of peanuts at the ready while she chewed the ones still in her mouth, Mother reminded me of a rodent. She started to laugh, a smile at first, then a guffaw, as if I had told a joke that was hard to get and she had needed more time to understand it. When she realised I was serious, Mother put down the peanuts, wiped her tears of laughter and took a deep breath. She then spoke calmly, with the confidence of a student who knows a subject very well, Your old room is in my home and in my home I am in charge, she said, visibly satisfied by the answer she had given me. Mother's home was always Mother's home, it was never our home. She pushed away the bag of peanuts and added, You can be certain of one thing, Eliete, that old woman won't be staying here, the last thing I need is to become her maid again, as if I hadn't been forced to serve her for over eleven years, they were the worst years of my life and believe me I know what a bad year is, I was more desperate to escape your grandmother's house than I ever was to escape my school at Senhora Santa, even though at Senhora Santa I was still a girl, I hadn't yet developed the thick skin that suffering gives you, when I lived in your grandmother's house I already knew that life is hard and even so I never suffered as much, you may have forgotten what we went through, I still remember very well how difficult it was, if it weren't for the promises I made myself I wouldn't have made it through, I had to get out of there before I died, do you remember how many times I swore I would get out of there?

How could I have forgotten? While we lived in Grandma's house, there wasn't a single New Year's Eve when Mother didn't swear that in the coming year she would get a better job than the one she had in the bridal dress shop, a job that would allow her to move us out of Grandma's house, there wasn't a single New Year's Eve when Mother didn't take me by the shoulders, I swear that this time next year we'll have our own house, but listen to what I tell you, Eliete, you also have to want to leave this house, you have to really want it, do you know how to really want something? Mother would poke me in the middle of my forehead with her index finger, This is where you get everything you want, nothing happens to us if it doesn't happen here first, do you understand, Eliete? If you really want something, if you're sure it will happen, then it does happen, this year we're leaving this place.

I felt important that first time Mother asked me to really want it, Mother's request was proof that I was old enough, that I could be her partner in the grand project of having our own home. It's true that Mother was already taking me along to films that bolstered her hope when it was beginning to fade, but I was merely Mother's companion, I wasn't expected to do anything, other than watch the film with her. That was an easy task, even if I didn't like the film, which was often the case when Mother chose romantic films that made her cry, but to really want something, no, that wasn't an easy task, I didn't know what to think about, and even when I felt I knew, I couldn't think about what I should be thinking about. I would close my eyes to try to concentrate, I imagined us, me and Mother, in the new house, but if I imagined too long I would realise that the new house I had in my head was one of my friends' houses or, more often, Grandma's house with different furniture, different decorations, a different colour of paint, I imagined us leaving Grandma's house, that was what Mother had said, You have to want to leave, you have to really want it, but then I imagined Grandma becoming sad so I would open my eyes. I soon realised I didn't know how to really want something. Throughout the year, instead of helping me to concentrate, the growing pressure of Mother's finger on my forehead seemed to open a valve that slowly released the enthusiasm I felt about my responsibility at the start of the year. It was my fault that Mother couldn't get a better job, that we couldn't leave Grandma's house. Mother must have known this, she must have realised that I didn't really want it. And so, perhaps less to ask for my help, and more to punish me, at the next New Year's Eve, You have to really want it, Eliete, and me terrified with Mother's index finger boring into my head. And next year's New Year's Eve, and the next and the next. In the end Mother managed to get us out of Grandma's house, but I still didn't know how to really want something and Mother continued to work in the bridal shop I liked so much.

The shop was in the Parede district, where, as a girl, Mother used to take me on Saturday mornings. I liked everything there, the mannequin brides with half-open lips and hands posed as if in conversation, the velvety blue carpet with its two golden stripes running lengthwise towards a circular hall, the antechamber outside the fitting room, the ivory coloured wallpaper with its patterns of heavenly angels and ribbons, the smell of jasmine that stayed in our clothes, the swish of silks and taffetas, the cupboards filled with garlands, gloves, veils, tulles and tiaras, I liked everything, but I was especially fond of the fitting room. It was covered in mirrors so brides could see themselves from every angle, it had a circular platform that, when activated with a small switch, would make the bride turn slowly like the ballerinas in music boxes. I was certain that I would, one day, be one of those ballerinas, *Amour et Bonheur*, my whole life waiting for the day when, at a grand wedding, I would marry the love of my life with a *robe de mariée* made *sur mesure*, my whole life waiting to be happy ever after, a time when happiness was French, *Amour et Bonheur*, certainly preferable to the English *Love and Happiness*. But the most surprising thing about the bridal shop was the vanishing of Mother with her crude gestures and expressions, everyday Mother. In the fitting room, Mother became the perfect seamstress narrowing waists and adjusting necklines, the green pin cushion attached to her wrist. Mother looked pretty as she marked the lining fabrics with chalk, slid the sharp scissors, aligned hems, and laid out on a long wooden table the billowing dresses that murmured quietly as she smoothed them down. Mother wasn't as skilful as Dona Herlanda, the shop owner, at fitting brides with veils and hairdos, something blue for good luck, the brassiere to defy gravity, the waistband to make tummies disappear, but she was very skilful at turning tubby, ugly, misshapen and acned women into the beautiful brides that Saint Inês, the patron saint, with her lily and her lamb, blessed from the portrait that hung on the wall.

When she was in a good mood, Mother allowed me to touch the dresses, and I did it with the same care and reverence I might use when touching a relic. Ours will be even prettier, said Milena, one time when she came along with us to the bridal shop. I agreed, even if I couldn't imagine dresses more beautiful than the ones displayed there. I feigned interest in the details of Milena's dress to avoid talking about mine. I didn't want to reveal my lack of imagination, no-one needed to know that I was so tragically tethered to humdrum reality, not even my best friend.

Even though I didn't manage to really want it, as Mother asked me to, I did want to leave Grandma's house. I was lured by the promise of having a room of my own, and therefore bringing an end to the daily battle with Mother about turning off the lights and switching off the radio. At Grandma's house I always slept in Mother's room, the room that was once Father's, then Father's and Mother's when she was pregnant with me, then for the three of us, then Mother's and mine, and finally no-one's. Mother never forgave Grandma for not turning Senhor Pereira's study into a bedroom for me, I don't know what he was doing in his study that could have been more important than me and your father being comfortable, I think the old woman did it on purpose, Mother said every time she talked about Grandma's house. It was Senhor Pereira's house, but we always called it Grandma's house. Whenever we finally moved to a new house, I would no longer have to witness the hostility between Mother and Grandma, so noticeable even in their smallest gestures. In Mother's own house, I'd have a desk of my own where I could display my eraser collection and I'd be able to watch television as long as I wanted to, I might even spend the whole night staring at the television test card if I felt like it. And I wouldn't have to eat everything on my plate, or avoid meat on Fridays, or go to Mass on Sundays. But, for all of that, Mother could have poked my forehead for years and my desire to leave would never have weakened had the boys from Torre not showed up outside church one day. It was a summer of wildfires, on a day of more than forty degrees, when clothes left on the line were covered in ashes. I didn't exchange a single word with the boys from Torre. I saw them arrive on their bicycles, shirtless, young gods performing stunts, skin darkened by the sun, long hair, muscular bodies, frayed shorts, dirty trainers. I shouldn't go near them. I mustn't go near them. Suddenly, it was easy, very easy, to really want Grandma not to be breathing down my neck or Senhor Pereira not to be lecturing me about what all boys wanted. I never saw skies as beautiful as those smoke-darkened skies. I knew it was wrong to see beauty in wickedness, but I didn't know how not to see it. I never knew. Over the years, I crossed paths everywhere with the boys from Torre, at the beach, at the cinema, on the town streets, and I never forgot those wide smiles brimming with happy futures. Nor did I know where those cheesy phrases repeating themselves in my head came from. Perhaps I wasn't so different from Mother, perhaps I was only sadder than she was, because I knew not to think like someone in a photo novel. Much less live that way.

Conversations with Mother about the time when we lived in Grandma's house were a perverse game, a game of combat in which Mother's objective was not to win but to lose, to have lost disastrously. It was as if, at the vaguest mention of Grandma, a bell sounded that made her jump into the ring, eager to add new wounds to the old ones she had always nursed. If I was slow to agree that we had been unhappy in Grandma's house, if I failed to remember all the terrible things Grandma inflicted on us, if I mentioned anything good that Grandma had done, that was immediately considered an aggression against her and the new wounds hurt even more because it was her own daughter inflicting them. So I let her demonise Grandma as much as she wanted, your grandmother this, your grandmother that. I would remain silent or, when Mother took my silence for disinterest or disagreement, I would echo her in monosyllables, yes, yes, right, right.

You called me to the hospital, hoping I would feel pity for the old woman, do you think I'm that stupid, Mother said, and turned away ostentatiously, looking for a moment like the cheap replica of the sphynx she had bought many years earlier at the Estoril Craft Fair and that, ever since, had been climbing up the shelves with the photo novels and the Heinz Konsalik books, until it was placed at the top, where it started gathering cobwebs. I didn't mind Mother's hostility, I preferred her aggression to the moaning and the self-pity. I didn't reply, but Mother charged again, Don't put on that superior air like I'm ignorant, I know exactly what you're trying to do, but you're barking up the wrong tree.

Perhaps Mother was right. If so, she had known long before I did what made me tick. Perhaps I had a protective mechanism that made me act unconsciously in self-defence, a mechanism that was responsible for my unexpected behaviour, like asking Mother to meet me at the hospital or agreeing to come up to her flat. Even I found it difficult to believe that there was no ulterior motive in both of those decisions. It was obvious that I was trying to be relieved of some of the help I would have to offer Grandma, even before I knew whether she would need any help. Perhaps Mother was right and it was true that mothers are condemned to know the worst about their children, recognising, even before the children do, their vilest intentions. Or perhaps it had nothing to do with motherly wisdom, perhaps I was simply predictable, as predictable to Mother as Mother was to me.

The pain of losing her son gave your grandmother an excuse for everything, Mother continued, except the old woman forgot that I was also suffering from the loss of a husband, and, on top of that, I had a fatherless girl to raise. Grandma had apparently forgotten that when her son died, Mother's husband had died too, and Mother had forgotten that when her husband died, I had lost my father. In truth, for me, Father died twice, but I always struggled to believe in his death. Perhaps because I never saw Father's dead body.

The first time Father died, we were living in Grandma's house and I didn't yet know what dying meant, death was something that happened to animals, something that served a purpose. The chickens in the coop had their throats cut so we could have chicken soup, mosquitoes and flies were sprayed with insecticide to stop the former from buzzing and biting, and the latter from landing on the food, slugs were squashed underfoot because they were disgusting and they left holes in the cabbages and tree leaves. I didn't know that people could also die, and it made no sense, because dead people served no purpose.

It was night, I was with Mother, Grandma and Senhor Pereira in the dining room, we were watching Games Without Frontiers on television, when there was a knock on the door. We had just had dinner, Mother and Grandma had cleared the table, leaving only a place set for Father. The affairs of the Revolution often delayed Father. Senhor Pereira was in an armchair and I in another, and Mother and Grandma were still at the table, watching the programme from where they sat while they waited for Father. Portugal hadn't yet joined Games Without Frontiers, so Mother cheered for France, *Amour et Bonheur*, while Senhor Pereira supported Germany, because Germans were a civilised people who didn't ally themselves with barbarians. Grandma didn't express any preference and Father, the few times he was at home while the games were on, found them uninteresting. I felt compelled to go along with Mother, declaring our allegiance to the country of love, but secretly I was rooting for Yugoslavia, which was a newcomer to the Games, and had Father's sympathy.

When there was a knock on the door, Mother got up in a hurry to be the one who walked down the corridor to open the door for Father, who had probably lost his keys or was having trouble finding the keyhole. But, instead of returning with Father, Mother started wailing. We all ran, Is it Antoninho? Grandma could say nothing else, is it Antoninho? Mother came to find me, grabbed me in the middle of the corridor and bundled us, me and her, into our bedroom. She held me, clinging tight and unable to stop sobbing, Papá died. I learned then, at once, that humans could also die and that the purpose of their death was the suffering they caused others. Before that night I hadn't known that there could be pain, serious pain, without the body being hurt. Grandma's and Mother's bodies were intact, but they were crying more than I cried when I fell in the garden and landed on my face on the concrete patch, cracking my front milk teeth, or the time I pulled Bardino's tail so hard he scratched me and left a scar on my arm. That night, death had come knocking on our door and there she was, at the end of the corridor, introducing me to new types of pain. I saw her before Mother pushed me into the bedroom and locked us up inside. With the house door open, the light of the moon drew the silhouette of two men with hairstyles and trousers very similar to Father's, framed by the doorway, as if Father had somehow unfolded into those two shadows before disappearing forever. Mother explained to me later that two of Father's comrades had come to say he had been in an accident, the Ford Taunus had driven off Avenida Marginal, on that curve by the Mónaco restaurant. Or perhaps it was Grandma or Senhor Pereira who explained, because at that moment Mother could only cry. Don't go anywhere, she said, as soon as we heard the noise of the front door shutting. Mother went to speak to Grandma and Senhor Pereira and I remained alone in the room unable to understand their cries, their voices and their shouts. It seemed to me like they went on for hours, but it must have been only minutes.

Despite the fact that Mother, Grandma and Senhor Pereira never wanted to talk about Father's death, my memories of that night coincided with theirs up to the moment when I was left alone in the bedroom. But from that moment onwards my memories diverged irreparably from theirs. To have remained alone in the room, knowing that Father was dead, even if I didn't yet know what it meant to be dead, not only turned seconds into hours, but also erased three days of my life. The next moment I remember was Mother hurriedly putting my clothes into a travel bag and bundling me into a car that Senhor Pereira drove out of the garage with such haste that he scuffed the wall paint, yet, when years later I insisted on talking about this, Grandma and Senhor Pereira assured me that wasn't how things had happened. It was true that Senhor Pereira had driven me to his village so I could have a change of scene, that I cried almost the whole way, that Grandma and Mother had joined us a few days later, dressed in black from head to toe, all that was true, except that the trip to the village hadn't happened on the night of Father's death, but three nights later, when Grandma decided I shouldn't continue to witness the grief that had overcome Mother.

It frightened me that three days of my life had disappeared, that no matter how much I tried I couldn't rescue a single memory of anything that had happened in that time. Everything I couldn't understand felt threatening and the blackout, as I came to call it, terrified me. It was natural that the shock of Father's death had caused a short circuit in my brain, if I could compare the brain to an electric circuit, but it was strange that I remembered everything so clearly up to the moment when I was left alone in the bedroom and that I didn't have a single recollection of Father's funeral and wake. Where had those three days, containing such important moments, gone?

In my early adulthood I read everything I could find about traumatic shock, trying to understand why I had stitched together two moments that were in fact separated by a three-day interval. For years, I believed that I would end up recovering those days in the same way I had lost them, that when I least expected it something would happen that might cause a reverse short circuit, something as commonplace as a high fever, a serious fright, a drunken binge. I even tried hypnosis, but nothing happened. I only stopped trying to reverse the blackout when I became pregnant with Márcia. When I saw the changes the pregnancy caused in me, I understood that bodies are steeped in a complexity that only fools would claim to control, and I stopped trying to understand the mysteries of their workings. The three days that had disappeared were hidden within me, as a house's foundations are hidden beneath the floor, and I didn't need to worry, they were certainly more integral to me than destructive.

On the day of Father's second death, the day I followed Mr Readers' Circle back to his home, we were already living in Mother's new flat. That day, Father didn't die for anyone else and perhaps that is why his second death hurt me more, pain endured in solitude is always more violent because it has no company to soften it. Father's second death was so painful, that it retroactively contaminated the first one, imbuing it with a pain it would have been impossible for me to feel at the age of five. At that age, I was only just learning what pain was and my unique fatherless status had its perks. As I was the only one who exhibited the strange quality of not having a father, I was given preference when playing, I was picked first when sides were chosen for duck-duck-goose or dodgeball, there was no birthday party I wasn't invited to, even the ones for children who lived in some of the posher neighbourhoods or whose houses were on the way to the camping ground and, at school, teachers hardly ever scolded me for not handing in my homework or not understanding the lesson.

At the time of Father's second death, being fatherless was no longer a novelty and no person or thing could save me from a greater pain. The Father who died the second time was no longer a clearly and vividly visualised Father, but a Father created by me as I began to embellish my need for a father figure and to channel my unrequited filial love. Perhaps that is why I told no-one about Father's second death.

At Mother's flat, the man from the electricity company would come into the hall to read the electricity meter and calculate our bill, the man from the water company did the same with the water meter beneath, the man from the gas company brought us the gas tanks and was the reason Mother shouted at me to be quick when washing my long hair. There were also the occasional visits, the man selling towel sets to be paid in instalments, the man who sold blinds, the night watchman and, among these other men, the man from the Readers' Circle, whose visits to Mother's house were difficult to anticipate, we never knew how soon or how often after dropping off the quarterly catalogues he would come by again asking if we had placed an order. Mother liked the mawkish Konsalik novels, I liked the books about unsolved enigmas like the Bermuda Triangle or UFOs. Despite the unwritten rule that Mother and I should take turns to choose from the quarterly catalogues, there was always the chance that we would say to each other that it was a shame to be so strict, citing some unmissable quality about a Konsalik novel or a book about alien abductions. When he came to take our order, the always affable man from the Readers' Circle, who when dropping off the catalogues might sometimes suggest some title or other, would limit himself to reading out our choices, as if my handwriting required some additional effort. I always filled out the order form, even when it was Mother's turn to choose. Unlike most of the other men who came to Mother's house, the man from the Readers' Circle never went past the front door. He would come with the catalogue one month, then return repeatedly until we had made our choice, and the following month he would come back with the chosen book and take our payment. Mother always failed to have the exact amount, so getting the correct change was often a problem. At the end of every visit he said goodbye with a serious nod, picked up his enormous leather folder and knocked on the door of the neighbour, who was also a member.

That's why I was left floored and stunned when I saw Mother and the man from the Readers' Circle at Docerina, both of them seated at the table nearest the entrance, drinking beer. As soon as I composed myself, I hid beneath the awning of the shoe shop across the road, waiting for my heart to recover and my ideas to unscramble. What was Mother doing at the pastry shop with the man from the Readers' Circle, instead of being at work at the bridal shop? Of course, Mother could have asked me the same question, I should have been at home, studying, instead of going to Cascais to eat Docerina's chocolate pyramids. They were the largest and the best chocolate pyramids in town, but that didn't justify me disobeying Mother and walking around Cascais on my own, especially when I had to study to achieve the enviable life that Mother had observed in some of her colleagues' daughters. I was half-hidden under the shoe shop's awning, trying to find a reason for Mother to be at Docerina with the man from the Readers' Circle, when they got up to leave. The man from the Readers' Circle lightly patted Mother's buttock, his hand brushing her discreetly but in a way that could only be interpreted as a gesture by a husband or a lover. They ambled slowly up the road and stopped in front of the Fim do Mundo, perhaps considering whether to have another beer. Only then did they disappear among the crowd of people swarming by the bus terminal's entrance.

I didn't tell anyone what I had seen at Docerina, not even Milena. I refused to see what I had seen, and to think what I should have thought, preferring instead to fabricate an intricate story about Soviet spies, the man from the Readers' Circle was in fact Father, who instead of dying had abandoned his mission and had to change his identity, as it often happened in films. Father wasn't a revolutionary, but a fearsome spy. He had faked his own death to save us from being in danger, but he loved us so much that he disguised himself as the man from the Readers' Circle to spend a bit of time with us. So then it all made sense, the man from the Readers' Circle and his reserve and formality, him and Mother ambling up the road as if they had long known each other, me not seeing Father's dead body when I was five. The next time the man from the Readers' Circle came to visit, I would be looking out for the evidence to confirm my theory. The fact that Father from the Readers' Circle looked nothing like Father from the portrait was also understandable, seven years had passed, and besides everyone knew that these sorts of spies had to change their appearance regularly, so the lack of similarity between the two didn't undermine my theory. As for Father not interacting with me beyond exchanging two or three sentences about the UFO books, it seemed obvious to me that it was to protect me and that he would have to continue acting that way until the day when he could disclose his identity, when we would fall into each other's arms.

Who knows how much longer I would have believed that tale, had I not been on Mother's roof terrace the day I spotted Father walking down the nearby street carrying a supermarket bag in each hand, instead of his usual leather folder full of book titles. I saw him head towards the new square, then turn right into one of the side streets. I went down the staircase of Mother's building with all the agility that my twelve-year-old legs would allow, and I followed Father at a safe distance all the way to the white buildings. When he walked past the third building Father knocked three times on the window of the ground floor flat. That knock was, surely, a code. A moment later, someone opened the door to the building. I drew closer as soon as Father entered, the door was locked but I was hopeful that, despite the drawn curtains, I might catch a glimpse of the spies' headquarters through the window Father had knocked on. The curtains were translucent and, instead of the tables strewn with cigarettes, documents, typewriters and surly men from spy films, there was a table set for lunch not unlike Mother's table, a woman more beautiful than Mother and two horrid children who appeared to be roughly my age. Everything started to look blurry, but, no, I wasn't crying. I didn't cry for Father's first death and I didn't cry for his second death. I ran away from the place, that's all, I ran away as fast as I could.

Had I planned my actions consciously that day at the hospital, I wouldn't have expected Mother to welcome Grandma into my old room, but whatever was causing my uncharacteristic behaviour that day stopped me from offering the usual yes, yes, right, right, and instead made me say, I'm not interested in a pity competition, but you accuse Grandma of forgetting you'd lost a husband while you forget she also became a widow at an even younger age than you did. Mother didn't wait for me to finish talking before she countered, That's the last thing I needed, you reminding me of that ridiculous story about your grand-father the travelling performer, don't make me laugh, your poor grandmother, my heart bleeds for her, if you really want to know, I feel no pity whatsoever for the old woman, you reap what you sow, I'm not surprised she's lost her marbles. Mother appeared to be relishing what lay in store for Grandma, she would stop making sense, she would forget everything, she would behave foolishly, when the head went there was no way back, Grandma couldn't continue to live alone, she would need someone to take care of her, she would need to be looked after every second, she would become more helpless than a baby, a giant baby, sick, ugly and smelly, a burden.

Your grandmother doesn't deserve you ruining your life for her, don't forget she didn't even give you your own room, be careful what you get into, at your age you should be enjoying life, you don't want to throw that away, do you? Mother wanted to persuade me that my life would be destroyed by a hurricane stronger even than Hurricane Gilberto, the hurricane that struck the first night we slept in Mother's new place. That first night, as we were making my bed, from the living room came the sound of the black and white television, still showing images of the chaos that Hurricane Gilberto had left in the places it had passed through, roofless houses, fallen trees, waves dragging boats out, when Mother asked, as she stopped stretching out the blankets, I wonder who names hurricanes? So many things happened on the day Mother finally entered a flat she could call her own, almost eleven years after my birth forced her to live in Grandma's house, and when I thought about that day the first thing that came to mind was Mother's question, I wonder who names hurricanes?

Hurricane Gilberto had destroyed everything in its path, but Grandma's unexpected return to my daily life wouldn't cause any major disruption, Grandma might be depressed, the consultant had warned us about that, but all it would

take was for Grandma to take her medication and everything would be as it was, Grandma wouldn't need me in
a way that was different to how I wanted her to need me.
No, Grandma's disease wouldn't be any sort of hurricane,
nor would I be giving up my life. I had spent the past twenty
years lost from myself, busy with raising the girls, first
Márcia, then Márcia and Inês, at one point both were in
nappies, I would use the weekends to change the sheets
and do four loads of laundry, not to mention Jorge's shirts,
which always needed special care, I had spent the past
twenty years stuck in dead-end jobs, sitting in traffic or
standing in supermarket queues, letting my thighs get fat,
neglecting my hair colouring, spending my weekends on the
sofa in "Nikey" and "Avivas" tracksuits, eating two-for-one
chocolates, falling asleep halfway through films, I had spent
the past twenty years missing out on the fashions that I
saw in shop windows, hating the summer because it forced
me to uncover my embarrassing body parts, putting off my
plans to straighten my crooked tooth and to start doing
regular walks, I had spent the past twenty years envying
women who recover from their pregnancies in a few weeks,
the ones who wear high-heel shoes with the elegance of
ballerinas, the ones whose legs are already bronzed in
March, who travel unaccompanied, who can talk about
any subject, who ride motorcycles and know karate, for the
past twenty years my life had been on hold and now that
I could pick it up again, now that I could once again concentrate on my own plans, because our forties were the new
thirties or even the new twenties, now that I could enjoy
those brunches that Milena kept talking about and drink

61

mojitos at sunset as if night would never come, now that I had resolved to learn aromatherapy and Mandarin so I could sell houses to the Chinese, to correct my posture and to plant parsley, rosemary and chives in the raised beds near our building's storage units, Grandma wouldn't derail my plans, Grandma had always spared her much-loved and only grandchild any trouble and would surely continue to do so. If you want my advice, said Mother in a false attempt at reconciliation, when she is discharged, take her to her own home and hire someone to go and look after her, there's nothing like one's own place, it won't be easy to find someone to put up with her, but there's no harm in trying. Mother started sweeping the peanut shells off the tabletop with her hand, as if the task of putting the shells into the plastic bag required all her concentration. Every now and then, drifting up from the ground floor, chords of happy music brought to my mind the faces of the first generation of Indian tenants who lived there and, with them, the circles of light dancing among the pine tree tops in the old valley, the voices of the resin tappers with their iron gouges and tin cups, Milena and me collecting wild berries, our hands tinged purple. Don't worry, I'll manage, I said, getting up and rearranging the chair. I put into my gestures the same elegance and formality I used when meeting with my boss and with the agency's managers.

Mother followed me to the door. In Mother's tired footsteps I could hear, as if from the future, my own tired footsteps, Mother was a preview of the decline that lay in store for me. In Mother's limping body, my own limping body, in Mother's wheeziness, my own wheeziness, in the hairs on Mother's chin, the hairs on my own chin, the hairs signalling my infertility to all males. With my departure now imminent Mother went on the offensive again, I'm sure that, when you calm down, you'll see that what you're asking of me is unfair, you cannot expect anyone to take over your duties. Mother should have known to stop, she should have understood that I wasn't being my usual self. If she had, perhaps I wouldn't have said, What I'm asking for isn't absurd, and you shouldn't think of it as an imposition, to let Grandma stay with you for a few days would be minimal payback for all the help she gave you. I knew I was sticking the knife into the place where it hurt most, You can believe whatever stories you tell yourself, that you were Mother Courage raising a daughter single-handedly after her husband's early death, but you know it was Grandma who raised me, if Grandma was as evil as you say she was you should have gone to your own parents' home, maybe you would have been treated better there. Mother opened her mouth, but then shut it again without saying anything. We remained face to face for a few long seconds and Mother didn't do what she usually did, the melodramatic gestures, the high-pitched voice, the quiet tears, none of it. You know very well that my parents couldn't take us in, she finally muttered. And, with no hint of emotion, she added, It's not your fault, your father was just the same as you, it's in your blood.

Sometimes I thought that we had all come into the world with the sole purpose of bringing things home, things that had no use other than to clutter wardrobes, shelves, boxes, under-the-bed drawers, the larders and, that most sacred of places, the storage unit. Ours was on the ground floor, down the corridor next to the service lift, through the iron gate leading to the large rectangular patio with the storage units arranged along the back and the side walls. The units, painted in pink, were variously sized according to their capacity, and had green metallic doors. Some of the more cautious owners had added door latches, and it was rare to have a building committee meeting where at least one of them didn't suggest replacing the doors, arguing that it would be very easy for delinquents to break in with the existing ones. The replacement never happened, there were often more urgent works to be undertaken, or, if not, the other owners, including us, just shrugged our shoulders about the danger, there's never been a problem and those are the original doors, we would say by way of excuse, as if the proposed replacement might take one step too far the many architectural changes to which the building had already been subjected. It was almost seven o'clock on another nice summer evening when, having emptied two drawers in Márcia's chest of drawers, I carried some junk-filled bags down to the storage unit. Grandma wouldn't be staying long in our flat, but she would need somewhere to keep the few things she brought with her, above all she would need Márcia's room to once again become a room instead of the improvised storage space that, in her absence, we had turned it into.

It was Jorge who suggested that Grandma might come to stay with us, when I told him that the doctors had warned against her being alone, at least until she was seen by a specialist. She can stay with us a few weeks, Jorge agreed, and the following day I proudly told the doctors, nurses and hospital assistants that, as soon as Grandma was discharged, I would take her home with me. I didn't say what Jorge always added, It will only be a few days. At first, I understood Jorge's words to be a form of kindness, he was trying to say that there was nothing to be worried about, no need to thank him, but I soon realised my mistake, it was in fact a cautionary note, a warning, Let's make sure it's only a few days, don't think this can just drag on. I didn't want Grandma to live with us any longer than her recovery needed, but it hurt me that Jorge was planning our future according to his own wishes, acting in a way that prevented me from expressing my own, so that even if I wanted or felt an obligation to act in another way regarding Grandma, I wouldn't be able to. Even though Grandma's stay at our place was going to be short, Márcia's room had to be in a suitable state and so, at seven o'clock on a Sunday evening there I was shuffling between the untidiness of Márcia's room and the untidiness of the storage unit.

Family arguments about what we kept in the storage unit were frequent, because each one of us, wanting our own possessions safely stored and easily accessible, was deaf to any suggestion that a particular thing would hardly ever be used again and so continued fighting for the best place to keep it. My relationship with things was similar to the one I had with people, a brief acquaintance might quickly awaken affection or at the very least possession, and then it wasn't easy for me to get rid of anything I had considered mine, even for a short while. Not so much because I thought it might be useful, but because I didn't want to lose something that I felt affection for or had been mine or had served a useful purpose, I didn't want to lament hasty losses that might later come back to haunt me. Collecting before definitively and dispassionately moving on. That's how it was with people, perhaps that's also how it was with things.

For one reason or another, over the years, we had accumulated junk, junk and more junk, until there was hardly any space. Beneath it all, like the foundations of the precarious structure growing in the storage unit, were the unused tiles from when, a long time ago, we had redone the small toilet, and cans filled with left-over paint we had kept thinking that it might be useful to paint a spare room, because the future would surely be filled with spare rooms in need of a coat of paint. On top of this base, we piled the rest of the junk, most of it in boxes of many sizes and plastic bags of many colours and provenances. Upon arrival at the storage unit, everything lost its identity, forming a compact but mobile mass, occasionally releasing pieces that once again acquired their individuality, like Jorge's fishing rod, stacked near the entrance, and falling on top of me with every move of the storage unit Tetris, as I tried to make space to stash away the things I had brought down from Márcia's bedroom.

Seven o'clock on a summer evening and me breathing from the belly to calm myself, the only lesson I remember from the yoga sessions I attended while pregnant with Inês. As a relaxation technique it proved to be powerless against the chaos within the storage unit and the chaos of memories I was dragged into every time I opened a box, trying to establish its contents and find the best way of adding the new junk to the old, without damaging any of the things that would probably never be used again. I caught glimpses of my life, some sharper, others duller, some shinier, others drearier. As I opened a box, my Banco Português do Atlântico address books, and me, at the start of every year, at Mother's flat, in my bedroom, sitting at the fake pinewood Moviflor desk, copying the list of names and phone numbers I wanted to keep from the address book for the year that had ended into the new year's address book. We started getting the black address books from the BPA the day Mother took out a loan for the flat. The address books were a little freebie that the bank gave its customers in compensation for keeping them captive until the loan was paid or until death did them part. Mother was only supposed to get one per year, but she always found the way to identify a bank clerk who might succumb to her pleas and slip her an extra address book that she would pass on to me, a man or a woman about whom Mother would say, so nice, there are still good people in this world. Letters A and C in the address books had the most names, followed by letters L and M. In 1988, I almost filled all the pages and, judging by the notes in the address book, it was the year when I was most popular, I wrote the letter "I" in front of the names of ten boys. I had agreed the code with Milena, who also used it in her own address books. Boys we were interested in were marked with an "I", the boys we should forget had a cross next to their name and the ones we were undecided about were given a question mark. The girls needed more symbols attached to their names: exclamation marks, numbers, money signs, squares, circles, different types of brackets, various letters. I could no longer decipher the annotations, partly because their exact meaning had changed over time, but I could still remember that we ranked girls based on how much we liked them, which depended on two main criteria, the type of clothes they wore and whether they had shown any interest in the boys we were interested in. I could no longer visualise the faces belonging to many of those names, for some of them, including boys marked with an "I", I had only a name and a phone number, who was Mario, 266486? Was I also in a box somewhere in his home, now only Eliete, 280723? In all my address books, Christopher, the photographer, was the first name under the letter C, full name and address, no "I" and no cross and no question mark, a name that moved on from year to year and whose face I couldn't remember because, for me, Christopher never had one. The abbreviation for best friend was written next to Milena's name in every address book, and Milena did the same with my name in her address books. It wasn't just the misfortune of being average in everything, in our beauty, in our intelligence, in our homes and our families, that united us, there were so many average girls, there had to be something else. Perhaps it was the coincidence of living in nearby buildings and of having a similar destiny, not the long-term destinies of our lives, those would diverge, even if never enough to make us lose contact with one another, but our day-to-day destinies back then, the same secondary school, Tchipepa ice-cream parlour, where we went to eat cakes topped with whipped cream, Tamariz beach, the 2001 nightclub. We spent years traipsing, together, across the depressing new square on the way to the minibus stop, then trying to keep our balance, holding on to each other, despite the swerving and sudden stops on the way to the train station, where we caught another mini-bus, towards Torre, and once again the balancing, the swerving and the sudden stops all the way to the bullring, which was next to the school, in Bairro do Rosário, a neighbourhood where wealth was displayed discreetly in sober residences with uniformed maids cleaning windows and gardeners shearing their way through the quiet spring and autumn mornings. I was sure that Milena wanted to be one of the girls living in those houses, a posh girl, but she never admitted it. I too wanted to be a posh girl, genuinely posh, and I always kept it to myself. We shouldn't have wanted to be one of the posh kids from Linha, we should have hated them, we, who belonged to the huge mass that those types of kids despised, we, the people, that abstract concept they had heard about on the television, we, the riff-raff, the plebs, the ones with no silver spoon and no family name to rely on, the abominables, the nobodies from the ugly suburbs of Cascais, we should want to finish them off, instead of wanting to be one of them, we should be glad to have avoided the weirdness of cross-breeding that, so often, made their faces ugly and their bodies crooked, there were few of them and they bred among themselves, there were many of us and we would breed with whoever we could. Even though they had always known about us, the posh kids still looked at us with the same surprise they might have shown if their pets had suddenly taken over their lives, dogs learning to read, chickens going to the disco, pigs spending time on the beach, cows driving, they were surprised to find us taking over the spaces that had once been exclusively theirs. The surprise was certainly hereditary, because those posh kids in our generation, unlike their parents, grandparents and great-grandparents, had only ever known a world that was permeable to our presence. Those poor posh kids in their blue blazers and golden buttons, their neckerchiefs and buckled shoes, helpless witnesses to the vanishing of the world they once knew. Not that the new world was better and fairer, not at all, it was merely a paradigm shift, as the talking heads on the television always said about everything and anything.

The posh kids were banished to the past when, rooting around in another box, I found one of my poetry note-books. Suddenly, on the storage unit's mottled tiled floor, my hesitant and adolescent handwriting, *For Marco, The walls crumbled, I am still imprisoned, Night does not extinguish the fire, Come, eternal belated morning, Trembling moon, you are nothing more than . . . ,* then a blank space waiting for the next word, the right word, me and my naïve belief that the right word existed, even if I could never discover it. *Trembling moon, you are nothing more than . . . ,* and me tripping over boxes and over the past, a past unlike the one in Mother's flat that hurled me against the present and saddened me, in this past every recollection seemed to have gained the peace of its definitive place, my poetry notebook open on the floor and Marco and me embracing on the rocks of Inferno beach, in the alley near Rainha beach, in the hidden-away parts of Guia beach, Marco with his grand dream that I so admired, to perform for thousands of fans with a guitar just like the one Bryan Adams had, a Cherry-Red Fender Stratocaster, Marco who asked about my dreams, who was certain I too had dreams, Everyone has dreams, he would say, and me, after much thinking, would come up with a list of humdrum wishes, stop wearing glasses, pass my exams, find a job, get a driver's licence, buy a car, What car, Marco asked, doubtful, I don't know, maybe a Ford Taunus? I ventured, knowing that this would be the wrong answer, that I should say one of those complicated car names with letters and numbers that Marco often talked about. That is what everyone wants, Marco would protest, those aren't dreams, a dream is something that is yours alone, think about something that only you can do, a way of leaving your mark on the world, I thought about it, I thought and came up with nothing, I insisted on the driver's licence, the car, the job, a

71

house, a husband, a week's holiday in the Algarve, healthy children, perhaps Marcos wanted to hear me say, I want to have children, a child is a mark we leave on the world, isn't it? Mother had me when she was more or less my age and now I too was a young woman, now everything could happen. Frustrated, Marco temporarily gave up on finding me a dream and focused instead on his more immediate desire, he unbuttoned his trousers, pulled my hand into his pants, See how I like you more every day. I never had the nerve to ask him how his stiffened cock might be a measure of his growing love, and that mystery took up more of my thoughts than the dreams I was unable to conjure. Once we got past his instructions for how to handle his cock so it would show his growing love, and the promises of love he made while I followed his instructions, because girls liked to hear boys' promises of love and boys liked girls to be obedient, Marco would go back to his dreams and the photograph of the Cherry-Red Fender Stratocaster he kept in his wallet. I never met anyone else who used his cock as an instrument to measure love quite as categorically, or who carried a photo of a guitar in his wallet.

The first time he asked, Do you want to see the photograph I have in my wallet? I was certain that he had cut mine out of one of our yearbooks and my heart leaped with joy, Marco's cock was, indeed, like an oracle, he truly and madly liked me. I closed my eyes for a moment to better savour, when I opened them again, the pleasure of seeing myself in Marco's wallet. Although I had always told Milena almost everything and had given her detailed descriptions of Marco's cock and how it worked, because Milena hadn't yet been introduced to one, I couldn't have found the words to describe my disappointment, even if I had wanted to. In reality, Marco and I were not dating, we were just going out, to date was tacky, and romance was a forbidden word.

After a few weeks of going out, Marco decided to find me a dream, insisting that no-one could live without dreams. If you liked singing, Marco said, you could be the lead singer of the band I'll have. I explained that I had never even been chosen to sing Christmas carols at Sunday school, despite the group being so large as to charitably include almost everyone. Maybe a dancer, Marco suggested, but he would himself drop the idea when he remembered my clumsy moves on the 2001 nightclub dancefloor. Maybe film, you're always at the cinema, how about an actress, a Hollywood actress, like the ones at the Oscars? I'm too short, I would reply, as if that were the real problem, and my English isn't good. How about painting? There are some very famous painters, Marco added, with some uncertainty, because he could barely remember one and only then because that painter had cut his ear off. That, too, wouldn't work, it was clear from my art and design grades at school. Writing? Anyone can write, Marco said, as satisfied as if I had discovered new ways to handle his cock, you could write poetry, girls are dead keen on that. I wasn't hugely excited by this, but to avoid being accused of not trying, I started writing poetry in the lined Hello Kitty notebooks that I bought at the stationery shop, on Rua da Polícia, next to the pharmacy where Mother bought her counterfeit

Bien Être. Marco, who had never read a poem, invented for me the dream of becoming a poet and, almost thirty years later, pages and pages of bad poetry were still there in the boxes, *Trembling moon, you are nothing more than . . . ,* a blank space for the word I never found, the word that might allow me to finally bring the poem into existence. No matter how hard I tried I was always at a loss for words. But while my own dream dwindled, Marco's continued to grow, only a few months later he no longer just wanted to play the guitar, he was going to be the front-man for a band like the Rolling Stones, go on world tours, make so much money that he would live in the most expensive suites in luxury hotels, fill his bath with champagne, he would have a collection of convertible cars, Marco's dream grew grander by the day while mine languished in the verses that lacked the words that would save them from the anonymity of a Hello Kitty notebook.

A few years before that evening in the storage unit, I had come across Marco on Facebook. I hadn't seen him since the end of secondary school, but I found out, browsing his profile, that he had married a chubby woman who, in one of the photographs on her timeline, wore tiger print Lycra tights and counterfeit sunglasses. He looked fat, had two teenage sons, one dead-eyed and the other bow-legged. Thank goodness we had Facebook to show us that, regardless of the dreams we may have cherished, we all ended up the same, old and fat, too bitter about the small defeats life had handed us, too opinionated, quarrelsome, alone. Among the thousands of photographs that Marco posted over the years, not a single one of a Cherry-Red Fender

Stratocaster, Facebook arrived too late to immortalise his dream. I didn't send him a friend request.

I had put away the poetry notebook when I noticed that Jorge's ZX Spectrum was at the bottom of the box. I knew he had been looking for it for some time and that he would be happy to see it again. I used my phone to take a photograph of the old machine and sent it to Jorge. As soon as I closed the box, I cursed the fishing rod that once again fell on my head. The fishing rod hadn't been used more than three times, because in the end Jorge realised he didn't like having to wait for the fish to take the hook, he didn't like the beer getting warm in the icebox, the slippery live bait, the rubber boots, the rocks, the wind, and that is how the fishing rod and the days of peace and communing with nature went into storage.

Next to Jorge's fishing junk was a rucksack for rock-climbing that once belonged to Inês, who discovered she suffered from vertigo when she was three metres off the ground, an exfoliator from Lidl that Márcia used to get rid of the tiny spots that blemished her luminous skin, the wind chime I had bought because of a film whose title I could no longer remember and that came in one of the ten-film bundles we used to rent from the video club in Bairro da Asunção. In the film there was a balcony decorated with many wind chimes, their melodic tinkles stoking and setting the pace for the lovers' passion. Years later, I bought a wind chime in a novelty shop at the Riyadh Shopping Centre, hoping that it would have a similar effect on our balcony and in our bedroom, that Jorge and I would be moving our bodies together to its sweet sound and its slow tinkles. For weeks the wind chime remained wrapped inside a bag in a corner by the entrance, because we were always missing something we needed to hang it up, the drill bit, the plug, the hook, the will, until finally one Saturday, Jorge climbed onto the stepladder with the power drill. But instead of being caressed by a soft Florida breeze, our balcony was lashed by furious gusts of wind, turning the melodic tinkling from the film into a wild and incessant concert for percussions that only jangled our nerves. We put up with the racket for a few days, surprised at not having noticed how windy our balcony was, but after coming across some of our neighbours' grouchy faces in the lift, Jorge climbed up the stepladder again. The wind chime went back into the bag, this time abandoned in a corner near the balcony, awaiting a calm night when it might once again return to the heights to finally delight us. Rain came along instead of calm nights so the wind chime went into the storage unit. There it remained, in anticipation of the beach house we would buy one day, a beach house or a country house where, in the stillness of the front balcony, the wind chime would ring sleepily in the breeze. In the storage unit, it was one thing lost among many other things, in anticipation of a life that was not yet our life, but that we hoped might be, a thing awaiting the day of triumph when one of us would exclaim, it was worth holding on to you! Until we reached that other life at least we would be able to return to that one thing and recover it among all the others. That was how it was with things, perhaps that was also how it was with people.

I paused. I was too lazy to go upstairs so I sat on the

gravel floor, with my back to the storage unit's outside wall, not caring that the neighbours would see me defeated by the task of tidying up and defeated by the past. I pulled out my phone and, before sending Jorge the photo of the ZX Spectrum, I had a peek at his Facebook. I was still in the habit of scrolling through his timeline even though, for some time now, I had done it more serenely. At first, I was very jealous of the likes and the messages exchanged between Jorge and some of his women friends I didn't know. Even if they were only virtual friendships and would remain that way, I was more hurt by Jorge's interactions with them than I was the day he took Inês, cheeky Inês, into work. It rarely happened, it was usually me staying at home with the girls when school was shut, it was either me or their other grandmother, because Mother always had an excuse not to spend time with her granddaughters, Dona Herlanda had given her some last-minute task, she was scared that they might hurt themselves or fall off the balcony, she didn't know what to do with the girls because I didn't allow her to bond with her granddaughters, she was tired or had a cold and didn't want to pass it on, and, finally, the truth, I just can't be bothered. As I put her to bed the day Jorge took her to work, Inês asked me, What is hot stuff? still wearing her eyeglasses for correcting her lazy eye, the butterfly wing rucksack she liked so much at the foot of her bed. I explained that hot stuff was something that burned but Inês was confused because her father's work colleague had been fussing over her, she was even kissing her and Inês didn't get burned, even though Inês' father was saying to the lady that she was hot stuff. When I

77

went back to the living room I kicked off and for a few days didn't speak to Jorge, how dare he flirt with his work colleague in front of our daughter? How dare he let his work colleague touch my child? And yet, the flirting witnessed by Inês bothered me less than Jorge's virtual chit-chat with his lady friends, or those strangers he started calling friends when he signed up to Facebook. I didn't know what hurt me most, whether it was Jorge showing interest in other women, knowing full well I could see it, or the humiliation of our common friends witnessing it. It looked like my suffering would never end, every day there were new posts, new likes, new photos, new friends, I could read the conversations, study the emojis, the timing of responses, I could browse the women's profiles, just look at that slag, I heard myself saying in Mother's voice, and not even that stopped me. Over time I got used to it and stopped making a scene, I was quick to adapt to things I couldn't change. But I was never immune from the happiness that the slags displayed in the profiles, the infinity of other lives that, suddenly, became available, I worried that our life, mine and Jorge's, a real unedited life, might not withstand the pressure of virtual lives, I worried that other women's retouched bodies would triumph over mine, the imperfectly real body in all its substance as it lay down next to Jorge every night.

Jorge had published a selfie with Inês some ten minutes earlier. They were on our front balcony, the one that still had the hook for the wind chime but from which nothing ever hung. Jorge was raising a beer and Inês lifted a pink-coloured smoothie topped with whipped cream and decorated with one of the little paper umbrellas I had brought back from the holiday in Tenerife. They were sitting on the small hammock and smiling for the photograph. Inês was still wearing her beach clothes, a transparent tunic over her flower-patterned swim suit and rubber flip-flops. In the background, nicely framed, was the Sintra mountain range, and it was easy for me to see the satisfaction Jorge took from depicting the idyllic father–daughter relationship in the afternoon's golden light. The more I looked at the photograph, the more irritating I found everything about it, Jorge's inane grin, the disgraceful complicity between father and daughter, the message, in English, *I take nothing for granted, I now have only good days and great days*. When I looked at Inês, I thought about the sentence I had tapped into my phone the day before, I miss being young in summer. I missed being young in summer, walking by the ocean, from Tamariz beach to Cascais. I would walk along the seawall, saving up the train fare that Mother gave me reluctantly, With so many beaches in Cascais, what's so special about Estoril? she asked, those few times when she agreed to open her concertina wallet and take out a twenty-escudo note. Back then the seawall was still a solitary place, useful only to temper the waves' fury and as a haven for exhibitionists, fishermen, amateur thieves and careless tourists, it smelled of the sea-breeze that, sometimes, became a strange fog clouding the view of the coast as it curved in the distance as far as Cascais. To travel on foot was still something for the poor, walking was for those not wealthy enough to drive a car, and the thieves in the area were not yet professionals, who would want to be a professional thief in a place that was almost deserted. So thieves back then would wait for careless tourists with the same patience with which fishermen, sitting by their rods on the edge of the seawall, and more persistent than Jorge, waited for a tug on their lines. The seawall didn't yet have cafés or lounges with pouffes or sunset bars, the seawall was just the seawall and the sunset was just the sunset, it wasn't yet an event celebrated and shared in thousands of photographs. At that point, everything could happen to me, I was a young woman and the men I came across liked my long hair à la Cindy Crawford, dark, strong and silky hair like in the television adverts, deceptively alluring. Men became aroused by the beauty of my hair, only to become disappointed by my face. Not because I was an ugly girl, but averageness was even less alluring than ugliness, very few could fail to be disappointed by my skin that wasn't quite dark, but not fair either, yellowed skin, dull, by my hooked nose with its wide nostrils, by my eyes so banal in their almond-shape that they made me look lethargic. Even so, men catcalled me and I felt it was my fault, by going on foot to the seawall I had ignored Grandma's warnings and Mother's orders, and because of that I had to put up with whatever the men said to me. But guilt was soon overtaken by relief, because the worse thing of all would have been for the men not to catcall me. If the men catcalled all the other girls but not me it would have meant there was something wrong with me. Even if I was scared by the desire darkening the eyes of those men, some as old as Father would have been had he not died, I felt relieved when I heard them say what they wanted to do to me. Relieved and guilty. And all the more guilty the more relieved I felt.

Once I was in my thirties, it didn't take long for Mother to start criticising my hair. It was at a birthday party for one of the girls, I can't remember which, You're too old to wear your hair so long, it looks like a horse's mane, Mother said, with her short hair curled in like Doctor Helena Russell from the TV series Space: 1999, and some years later, Jorge, as we were getting ready to attend a meeting about a time-share in the Algarve, Maybe such long hair isn't a good idea anymore, and finally Inês, None of my friends' mothers have hair as long as yours. So the day finally arrived when my hair in the style of Cindy Crawford ended up in a small pile on the floor of the salon, next door to the bakery that, on Saturday nights, sold cakes secretly through a hole in the wall. There appeared to be a sadism in the satisfaction with which the hairdresser cut away the youth I had been so determined to preserve and which, unlike my hair, would never grow back again. Not content with that, he dared to suggest that I should get highlights, at a certain age all women go blonde, he said, smiling, and me thinking, fuck off, which came out as, I won't have time to do it today. Unlike Milena, I was never able to use swear words, even if I said them in my head and, very often, wanted to say them out loud. I felt I was welling up, I said I had developed a sudden allergy to hairspray and never again returned to that salon.

I stood up, leaning against the rough wall. I hurried back into the storage unit and tried to take a photograph of the boxes, choosing an angle in which my legs could be seen. The photograph would have to meet two challenging criteria, first my legs would have to appear to have been accidentally photographed, and second, they would have to appear to be slimmer and more toned than they really were. After experimenting with various filters and croppings, I achieved a perfect photograph of my legs, a photograph that didn't appear to be a photograph of my legs and where my legs didn't appear to be my legs. I posted it with the message, working hard, adding a tired face emoji. I thought of writing a reply to Jorge's post that would make him feel bad, a cute comment so that he and Inês would feel guilty about not helping me, but looking again at Jorge's Facebook profile I noticed that some unknown woman had already commented on the photograph, Your daughter is gorgeous, she takes after you, followed by a winking face emoji.

Instead of posting a comment, I decided to browse the unknown woman's profile. Do you know Isabel Sousa? To see what she is sharing with friends, send her a friend request. Whoever Isabel Sousa was, there wasn't much to see in her profile without being her friend. Her face was half-covered in her three profile photographs, a hint that she might not be very attractive. She had shared songs, some of those beloved quotes that the Internet is filled with, Improbable does not mean impossible, The world needs people who are crazy – crazy for one another, photographs of beaches and sunsets, Christmas trees and French toast, popular saints and sardines. The comments to her photos came mostly from other women, Gorgeous, Amazing, Happy holiday, You deserve the best, So good to see you happy, and lots of hearts, flowers and dolls. I kept browsing until I found a photo album with the hashtag #tableforone, the euphemism for single women. Another one of those hussies on the hunt, I thought, calling herself #tableforone, but I bet the bed was for two. If I found the coyness of Jorge's new friend reassuring because it suggested that she might not be physically attractive, I was disturbed by her apparent availability to other women's husbands, I felt sure she was one of those women who brags, Married men are not off-limits. I browsed her friends' profiles, they were the sort of women who said goodbye using asterisks or xxx as kisses, the few posts I was able to read were like the ones in the #tableforone folder, song lyrics and self-help quotes, to see any more I had to send a friend request. What do these people have to hide, I wondered, who wants to know anything about their lives? They must think of themselves as celebrities. If there was one activity I carried out with great diligence it was being a Facebook detective. Scrolling through the comments to photographs, I jumped from one profile to another and another, until I found a friend in common with #tableforone, who interacted frequently with Jorge. Bingo. I realised she worked in computing, she must be the new work colleague that Jorge mentioned some time ago. I clicked again on the profile photographs. #Tableforone lady seemed to have curly hair, fish-eyes, thin lips, fake jewellery decorating her double chin. She is fated to booking a #tableforone and getting compliments from her friends, I reassured myself. Even so, I had to mark out my territory and my cute post should do the job, Am I not the luckiest woman to have a family like this one? Jorge and

Inês might not notice the irony, but what mattered most was that the rest of the world, who didn't know what was happening, would think of me as a lucky woman, especially #tableforone. And how would they not consider me a lucky woman, I was more interesting than the other women who shared my interests. In fact, none of them could get as many likes and comments as the photograph of my legs had already gathered, and increasingly that mattered most, more important than what we did was the number of people who liked, or commented on, what we did. One of the comments, from a colleague in a competing estate agency who had invited me out for a coffee many times before, was particularly pleasing, *nice pins*, he wrote alongside the indispensable eye wink and rolling on the floor with laughter emojis. The comment, so hackneyed and so trivial, reconciled me with the world. I put the phone back in my pocket and got back to reordering. I was still upset about the depression that had scrambled Grandma's head, and to make matters worse at the start of summer, about Mother who refused to help me, about Jorge and Inês who had avoided the task of reordering the storage unit, but I felt better because a man, a man I didn't have the least interest in, had complimented my legs, a man who was very definitely married and had a whole litter of children and was flirting with me.

I was almost done with the storage. One more trip back to the flat and I would bring down what was left. As I re-entered life I opened Facebook again, an automatic gesture. Jorge hadn't responded to my post or my comment. He had, on the other hand, reacted with a smile to

#tableforeone's comment. The lift hadn't gone past the second floor and I had already responded with a smile of my own to the colleague who had complimented my legs, it took the lift longer to climb the six floors than it took me to scan Jorge's Facebook and flirt with my colleague. Outside of the virtual world, real life moved slowly. When I arrived at the sixth floor, I looked in the lift's mirror. I ran the tip of my index finger over the dark circles under my eyes foretelling my period, I looked out for the white roots in my hair, at the temples and on my forehead, I studied the looseness of the skin around my face, the dryness of my lips, the wrinkles on my forehead. Middle age, I thought. What did middle age mean, that I had little left to gain or to lose? The first half of my life was spent and what remained, all being well, was the half of my decline. Middle age also meant, I reflected, that my life was the result of decisions taken many years ago, it meant that I had never again rethought it, that the inertia, the force of habit and fear of the unknown had made me accept, often without realising it, the paths I was travelling down. In middle age, the time of choices was left behind, choosing belonged to adolescence, to early adulthood. Should I study sciences or humanities? Should I try drugs? Should I do what Marcos' cock wanted me to do? Should I take a shitty job or wait for the one I deserved? Should I move in with Jorge? Should I stop taking the pill? The adrenaline rush of choice, the stress of making decisions belonged in a distant past. There was nothing left to decide or to choose from now, life was packed and bundled, it wasn't easy to pick apart, it wasn't easy to unwrap. And it hardly mattered that death, my own death, had stopped being an abstraction and was now peering back from the mirror. On second thoughts, there might have been some mockery in the comment about my legs made by the colleague from the competing agency. I unliked it, exited the lift and entered the flat.

Jorge and Inês were on the living room sofa. I should have guessed that the image of the idyllic relationship between father and daughter would have lasted no longer than it took to take the photograph and post it on Facebook, they would have spent most the time on the sofa, each in their own corner, each entertained with his or her phone and earphones. The television, with the volume lowered, was tuned to a news channel showing a debate from the night before, while a question scrolled along the bottom of the screen, Should the United Kingdom turn its back on Europe? but neither Jorge nor Inês were watching the television and, had it not been because a current of air swayed the curtains, they wouldn't even have realised I had come in. Do you need help, Jorge asked, pulling out one of his earphones. Because I didn't respond, my silence was taken as a negative and he replaced the earphone and got back to his screen. With Jorge, silence created more misunderstandings than words. Inês picked up the remote control, This is so boring, and she switched away from the debate and the pros and cons of the United Kingdom leaving the European Union. Now the television showed a competition where some Germans, in twos and threes, strolled naked around a paradisal island, looking for love.

I opened WhatsApp and walked along the corridor. There on my screen, sitting on her bed in her pyjamas, was Márcia. She had her phone on her lap, and was wearing stripy socks and loose hair. With that plain look she resembled her grandmother, and seemed prettier. I'm back in your room, darling, I said, the last drawer, just a few minutes and I'll leave you alone. I pointed the phone's camera towards the yellow coat with two embroidered bees. What about this coat? I asked, sure that Márcia would be happy to see it again. That's hideous, throw it out, she replied, without hesitation. I don't know whether I was more unsettled by the speed of her response, or by being so wrong about it. When you were a little girl you hardly took it off, I thought you might want to keep it as a souvenir, remember those photographs from our trip to the Picos de Europa? I directed Márcia's gaze, which I held in my hands, towards the corkboard covered with photographs, You always wanted to wear that coat, do you remember that trip? We still had the pushchair, you and Inês went for a swim in a pond in that orchard by the side of the road, it was unbearably hot in the daytime and the nights were freezing cold, and the views, my goodness, they took my breath away, those mountains, do you remember that? Márcia seemed increasingly impatient, I can only remember the gecko, she said. What gecko? I asked.

Márcia hadn't yet said a word, and already the gecko trapped under the door had appeared in my mind. It was as if, for years, the gecko had applied in my memory the same camouflage mechanism that it uses in nature to go unnoticed by its enemies, merging chromatically with its surroundings, and the mechanism had suddenly stopped working at that precise moment, making the creature reveal itself at last. All those years, I had often seen the Picos de Europa photographs and they had reminded me of the vastness of the starry sky, of how much I missed my little girls, I had heard the stories of friends who had spent holidays there, I had walked past posters in travel agency displays, and in all that time never once, not even vaguely, had there been the memory of a trapped gecko. At that moment, however, all those other memories seemed a mere backdrop, the pattern against which I was able to see the contours of a body, the gecko's. The story of the gecko, a banal story, could be told in a single breath. One night, at the campsite, the girls had wanted to go to the toilets on their own, they had started wanting to feel they could do things without their parents. Minutes later they returned, breathless and distressed, because there was a gecko trapped under a door. When we arrived, Jorge and I thought the gecko was dead, but Inês noticed it was moving one of its legs slightly, it's alive, she shouted. Márcia started crying, the gecko is hurt, it must be in a lot of pain, and it wasn't long before Inês was also crying. The girls had no particular fondness for animals, and even less for geckos, but, by moving its leg, that gecko seemed to be asking for help and Márcia insisted that we should help it, that we should save it. Days were too long for the girls during our holidays, tiredness made them longer still, childhood, as ever, was too long in its brevity. Childhood is long but life is brief. Jorge freed the gecko and put it in a plastic bag, I will take it to the man at reception, he said. What will they do to it, asked Inês, always the more quarrelsome of the two. They will take care of it, there are lots of geckos here, they're used to dealing with them, Jorge replied, stumbling over his words, in a hurry to take away the gecko in the plastic bag. I don't know why you lied to us, it was obvious that dad was going to kill the gecko, Márcia said. That revelation, so many years later, through my phone's screen, Márcia's voice echoing weirdly and her face distorted by its proximity to the camera, turned a seemingly insignificant thing into something strangely serious and I almost cried. I'm sorry, I stuttered. What are you sorry about, Mum, it was a gecko, for goodness' sake, Márcia laughed. And then she told me about an Italian neighbour, good looking, educated, with a sense of humour, well dressed, knew how to cook, he would be the perfect man if she didn't already have a boyfriend waiting for her to return. Forget about the Italians, we miss you here, I said, and I tried to crack a joke about our local produce being best, but I felt desperately alone, as if the story of the gecko had made me suddenly and sharply aware of how every mind was a prison, every life, each one of us busy with our lives, living in our own heads, until, one day, somebody with a harmless plastic bag . . .

Can I throw this out as well, I asked before hanging up, showing her a pack of cigarettes, almost full, that I had discovered in one of the drawers. Pretending not to notice my disapproving tone, Márcia joked, Don't even think about it, that's worth a fortune, you can't imagine how expensive they are here. Because I found myself in that tearful and sentimental state, I felt tempted to reach for the words that Grandma always used, whenever she was sending me off into the world, but instead of saying God bless you, like her, I simply repeated my usual Lots of kisses, darling. Márcia disappeared, I pressed the side button on my phone and the screen went black.

I was finished tidying up Márcia's bedroom. I only had to put into the rubbish bins whatever needed to be thrown out and find space in the storage room for the last few bags of knick-knacks. I was trying hard not to hear the words that Jorge and Inês exchanged in the living room from time to time, and to pay no attention to why they were laughing. I felt like taking a cigarette out of Márcia's pack and lighting it up, but I hadn't smoked for more than twelve years. The craving for a cigarette reminded me that I should hide away the lighter that was in the bedside drawer, it wasn't a good idea for Grandma to have it nearby when she moved in, just in case she should become disorientated again. I picked up the lighter, I recovered the cigarette pack from the rubbish and sneaked out onto the balcony of Márcia's bedroom, where I stood with my back against the building wall.

Not a single window had its shutters lifted or its curtains pulled back, neither on the side of the old Avenida do Ultramar, now called Engenheiro Adelino Amaro da Costa, nor the other side, the old Bairro do Jota Pimenta, now called Avenida das Comunidades Europeias. Perhaps Jorge had been right in what he said, that time when Milena came for lunch and they discussed the strange Portuguese habit of always keeping windows shuttered. This is a vestige of the dictatorship, it lasted almost fifty years, a lot happened, people are still afraid, our dictatorship was not like other dictatorships, it pretended to be soft and that's what ruined us, making us distrustful, anyone could be a grass for the PIDE, the neighbour, the baker, the man at the coffee counter, the electric meter man, the work colleague, the doctor, the priest, a friend, danger was everywhere, it was natural for everyone to be afraid, Jorge explained. Milena disagreed, The past has broad shoulders, very soon we'll have had as many years of democracy as we had of dictatorship, and you're saying that we still keep our windows shuttered because we're scared of snitches, do you really believe that Jorge? His arguments with Milena were always heated and I liked to think that their robust exchange of views was really a settling of scores, driven by their jealousy at having to share my attention. To blame the past for everything is ridiculous, Milena said, just like it's ridiculous to see grown men and grown women still blaming their parents for everything, Freud screwed us up, there comes a point when it's us, not our parents, who make decisions, and it's in the present, not the past, that decisions are made, the past was made by others, but the present is made by us, even if we want to avoid it, hiding behind our parents and the past, even if we insist on being scared of something, we are scared of the soil, of the dust, of the open air, if the past has anything to do with that it's because we associate it with misery, with some wretched rural life, that's why we shutter our houses, concrete over our gardens, that's why foreigners have to come and teach us how to do a proper picnic, how to enjoy gardens and public squares. At that point the girls were not yet joining in the grown-ups' discussions, and my own laconic offering, It takes all sorts, which I tried to shoehorn into any discussion, and which instead of generating conversation generally tended to kill it, could hardly be considered a contribution. It wasn't that I disliked discussions or that I wanted to derail them, it was only that I was incapable, I didn't know how to get to the heart of things or how to change what I disliked, I accepted almost everything around me as inevitable and unchangeable. I thought it was best to keep quiet, but I always blurted out the same thing, It takes all sorts.

Despite the wall of closed shutters and drawn curtains around me, I was comforted by the thought that Jorge might be right, there might be someone to look out for me after all. I lit the cigarette. When I went to bed later Jorge would know I had been smoking, there would be no need for the snitch watching me from the other side of the building to go to the trouble of denouncing me, Jorge would notice the smell of tobacco on me, on my breath, even if I tried to conceal it with toothpaste, but I could always bet on him not saying anything about it, if there was one thing he was good at it was avoiding conflict, he could have been one of the UN's Blue Helmets or whatever they are called. Once, during an argument, I accused him of not caring about living in a state of rotten peace as long as his life was easy, expecting him to feel rattled and insult me in return. You have to calm down, he said, going back, unperturbed, to whatever he was doing. I took a final drag of the cigarette. I smiled as I recalled an old story that Jorge always told amusingly, about a husband who finds his wife in bed with another man and rebukes her, As long as I don't find you smoking. I thought about the doctor who saw

Grandma, about the colleague who commented on my legs, about the man at the Repsol petrol station on the old Avenida do Ultramar, about the men I had fantasised about for years, Jorge wouldn't find me with any of them, but he might find me smoking.

I checked my Facebook again. My boss had reacted to the photograph of my legs with a flexed bicep emoji. Despite being online, Jorge had still not reacted to my post or to my comment on his. I posted the photo of the ZX Spectrum with a caption, *lost and found*.

A car parked up in the little nearby square. Its occupants, a couple with a child, spoke animatedly as they got out. Everything was silent, so I could overhear them talking about the quality of the restaurant where they had just eaten. My gaze followed them until they disappeared into the neighbouring building. When I raised my eyes I noticed a gap in the wall of closed shutters. Somebody had switched on the light in a flat on the other side of the little square, it had been sold not long ago and I had missed the chance to sell it. I regretted my slowness, once again Natália, or some other enterprising agent, had pressured the old owners into selling the flat as soon as they declared their intention to return to the village of their birth. That was the way to do it, no-one in that line of business could afford to be soft-hearted, my boss was right, you snooze you lose, no such thing as a free lunch, if you want something you have to grab it.

The lit-up rectangle in the middle of the dark wall of closed shutters and drawn curtains revealed a young couple – the new owners, surely – in an empty living room, and I became the viewer in a film being screened only for me, a silent film, but in colour. The man stretched out a measuring tape and made notes in a notebook that he supported on his thigh. He looked comical as he balanced precariously on one leg. The woman swayed her hips sensually, as if dancing quizomba, while walking towards the man. She danced so well that I couldn't take my eyes off her, that woman's body was powerful as it danced. When she was near the man, he put down the notebook, held her by the waist and pulled her into the centre of the living room. They danced holding on to one another, slowly, and slowing down further. Suddenly, the woman let go and ran out of the frame. My experience of reading Mother's photo novels led me to expect some sentimental drama, the woman had discovered an unknown woman's lipstick on his shirt collar and had run off to avoid crying in front of him, the heroines in photo novels were always crying out of sight. The man remained standing, in the middle of the living room, but instead of looking in the direction of the vanished woman, he was looking out of the flat's window. After a few moments, I was sure of it, he was looking at me. I thought I recognised him. Were I not hearing Jorge's loud guffaws coming from the living room, I could have sworn that it was Jorge looking out of the only lit window in that dark wall, staring at me, still young, across time. And if that was Jorge, then the woman who rushed out of the living room had to be me. Right now I would be hiding somewhere in the flat, crying, waiting for Jorge to find me, but instead of doing so he would remain standing in the living room trying to catch a glimpse of future me.

Go after me, I wanted to shout at him, don't leave me alone, crying in the past.

Perhaps the man in that building wasn't Jorge, perhaps he couldn't even see me, perhaps I was watching a film and he was standing still during the interval. Or the film projector had broken down, as it sometimes happened at the Oxford or the São José cinemas. I wouldn't have been surprised if the little man with his tray of chocolates and sweets had suddenly appeared, or the usher who scolded the boys on the balcony. But no, the Oxford Cinema didn't have a balcony, the balcony was in the São José Cinema, and it was in neither of those that the usher expelled the boys from Torre for putting their feet up on the seats in front of them, that happened at one of the cinemas in the Jumbo Shopping Centre. Jessica Rabbit was singing while the boys from Torre, as they were escorted to the exit by the usher and the doorman, raised their arms, shouting out, like champions, and all the other children applauded them. In any case, there no longer was an Oxford or São José cinema and not even the ones at the Jumbo existed, everything had shut down. Every now and then, when I absentmindedly observed members of the Universal Church of the Kingdom of God gathering on the steps outside the old cinema, I could almost picture the audience for the matinée show at the Oxford, my old classmates, my old neighbours, Milena and me, Mother and me, I could still picture the blue carpet and the white leather seats, the bar with the curved counter, I could sense the smell of tobacco and hear the bells announcing the start of the film, but nothing could save the Oxford from oblivion. To have kept the buildings where the cinemas and cafés once stood hadn't been enough to spare them the oblivion they were fated to, the past of small things was always vanishing. Boring, Mum, the girls said whenever I told them about something that once existed in a particular place, long before they were born. They rolled their eyes, like I rolled my eyes when Mother told me about things that existed before I was born. Perhaps that is how it had to be, perhaps the next generation's survival requires it to start with a clean slate and there is no point in the older generations telling stories with which, more than saving the ancient soul of a place, they sought to save themselves, stories that begged, don't let us die, not even when our bodies have ceased to exist.

The woman reappeared in the lit-up rectangle and the man moved again as if someone had fixed the film projector and the session had resumed from the same frame where the machines had become stuck. She brought a bottle of wine and two large wine glasses. How had I not considered the possibility that she had gone to the kitchen to find something to drink, I wondered, had I forgotten how things work?

In the early years of our life together, that was also how Jorge and I avoided disagreements, we drank wine like fish and, on Saturday mornings, we slept in until late. The sun slanted in through the kitchen window and dimmed the tiles' old ochre. We didn't yet have enough money to remodel the flat, money was tight for everything. We had breakfast at the large dining table, we made toast, juice and eggs, and there was always a marbled sponge cake baked the night before. After the girls had gone to sleep in their beds with headboards I had painted myself, using stencils I bought at the Printemps Shopping Centre's final clearance sale, I would go to the kitchen, put the cake bowl on the granite countertop, pockmarked by previous tenants, melt the butter, mix it with sugar, add egg yolks one at a time, the sieved flour and yeast, the whipped egg whites, I would get my hands dirty as I buttered the cake tin, split the cake mix in two parts, adding the powdered chocolate to one of them, I would ask Jorge if he wanted to lick the bowl, he claimed to be a marbled sponge cake expert, Well, Dona Eliete, next time you'll have to add more chocolate, well, Dona Eliete, you may have overdone it with the flour, and we laughed. The girls sang jingles happily in the living room, we were proud of their growing independence, the girls knew things we hadn't taught them and laughed at jokes we didn't get, the girls sheltered from the world's evils in their pyjamas and fluffy slippers, hair frizzed, hands waxy from the crayons, the girls had grown up so fast, one day they were crawling, the next they were walking, then they were speaking, then they were challenging our instructions, then they were lying to us, then they were keeping us at a tragically insurmountable distance, the girls back in that time of the old ochre coloured tiles, still so attached to us that it seemed impossible they could strike out on their own, it seemed impossible that they could ever disappoint us, that we could ever like them less, even if it were for brief moments, it seemed impossible that one day I would fill my Saturday mornings with chores, would get rid of the large breakfast table to make space for the chest freezer, would be buying marbled sponge cake from the supermarket in plastic packaging with best before and use-by dates, one day there would be fewer things to do, but I would have even less time, one day the girls would have grown up, they would have found houses and jobs, there would hardly be anything else to do, but I would have even less time. And it would all make sense. Time was slower the more I lived within it instead of living in the future or in the past. The more caught up I was in the present, the slower time passed, the happier I was. Like that hot afternoon years ago, and the four of us indoors, Jorge, the girls and me, almost naked on the unmade bed, bodies in a sleepy tangle, through the half-open window the breeze brought in flutters and threads of sounds made by winged things, birds, voices, insects, songs. During those days, in that home, there were moments when time stood still, stopped completely, moments when I felt immortal, I became immortal. To be fully happy was a way of experiencing immortality. But since happiness is short-lived, immortality, too, was mortal.

When Jorge and I were all about sleeping together, and about the phone calls to arrange the sleeping together, I was already happy to have him, but I lived in the future, in a future in which he would be mine. So in those days I was very mortal, there were moments when I thought I would die, because I felt so mortal. I was in love with Jorge, who wasn't in love with me, and that divergence caused me not to be able to sleep, it made me vomit, it made me feverish, it made my legs weak like a newborn calf. Nothing had ever hurt me so violently until then as my love for Jorge did, for as long as it was unrequited. I wrote him poems and more poems, hoping I might diminish my suffering by putting it into words, but it seemed like the words re-opened old wounds that, together with the new one, plunged me into a despair that might only be soothed by a call from Jorge inviting me to come over to his house. The telephone was red and stood in the entrance hall of Mother's flat, on a half-moon table with a granite top and what Mother described as French-style gilded iron legs. When the phone rang it gave me such a jolt that it was hard to tell which was louder, the phone or my pounding heart. I would count to ten before answering, I didn't want Jorge to think I was just waiting by the phone, even though, in fact, that was exactly what I was doing. I would pick up the receiver but very often, instead of the voice that I was longing to hear, it was the voice of Dona Herlanda calling about some emergency with a wedding dress, or Grandma calling to know how I was doing, or Milena calling to gossip about our friends and to invite me out. I would try to dispatch the unwanted voices as swiftly as possible so the line wouldn't be busy. I despaired when Mother was stuck to the phone, I was certain that Jorge had called and, because I failed to pick up, he would never call again. Ask him if he likes you, Milena would nudge me, and I would explain once again that Jorge and I were only sleeping together and that sleeping together had its rules, the main one being that there must be no questions, going to bed together started and ended in bed, it didn't involve romantic breakfasts, calls to soothe the longing, meeting one another's families and friends, walking around holdings hands. You must be stupid, Milena said exasperated, your problem is that you lack self-confidence, if he didn't like you he would have found someone else. Perhaps Milena was right and Jorge was already in love with me, but I was never bold enough to ask him. I avoided asking him anything for fear of the answers, and his own questions, a simple question such as, what are you doing over the holidays, led to days of conflicting interpretations, Jorge meant to say that he would like to go on a holiday with me, he was worried about me going away, he was keen to be rid of me, he was planning to take a holiday with another girl and didn't know how to tell me, the interpretations becoming increasingly dire. The funny thing was that Jorge's questions were meant largely to cover up the awkwardness that lingered after we had done the sleeping together. It remained that way for over a year, I loved Jorge, who didn't love me back or didn't show any signs of it, so he needed me to do the loving. I was worried about being replaced by another girl, I was sure that Jorge needed nothing more than to be loved, and there may as well have been others who would love him the way I did. I didn't think of him as being cruel, malicious or a player, and even if I couldn't say it to anyone, because I couldn't translate my thoughts into words, I understood how difficult it was to give up someone loving you and expecting nothing, or almost nothing, in return. I loved him without measure. When Jorge wasn't by my side even the things I liked suddenly seemed uninteresting, it bored me to walk around the square even if the afternoon was magnificent, the smell of freshly baked bread made me nauseous when I couldn't share it with him, the wild sea was just noise, the shade beneath the trees was depressing, the flight of birds was tiresome, the colour

100

of flowers was vulgar. Before falling asleep, in those brief moments when I was no longer myself, those brief moments when, as a teenager, I dreamed of miraculously being able to do the front crawl, I contrived revenges inspired by soap operas, I would find a man who would fall head-over-heels and then Jorge, faced with the inevitability of losing me, would beg me to stay with him, would even swear that I had always been the love of his life. In those brief moments before falling asleep, I cruelly rejected Jorge's love and revelled in the suffering it caused him, but then daylight arrived bringing me back to reality, I loved Jorge who did not love me back or even suspected that I har-boured fantasies of revenge that only made me feel guilty, and so my love grew even more. Jorge, oblivious to my torments, had a happy life, he lived on his own in a flat he had inherited from his fisherman grandfather, single bed-room, living room and a minuscule balcony, on Largo de Alvide, opening onto the roundabout that the posh boys screeched around in their fathers' cars on Saturday nights when they could be bothered to drive out to the middle of nowhere. He never complained about the flat being too small, about the single bed with its cast iron frame, about the old wardrobe with a mirror so tarnished that it hardly reflected us, about the sofa with the broken springs and the torn upholstery, about the minuscule kitchen with a camping stove and a leaky fridge, about the balcony where nobody fit. He was already working as a coder, in that indecipherable language that ran in green lines across his computer screens, with its funny bleeps, and he spent almost all his time at home. What does Dad do? the girls asked when they were small, hoping that their father might be a fireman, a doctor, a pilot, anything they could recognise and other children might envy, Dad is building the future, Jorge would boast loudly, but the girls didn't care about the future, they wanted him to be a policeman, a chef, a football player. After the girls were born, Jorge stopped freelancing, he sold his soul to the devil, as he often said, and started leaving home at seven in the morning and coming home around eight at night, and wearing a suit and ties when he had big meetings.

When we were still all about sleeping together and calling one another to arrange the sleeping together, I spent most of my time with Jorge in silence. The devil that once led me to ask all those questions that so worried my grandmother now made me concentrate on a single question, a question that consumed me so entirely that it seemed impossible for me to keep it in. I worried that, while talking to Jorge about anything else, the question would leap out of my mouth like spit and I would hear myself asking him, Are you mine? and then, unable to avoid it, I would fill the awkward silence that would certainly follow by nervously reeling off my perceived shortcomings, a boring and badly paid job, being ashamed of Mother and of Mother's home, my crooked tooth, boys not liking me, and so on. As if Jorge had a perfect smile, as if girls were throwing themselves at his feet, as if he had a magazine-worthy house and a highly desirable job. But Jorge's shortcomings made me love him even more. I loved him more because he ate only bread and preserves, because he bought wine and beer at wholesale price from the restaurant owner down the road, because he didn't like motorcycles or cars, because he bought cheap clothes at the flea market by the bullring, because he didn't care for the yuppies, punks, surfer boys, nerds or any of those tribes and their rules. I even wasted time trying to work out whether he was desirably free or happily excluded, but I gave up before arriving at a conclusion.

If I had to place a bet, I would say that Jorge started falling in love with me when I told him about my ordinary dreams, a home, a good man, healthy children, a car, family Christmases, dinners with friends, holiday photo albums, a normal life. Unlike Marco, Jorge didn't need dreams. Milena always said that Jorge and I would end up together because we were birds of a feather, and she was right. When Jorge fell in love with me, I started spending every night at his place. During the daytime, I would show around a handful of tourists, just a few, very few, because back then almost nobody was interested in seeing where the land ended and the sea began, and at night we slept in the single bed, my head on Jorge's chest, until my heart synchronised with his. Years later, Jorge started saying that he missed his fisherman grandfather's flat and I wanted to believe that he missed us in his fisherman grandfather's flat, but perhaps that wasn't quite true.

Where is it, where is it, Jorge demanded, barging into Márcia's room. I'm here, darling. When he came closer I teased him, stroking his chest as I pretended to fasten a shirt button. But why are you now referring to me as it? I joked, putting on the sing-song accent of the posh kids from the Linha. Jorge took me by the waist and hoisted me into the air, enjoying my joke, You're the best, now where is my long-lost treasure? It's in your hands, I replied. Jorge was delighted that I had found his first ever computer among the clutter in the storage room. That night we fucked.

Hey, pretty lady, have you ever seen the sea? I'm not taking you into town, too many people and too much noise, but I'm taking you somewhere close by, a villa by the seaside. He called me a pretty lady, me, a widow, still mourning your grandfather, and Senhor Pereira treats me like I was a fifteen-year-old.

Grandma hadn't stopped talking since she got into the car. Inês and I recognised her voice as soon as we entered the hospital corridor leading to the room where she was waiting for us. She was sitting on the bed, the small bag with her belongings to one side, arms crossed over her lap, a white head bandage giving her a comical air. She stood up as soon as she saw us, greeted us as if it were some festive occasion, locked arms with Inês, not before saying to her, You've become a magnificent girl. She said goodbye to the other patients and wished them a speedy recovery, then asked one of the nurses for her address, She was a guardian angel, Grandma said, so she wanted to send her some lemons and some parsley plants, From my garden, Grandma explained, they don't need anything other than water, sunlight and the will of God that makes everything grow. Her cheery chattiness and her shows of affection were even more surprising than her rapid recovery. As the nurse explained how to change the bandage, I could hardly recognise the stern and austere Grandma in this beaming old woman clumsily interrupting the nurse and promising to send her some prayer cards that would protect her.

Seeing Grandma as overcome by happiness and enthusiasm as a child who finds the right company to play with, it occurred to me that she had been missing the friends she never really had. From her front gate, Grandma used to talk to the neighbour across the road, Dona Cecília, who had died a couple of years back, and she exchanged vegetables from the allotment with Dona Maria do Céu, whose ungrateful children, she said, had her in diapers. There were also the church acquaintances, who had gradually given up on their religious duties due to circumstances beyond their control, serious illness, relocation to care homes, or death. But neither the neighbours nor the church acquaintances were close to Grandma or even visited her at home. The only time I asked her why we had no visitors, Grandma replied, With a friend as with a horse, keep the reins loose of course, and that was the end of the conversation. Until the morning we went to find her at the hospital, I would have sworn that Grandma was a woman of few laughs and few words, but the smiling and talkative little old lady was proof that I was wrong. It might have been simply that Grandma, for some mysterious reason, had kept her more affable side hidden, or perhaps that little old lady was, in fact, a brand new Grandma. Both theories were unsettling, but the latter was scarier. If Grandma had changed so much, there was nothing to stop her from changing again.

Once in the car, Grandma put her rapid recovery down to a miracle performed by Our Lady of Fátima, to whom she had promised a votive wax head and two rosaries prayed at the tiny Aparições chapel. So you think there's someone in heaven keeping tabs on your vows, Inês asked, trying to wind up Grandma, and I braced myself for yet another telling-off for not baptising the girls and for not signing them up for Sunday school, therefore keeping them from learning about the marvellous mysteries of the divine, but Grandma let the comment slide, and once again talked about the terrible fright of finding herself in hospital with a gash on her head. I was hoping that she might be able to explain what had happened the day of the fall, but my hopes were dashed when I realised she couldn't even remember having walked out onto the street in her night-gown. And yet, she was aware of everything that had happened at the hospital. It was as if she had suffered a blackout like the one I had when Father died. It had been a shorter blackout, but with no obvious trauma to cause it, which made it harder to explain.

I was also wary that Grandma had so easily consented to stay with us, I'll just have to fetch a few things I might need, she said, as if her moving in was just another of those times when I asked her, as I had done over fifteen years, to come and stay with the girls so that Jorge and I could go out for dinner and a film. She never stayed any longer than was strictly necessary, I like to be in my own home, she said. Drugs can have some surprising secondary effects, Jorge had said over dinner the night before, after I told him about Grandma's change of disposition. Inês remembered a

YouTube video about a Swiss man who started talking in foreign languages after falling off a cliff, Maybe Grandma's fall had a similar effect, she said. For Inês, all knowledge of the world came from the Internet, that place made up of everyone's voices, billions of voices talking to one another, a place that mocked the divine rage that had once condemned humans to speaking many languages after trying to build a tower tall enough to reach heaven. Now every human wanted to be able to reach all other humans, an even more extravagant ambition.

As Inês tended to dodge family obligations whenever she could, I was surprised to hear her ask, Do you think Grandma would be happy if I went with you to collect her from the hospital? Her kind offer caught me off-guard, it would never have occurred to me to ask Inês to join me in that task, I usually did my best to avoid her spoiled and insolent refusals to help. Taken aback, I said only, Of course, Grandma would be very happy and I would be too. I said nothing else, because almost anything could trigger an argument. I'm going to get ready, she said, animated, as if going to fetch Grandma was something to get excited about. We were having breakfast in the kitchen, Inês was cutting a peach into thin slices and placing them carefully in a turquoise-coloured bowl. Who is this girl that wakes up early, has fruit and cereal with no added sugar for breakfast, and arranges her food so beautifully? I asked, with a smile, Where have you hidden my daughter? Inês could have shown her annoyance by raising her right eyebrow, but instead she pretended to find my joke funny. When she had finished decorating her cereal bowl with a sliced and fanned strawberry and a pair of physalis fruits in the middle, she photographed it with her phone, Wow, amazing, do you wanna see what it looks like? I thought Inês might be trying to trip me up, perhaps she had found out that I had created a false profile on Instagram to keep tabs on her and she was laying a trap, I worried that she had found me out and would shout at me as loudly as she did when she caught me looking through her phone, You have no right to be looking at my things, she cried, before locking herself up in her bedroom, slamming the door noisily. And, indeed, I had no right to be looking at her things, or to be spying on whatever she did online. I couldn't even justify my behaviour as maternal concern, since there was nothing in Inês' behaviour to suggest she was in any danger or was unwell, but I could only verify that by looking at what she did. There were other ways of doing it, but I had to admit that I wasn't a good mother, or not one of those mothers who are also friends, companions and confidantes to their children and who know them like the backs of their hands and can always find the right words to encourage and help them. No-one could ever accuse me of not having diligently carried out my practical obligations, I had certainly covered the basic parts of motherhood. For as long as the girls needed my care, I always fed them at the right time and prepared their food, remembering that one of them didn't like fried fish, peas or coconut, and the other didn't like stewed fish or bell peppers, I never let them go to school without having showered, even if, quite often, that led to massive tantrums, I kept a clean house, I tried to make sure they got enough sleep, I was attentive to their gift lists for Santa Claus and their fear of the dark and of burglars, I signed them up for swimming lessons, music, yoga and singing, I ruined my weekends driving them to their friends' parties, I became exhausted from walking around the sales without buying anything for myself, I moved into their bedrooms when they needed me because they had a high fever, or diarrhoea, or a nightmare. No-one could accuse me of not being a good mother insofar as the practicalities were concerned, just as no-one could accuse me of not making an effort to remain close to the girls when they stopped needing my care. Except then our closeness also started to depend on their willingness and availability and, no matter how hard I tried, that willingness and availability were slow to appear, until I realised they never would. The fault was mine, it had to be mine, I had been around for a long time before I gave birth to them, it was surely my job to persuade them about the joys of the sort of relationship I hoped to have with them. I didn't know how to do it. I didn't even know how to suggest that we should nurture some benign happiness together. Sometimes it seemed to me that Márcia mistook happiness for melancholy, while Inês mistook happiness for incessant conflict. I felt that wasn't right, I didn't know much about happiness, but I did know that neither gloom nor constant discord were the way to achieve it. It was up to me to save them from tortuous forms of happiness and I was unable to do even that.

The consequences of my maternal shortcomings expressed themselves in many practical aspects of our daily life and one of them was the girls' quiet but determined refusal to confide in me. Whenever they were sad or worried and I tried to understand the reasons, they immediately avoided the subject, it was never a big deal. I didn't insist. Not because I was uninterested, but because I didn't know how to insist without becoming tiresome, a busybody, a nuisance. And the girls carried their problems and their sadness further away from me, as they had already carried away their tastes and interests. I didn't mind it when I stopped being an interlocutor for them on so-called women's issues, clothes, hair and so on, I blamed the mad pace of fashion, but I did mind, a lot, when they excluded me from other parts of their lives, friendships, loves, professional choices, political opinions, musical tastes, all areas where Jorge appeared to acquit himself so well.

The way I felt about Inês was the same way I felt about Márcia and vice-versa, there was nothing substantially different in the relationship I had with each one of them, although with Márcia it was easier for me to pretend I was a good mother. Márcia listened to my advice, even if she did so with more patience than due regard, and she seemed happy when I suggested that we got manicures together or that we baked scones on a wintry afternoon. Inês, on the other hand, made it clear that she was bored to death whenever I started talking about her future and, besides avoiding any of the plans I suggested, would often turn my words and actions into the trigger for painful confrontations. I was convinced that Inês had started arguing with me to show how much smarter she was than the rest of us, and then the arguments became a habit, and in the end the habit shaped her way of being. And yet I confess that it filled me with tenderness to look at Inês posing in her Instagram posts and to see myself in her, spat out, as Mother would say. It was obvious that my dusky genes had gotten the best of Jorge's, there were so many parts of me that I discovered in the girls with wonder and with worry. If it had been up to me, Inês wouldn't have inherited my average features nor would Márcia have inherited my average intelligence, even if I knew that the first was a worse punishment than the latter. Intelligence was never an immediate advantage, requiring as it does an interlocutor to recognise it, whereas beauty imposes itself, without hesitation, at first sight. And if that is how it had always been, if images had almost always been the start of everything, now they were, increasingly, the end of everything. And there was no way that Inês didn't know that. Having inherited Jorge's intelligence, or better, Jorge's intelligence sharpened, since he was far from being brilliant, Inês was condemned to be clear-eyed about the fact that her unremarkable looks would make her lose out to prettier girls in the opening round. The time spent dieting and in gyms was pointless, the one thing she had going for her was her terse manner with boys. Instagram showed me that Inês was popular with the boys. She wasn't one to break hearts at first sight, but the ones who did interact with her soon found themselves caught up in her web.

Spying on Inês' Instagram allowed me to know what she was thinking, who she was with or what she liked without annoying her, because Inês, who so skilfully avoided answering my own questions, put a lot of effort into answering her followers' questions. I suggested one day that we should be Facebook friends, but her reply came swiftly, What kind of loser would accept her mother as a Facebook friend? I was unable to reply, but I felt I had a legitimate excuse to keep spying on her Instagram account, which only the day before had shown me a photograph of Inês' hand interlaced with a boy's, with the caption, in English, *when everything you've looked for is right there under your nose*, ending with a flourish of teddy bear, flower and heart emojis. I was so busy trying to work out the logistics to make sure Grandma's stay would go smoothly that I didn't spend any time trying to find out who the boy might be. In any case, Inês' enthusiasms were short-lived, she would have moved on in no time, that was what she said to Márcia, without a hint of bitterness, when Márcia asked her about a sort of boyfriend Inês had once introduced her to, Oh him, I've moved on. As I had suffered the wounds of love so deeply, it pleased me to think that Inês' coldness towards boys was my revenge, and that the education I gave her made her so strong and independent. Inês freely chose whatever she wanted to happen to her.

When we left the hospital, Grandma asked that we drive along the Guincho road, which Senhor Pereira believed was the prettiest in the world. The first few times I heard her say that I thought how incredibly lucky it was that the prettiest road in the world should happen to run so close to Grandma's house. The gusts of wind bent the pine trees and battered the car. I was driving slowly. Despite Senhor Pereira having died almost twenty years previously, Grandma kept parroting his opinions as if she had heard them only the day before, so the Guincho road was still the prettiest in the world, even if Grandma's world was a minute part of the world Senhor Pereira knew from his time as a barman on the Companhia Colonial de Navegação packet boats. I imagined that he must have been a skilled and talkative barman, but I couldn't be sure. Despite asking me to drive along the Guincho road, claiming she wanted to see the ocean, Grandma was so caught up telling Inês how she met Senhor Pereira that she hardly looked at the view.

Hey, pretty lady, have you ever seen the sea? Marry me and I'll raise your boy like my own. Senhor Pereira made me that promise the day of the processions and, God rest his soul, he was true to his word. In fact, for him, my Antoninho was like God come down to earth, if Antoninho said something was white then it was white, if he said blue it was blue, there was no law more powerful than Antoninho's will. And how patiently he dealt with Antoninho's tantrums. He was much older than me, age doesn't only affect the body, it also gives us wisdom and patience. He was older than me, but next to him I seemed to be the older one. He had the refined air of a person born in the big city, he slicked his hair back with pomade from a can, he stopped by the shoeshine every other day. Whoever saw him walking down the street would have said there goes a doctor, pinstriped suit, lace-up shoes, wide-brimmed hat. I never once saw him spit on the floor. And yet he was born in a small village just like mine, if the rain was falling on Vimeiro it wouldn't be long before it rained on São Joaninho. Now people say that those were the days of misery, but who back then was thinking about misery when the water from the spring was pure and the plums ripened

114

in the sun? If there was time to think about anything, it was about how fortunate we were, not because we were rich, but because we had the chance to save our souls and there was no greater thing than the soul. Then the revolution came and everything changed. The revolution and the communists turned everything we had into misery. They wanted to destroy the rich and in doing so they destroyed everything. But what would be of the poor if it were not for the rich? After the revolution it was a free-for-all. They ruined everything, even the villages. They made everyone leave, people left for the cities to escape misery, except many became even more miserable there. And the thing about cities is that no-one knows anything about the misery of others, if you fall to the ground there is no-one to offer a helping hand, the poorest, the eldest, the neediest become invisible. In our villages there might have been hunger, but no-one died of hunger, not even those years when frost or the heatwaves ruined everything. There was always a hay barn to sleep in and scraps of food, even if they were just potato peelings. At home, there were eight siblings. When our neighbours didn't have eight children of their own they had at least six, or five, or four, and it was lovely to see those houses filled with all those children. We slept in the living room and ate from a single pot. When one of us had nits everyone had them, if there was a single piece of bacon it was divided up between us according to age. People weren't afraid of having children. Children died a lot, but the strongest made it through, and that was as it should be. Now that there are all kinds of doctors, enough food to go to waste and electric blankets, everyone is afraid of having children. Back then there were children all over the place, and it was a joy to see them on the streets chasing a ball made out of rags. Many lived to become grown-ups without ever having owned a pair of shoes, but one thing was always true, the dead were never without shoes at their wake. In one of the church vestry's wardrobes there was always a pair of shoes for the deceased, I often saw them being used for people who had never owned any. Only the tips of the shoes were left on display, so the deceased looked properly done up. Nowadays they burn the dead to save space in the cemeteries, they put the dead in an urn. An urn. How can anyone be so heartless as to deny someone their own piece of sacred ground? Not to mention the visits. No-one visits an urn, no-one lays flowers by an urn. My dead are all in the sacred ground of the cemeteries. Some back in the village, some here, but all in sacred ground. When there is no respect for the dead there is no respect for anything. I don't know what was wrong with our way of living, what was wrong with being left alone and ruled over, with getting from the earth whatever God wanted to give us.

I never knew what Senhor Pereira saw in me, maybe there was something he found charming, or perhaps it was a miracle from the Sacred Heart of Jesus, to which I had offered up my own Antoninho, a baby chubby and mischievous like no other in the village's memory. How I struggled to carry him during the procession, the street as steep as if it were going up to heaven and my legs wobbling like those of an old mule. But God never abandoned His people and at the top of the hill, near the church, there was Senhor

Pereira, 'Hey, pretty lady, have you ever been to the sea?' I still remember the look on the faces of all the nosey folk who are more interested in other people's lives than their own, looking at me in amazement. Senhor Pereira had a reputation as a bit of a skirt-chaser, he couldn't escape that, he'd had many women but hadn't committed to any of them. Up to that moment he wasn't one to commit, nothing held him, not even his village. As a child he used to visit the villages and hamlets with his father and as soon as he was old enough, and not a minute too soon, he went off to see the world on the packet boats. He saw so many beautiful things, he said, that sometimes he had to pinch himself to make sure he wasn't dreaming. He travelled the world, but there was nothing like the Portuguese world, which stretched from the Minho river to East Timor. He talked about people who wore feathers, about animals of all shapes and sizes, about roses made of porcelain, about a bridge called Dona Ana, my mother's name, Senhor Pereira was very fond of telling stories. He knew nothing about threshing or reaping or taking the cattle to pasture, but if anyone mentioned the waves, the stars and the winds there was no shutting him up.

The few cyclists pedalling alongside us, on the cycle path, leaned forward, battling gusts of wind. Three tourists ran to catch the bus while trying, in vain, to protect themselves from the wind that blew their clothes around and blasted their hats away. By the entrance to the Fort of Nossa Senhora da Guia, day-trippers gathered around the tour guide. I still knew by heart much of the information about that military fort, built in the seventeenth century, if I made an effort I could still hear myself saying to tourists, The fort was built after the Restoration, the Governor at Arms in Cascais was the Count of Cantanhede, The fort follows a rectangular plan with the battery looking out to sea and the accommodation facing inland, It has vaulted ceilings, topped by a terrace that forms a platform with a parapet, if I made an effort I could still repeat the monotone spiel I delivered to tourists, the things I held in my head, I drove on, the tour guide receding in my rear-view mirror as she gesticulated and battled the wind.

It was Mother's idea that I enrol in an International Relations course. Anyone who knows about foreign affairs will be guaranteed a plum job in the European Economic Community, she used to say. I don't know why I listened, why I paid attention to Mother, who never finished school and had always worked at Dona Herlanda's bridal shop. I liked to think that I had no choice in the matter, but I didn't have to look far to realise that I was wrong, Milena was proof that it was possible to escape the destiny that others had drawn up for us. Around the time when Mother wanted me to find a plum job somewhere in the EEC, Milena wasn't yet known as Lewinsky, as some of the other lawyers would later refer to her to suggest that she won her court cases on her knees in judges' offices, but she had already set herself a goal and was working hard to achieve it. You have to fight for it, Milena would encourage me, but it was as if she were talking to me about some other planet. After I finished my course, I spent a year waiting for the plum jobs in the EEC to materialise, or indeed anywhere else, calmly resigning myself to the idea that the plum jobs had been taken before they were even created. Also calmly, I agreed to the six-month course, suggested by the advisor at the job centre, that turned me into a tour guide and thanks to which, months later, I found myself walking tourists around Cascais, getting paid an hourly pittance. The course to become a tour guide had the advantage of being paid, but Mother was right, there was always someone making money, for instance the geniuses inventing courses that do little more than qualify people for future unemployment.

I was driving slowly because the wind was blowing sand off the dunes and across the road. Grandma had finally replied to Senhor Pereira's question on the day of the procession, Hey, pretty lady, have you ever seen the sea? I told him I had. And where did you see it, he asked. In that painting of Moses at the Church of São João, I replied, cocky, filled with the arrogance of youth. Instead of feeling intimidated in the presence of that elegant man, words flew out of my mouth. I had seen the ocean in that painting of Moses. When it was time to grind the wheat, the rye and the millet, we could spend up to ten days at the flour mill, so we then attended Sunday Mass at the nearby Church of São João. Near the altar, on the right, was the Moses painting. I can almost picture it, the parted sea, each side standing taller than the mountains, the wild stormy sky, Pharaoh's army drowning beneath Moses' long beard and staff. How terrified I was of that painting, the soldiers and horses sinking to the bottom of the sea. I felt sorry for the horses, it wasn't their fault, but they ended up at the bottom of the sea along with the chariots, the swords and the spears, and in the distance the sea was beginning to close again, leaving the Lord's chosen people in safety. The Egyptians were bug-eyed and in agony, crying out for help, but all was in vain, they sank like stones to the bottom of the sea, it was as if all those people were drowning again in front of me, as if I were hearing the screams of all those agonised souls, I knew that the souls of the drowned were left to suffer for eternity and I was frightened by them. When I was young I was frightened by everything. Then my Antoninho was born and I was never frightened again. As if my soul had been cured by his first scream. How could I have imagined what would happen?

I knew that Grandma was referring to Father's death and that was why her voice and her body were breaking, all of a sudden. Inês knew it too and was more skilful than I was in trying to distract her from the sadness that had come over her. Why did you call him Senhor Pereira when he was your husband?

Inês' concern for Grandma seemed genuine, even though she was clutching her phone and texting incessantly. Looking at her in the rear-view mirror I was struck, even more, by the similarities between her and the girl I had once been. Inês' agile thumbs appeared to be morphologically different to mine and to those of all humans that preceded us. I remembered learning, while watching a TV programme on the Odisseia channel years earlier, that whenever a swarm of mosquitoes felt a particular need, the following generation's bodies would evolve to satisfy it. Perhaps, ultimately, humans' capacity to adapt was similar to that of mosquitoes, who resist everything and adapt to anything.

If that was indeed the case, humans of my generation would have felt lonely and would have recognised the need to write to other humans. With technology offering a substitute for writing paper, in the space of a single generation humans would have emerged fully equipped with thumbs adapted to a new form of writing.

Inês' question managed to distract Grandma from the sadness caused by Father's death. I hardly knew Senhor Pereira when I came to live with him, Grandma explained, with a smile, my father knew him well and he gave his blessing, he knew I was in the right hands. At first, I called him Senhor out of respect. After all, he was older than I was. Senhor Pereira. I got used to calling him that. He was so educated, so well spoken, that when he got an idea in his head he could persuade anyone. But I didn't need much persuading to live with him, I followed him from the day he asked me and I continued to follow him until God took him from us.

And what about your first husband, Inês asked affectionately, did you also call him Senhor? Oh, with him it was different, with him it was very different, Grandma replied. She never said much about the travelling performer who, while passing through Vimeiro to liven up the celebrations for the patron saint, fell in love with the beautiful dark-skinned girl with braided hair, who looked on in amazement at the performance. Whenever they came up, Mother was dismissive of the stories about the travelling performer, Your grandmother thought her life would be different just because she was a pretty face, but how wrong she was. Only when talking about the travelling performer, who died shortly after he married Grandma, did Mother allow herself to admit to Grandma's enviable beauty, even if she tried to undermine Grandma by describing her as a "pretty face". Back then, no man would have wanted anything to do with a woman who had been with another man, it was a stroke of luck that the old man Pereira was willing to take her second-hand. I didn't pay much attention to what Mother said about the travelling performer and about Grandma's widowhood, and put Mother's scorn down to envy. It seemed to me that Mother envied Grandma's love story even more than her beauty, that there was too much bitterness or irony in her account of the travelling performer's starry-eyed decision to remain in that little village. In any case, it was unusual for Mother to linger over the tale of the travelling performer, preferring as she did to rehash her grievances against Grandma. One story she never tired of telling concerned the question Grandma had asked her when Father introduced them formally, How do I know that my son is your child's father? Whenever we had these conversations, Mother would pore over every irrelevant detail such as the rusty jalopy Father used to drive around, or the chores that kept Grandma busy in the kitchen, Senhor Pereira reading the newspaper in a deck-chair on the balcony, she described Grandma's house in great detail as if I didn't know it, as if I hadn't lived there. She did this to delay recalling that moment when Grandma had offended her so deeply, How do I know that my son is your child's father? When she got to that moment, Mother would start ranting, The old woman must have thought that I was acceptable, before that day I had only seen her twice and she seemed neither pleased nor displeased by me, but the moment she found out I was pregnant with you she became a snake. Mother emphasised the "pregnant with you" to make it crystal clear that Grandma's anger was directed at me and that, had it been up to Grandma, I wouldn't have been born. Over the years I always hoped that Grandma might refute Mother's harsh rants, all the more so because Grandma was always hinting that Mother hadn't been a well-behaved girl, a well-behaved girl would have reined in Father's impulses, Father's behaviour wasn't his fault, it was a weakness, Father had simply succumbed to the evil impulses of the flesh. I waited and waited, but not even when she clung to me crying after Father's death, fully aware that I was all that she had left, did Grandma ever change her tune about Mother's pregnancy, or even remark that every cloud has a silver lining.

Father's tragic death didn't put an end to the grudge between Grandma and Mother, on the contrary, it heightened their resentment. Senhor Pereira and I counted for nothing in their disagreements, we were reduced to the roles of witnesses or allies, even after Senhor Pereira was dragged into Mother's complaints that she and Father, a newly married couple, had never had a bedroom of their own, while Senhor Pereira had his own study, as if he were a doctor. It's not surprising that your father was playing away from home. By playing away from home she meant having affairs. Mother couldn't have really believed that Father had affairs because Senhor Pereira wouldn't relinquish his study so that I might have my own bedroom, but she declared it as if she believed it, and it was then that

Senhor Pereira and his mostly unused study acquired some prominence for a few minutes. When I'm no longer here you can do whatever you want with it, Grandma would say, if you find no other use for them, all that paper and all those books will be good to light a fire in winter. I couldn't begin to imagine what the girls thought when they went into Senhor Pereira's study, what they felt when they saw on every wall the traces of a world that started falling apart the year I was born and about which Senhor Pereira liked telling stories, showing his photographs of lion hunts, elephant tusks, of crafts made by African and Asian natives, as he liked to say. Senhor Pereira was already retired when the packet boats that gave him his bowed back and the unsteady legs of someone who can't walk on dry land were discontinued, but shortly before his death he was still talking about the *Império* and the *Príncipe Perfeito*, his favourite ships.

The day we went to fetch her from the hospital, Grandma's stories about the travelling performer were even vaguer than usual, although she had now added a mysterious ending, I can't help thinking that it was a sort of punishment. What was a sort of punishment? I asked. Grandma finally seemed to be noticing the Guincho road's scenic beauty and I couldn't tell whether she was paying attention to me or was following the trail of some thought I couldn't understand, when she added, Everything that we make up will eventually happen, sooner or later. We turned inland towards Grandma's house at the point where the Guincho road pulls away from the sea.

As the car rolled silently along the road that runs past the camping site, I remembered Senhor Pereira's old van chugging along the old potholed road. Mother and I had already left Grandma's house when the big roadworks project started, laying down asphalt and connecting Grandma's house to the road we were travelling along. There had never been such a racket in this village, born more than five hundred years ago when nine houses were built in a desolate landscape, withstanding the onslaught of sea-salt and wind. Not one of those nine houses was still standing. And, of the dozens of whitewashed houses built subsequently, no more than five remained, and three of them were abandoned, not even the tourists, who so liked to photograph the ancient and authentic Portugal with its towers, its arched windows, its bucolic tiled friezes, its grapevines and planters filled with pansies and daisies, seemed interested in poorly whitewashed houses. The oldest part of the village disappeared gradually at the hands of those who inherited it. The first generation built houses with conspicuously gated garages, black-tiled eaves and outdoor side staircases, trying to leave behind the modest places where they had been brought up, the second generation preferred apartment blocks with rooftop pools, which they built a few streets further down.

Were it not for the apartment blocks there would have been no need to widen the avenues, or to redevelop the square outside the Church of São Brás, with its old fountain and wash-house, or to lay tarmac over the unpaved streets and connect them to the main road. The companies hired to do that brought in African labourers, dark as night in the words of Senhor Pereira, to operate huge steamrollers that flattened small mounds, and another machine with metallic claws that pulled plants, roots, rocks and rubble from the earth's depths. Machines, shovels, pickaxes, legal and illegal migrants from Africa, dark as night, as Senhor Pereira would say, second-class whites, local council officers, businessmen and enterprising individuals, corrupt and opportunistic and even some who meant well, all joined the efforts to domesticate the landscape, flattening out the clearings where the other children and I swore each other a friendship like Tom Sawyer's, and wielded swords like Dogtanian and the Three Muskehounds, where the other children and I grew up and beat each other up as mercilessly as the future would beat us all up.

They are levelling the ground, Senhor Pereira said to me, during one of the Sunday visits to Grandma's house that, for many years, Mother and I felt the obligation to make. The steamroller passed by the garden wall, making the earth tremble and birds fly off screaming, and that was when Senhor Pereira said, They are levelling the ground. Then he explained what he meant, They are flattening everything, getting rid of accidents, he couldn't have imagined the impact the word would have on me, he couldn't have imagined that years later, pursuing the dream of becoming a poet, I would write "Levelling", a poem left incomplete like all the others. It took me a lifetime to discover that incompleteness might have been my only poetic gift, my laboured handwriting on the storage unit floor in that poem that starts with a word I was unable to find, possibly a verb, . . . *until all accidents are erased, the sadness of wilting roses, until there is nothing to slow the heavy steamroller*. My indecisive and adolescent handwriting on the

126

floor of the storage unit . . . *until there is nothing to slow the heavy steamroller*, and the question gnawing at me since that day in the storage unit. The poem was surely about me, because at sixteen everything was for and about me. It was still like that, but I now knew that there was a name for it, and the name was loneliness. But what to call the pain that seemed to fill every pore, to shape every bone, to discourage every smile, to darken every word, what was this pain that I knew so well even at the start of my life, at the start of my poem?

At Grandma's house, Inês hurried to get out of the car and open the main gate. It was a wooden gate, painted green, the hinges were rusty and the paint was flaking off. She helped Grandma get out of the car with great care. Perhaps Inês was trying to show me that she could be considerate but chose not to be considerate with me. The world does not revolve around you, Jorge had blurted out, a few weeks earlier, in the middle of a silly argument. He wasn't being malicious. We had been together for so many years that we no longer said things out of goodness or malice, we simply said them.

Bardino appeared, from the back of the house, as soon as Grandma arrived. I don't know how many Bardinos I had met, there was always a cat in Grandma's house and when it died it was replaced by another also called Bardino that inherited its predecessor's duties, namely, catching mice and some sun on the balcony with Grandma. The day of her fall, I had been to Grandma's house to make sure that she hadn't left the door open or a gas hob burning, and Bardino was nowhere to be seen. It had saddened me then to think that Grandma hadn't replaced her last Bardino because she was aware that her end was near, so I was relieved to see Bardino rubbing his sides against Grandma's legs. What have you been up to, you scoundrel, Grandma asked him affectionately. When Bardino made his way towards the main entrance, and sat there waiting for us to open the door, time seemed to recede and Mother was now sitting on the balcony, in a green plastic wicker chair, painting her toenails with Bardino by her side. Father came in from the street, kissed Mother and fussed over Bardino, a grey Bardino, different from the fawn-coloured Bardino now sitting by the door. Grandma's fall was always making time recede, after Grandma's fall time receded dangerously like the sea does before curling into a large destructive wave, the large destructive wave that was about to hit us all, mercilessly.

That evening, as I looked through Inês' Instagram feed, I saw she had posted photos of Grandma and Bardino and had even captioned them, showing gratitude for the day with the clasped hands emoji. I wasn't in any of the photos. Even though I felt excluded, I wasn't angry with Inês, that night I had another reason to be upset with her, perhaps to distract myself from it I had started to think about what my relationship with my past would have been like if I had been able to record it in thousands of images and videos. I couldn't answer that question, but I knew that my past would be different, it would be a past with hardly any margin for error, for mistakes, for the imagination that filled the gaps whenever I remembered the beginning of a story, but didn't remember the end, or when I was unable to put my memories into a sequence. Perhaps the ability to record things exhaustively was altering our memory in the same way that the invention of writing had altered it before, the exhaustive record of everything we did was changing us, and no-one noticed it because almost no-one ever noticed anything unless reality was staring us in the face and, even then, we preferred to remain blind to it. Occasionally, I imagined Inês clearing out her belongings, I pictured the storage unit at her future home and the objects falling out of boxes and onto her, the splinters of life she might glimpse. Inês wouldn't have the black address books from the bank or the Hello Kitty notebooks with permanently unfinished poems, envelopes with the contact sheets and photograph negatives like the ones Jorge and I still kept in the top drawer of the living room cabinet, Inês would have thousands of photographs in external and internal drives, perhaps it would be memory drives falling on her head inside her future storage unit, photographs that didn't occupy the same kind of space or meaning. If Jorge died, Inês would have thousands of pictures of him and would never have to worry about the negatives of his very last portraits being destroyed by floods. Almost everything in the lives of Inês and Márcia and their contemporaries existed in such abundance that it was difficult for anything to acquire value. And as almost everything existed with no physical presence, almost everything became like a thought that passed through someone's mind only to vanish swiftly, almost everything existed in an infinite virtual storage unit that was immune to gravity, in which nothing would fall on our heads.

I shooed Bardino away when he rubbed himself against my legs. I had two meetings later that day, I couldn't meet my clients with trousers covered in cat hair. Don't be such a moaner, Inês said. Watch your tongue young lady, I said, you're not talking to your friends. I'm not being rude, it's not bad to be a moaner, there are lots of things that I don't like and I moan about, just now there was a snail near the gate that grossed me out. Except I'm not being a moaner, I said, just to disagree with Inês. But it was true, there were many things I moaned about, animals, food cooked by others, the smell of the dirty laundry basket, stray hairs in the bath, daily life in general.

Nothing in Grandma's house belonged in the present. Everything was from another age, the furniture, the carpets, the crockery, even the grimy and tired light seemed to come from another age. Amazing, Inês said, as if she were seeing Grandma's house for the first time. Amazing. Grandma flopped onto the sofa with the floral upholstery. These have been very busy days, she said, as if talking about days filled with good things. Bardino jumped onto her lap with the dexterity of young felines. He was a handsome cat, with a lustrous coat and eyes striped with two colours. Inês sat down beside them to take their photo on her phone, the cat's whiskers gleaming in the sun, Grandma's hand on Bardino's back, the dust like gold dancing in the light. I don't know how many seconds passed as Inês composed her photos, but it must have been many. She propped up her phone, and lay down, pulling Bardino onto her lap, a gesture that was both accusatory and meant to prove she wasn't like me. Stroke him a bit, you'll see how soft he is, just a little stroke, Inês demanded. Fearful, I moved my hand towards Bardino, but I hadn't even touched him and already his hair was standing on end and his claws were out. He could sense my fear, my uneasiness, he could sense I didn't know how to handle him, the same inability that prevented me from knowing how to handle Inês, or Grandma, or life. I remained standing, not quite knowing how to stop my impatience from coming across as an aggression towards those two placid and drowsy creatures with their eyes firmly fixed, Grandma's on Bardino and Inês' on her phone. And then out of the blue Inês said, I had dinner with Nuno yesterday.

Grandma had no idea who Nuno was, so she would have had no interest in that snippet of information. It was to me, then, that Inês wanted to say that she had had dinner with Nuno, even though she seemed to be speaking to Grandma. After speaking, she turned her face towards the sun and closed her eyes. She continued to stroke Bardino, as if in a trance. Nuno, your sister's boyfriend? I asked incredulously. Uh-huh, Inês replied, giving in to the lassitude of her own words. That's right. But you don't like him, you never got on, I said, stunned, as I put together the information Inês had just revealed with the caption of her Instagram post, *when everything you've looked for is right there under your nose*. Keep up, Mum, that was, like, a million years ago.

Whenever he had a few too many drinks, Jorge always told the tale of his fisherman grandfather and the shipwreck of the trawler *Alvorada*. In that sense, the day of the European Football Championship final was no exception. At half time, and after ranting about the nil–nil draw, Jorge began telling Grandma and Milena about the shipwreck of the *Alvorada*, without either of them showing signs of having heard it before. Milena jumped in with the story of a fisherman she defended some years earlier, trying to move Jorge away from the tale of his fisherman grandfather, but her effort was in vain and Jorge carried on with the story of his grandfather who before the day of the shipwreck had never missed a single day of work, and would never miss one after, but that morning, in words of the grandfather that the grandson took such pleasure in repeating all those years later, It was God himself who made him oversleep and miss his appointment with death. He arrived late and flustered at Praia do Peixe only to find that his crew had left on the little trawler never again to be seen, as if the sea that sustained them had suddenly wanted to settle the debt forever.

I had lived with Jorge for more than twenty years. Most of the time I could guess where his conversations were going, his turns of phrase, the gestures he would use to add drama to a story, the way he would repeat certain words for emphasis, I knew inside out the stories Jorge usually told and, therefore, I knew that once he had finished the story of the shipwreck of the *Alvorada*, he would go on to talk about his grandfather's youth in Cascais, in the 1940s, as if alcohol had the power to unleash some unsettling connection between him and the grandfather, making him describe, as if he had seen it himself, the flotilla of boats of all shapes and sizes at Praia do Peixe, the fishermen mending nets on the sand, the baskets filled with fish that the fishwives hawked at the mansions on Avenida D. Carlos I, the rich women coming to bathe with their maids walking twenty paces behind them, loaded with food and changes of clothes for their mistresses, the gamblers at the Casino da Praia, that once stood where the Hotel Baía is today, the dandies fortifying their lungs and bones as they promenaded by the water's edge in swimsuits up to their chests. I couldn't, however, have anticipated the number of stories about storms, sea monsters and mermaids that Jorge would tell, praising the courage of the fishermen who were subjects, first and foremost, of the sea, that capricious emperor that gave them everything and took everything away, because the number of stories was determined by Jorge's alcohol consumption and the alcohol consumption was determined by the importance of the football game. I knew, however, that on that day there would be many stories, Portugal was playing in the final of the Euros for the second time, twelve years after filling our stadiums and suffering the humiliation of a home defeat to Greece.

After describing how wonderfully simple life was in Cascais, back in the 1940s, it wouldn't be long before Jorge put his arms around me and said that his presence in this world had been touch-and-go, If my grandfather hadn't overslept, you would never have met me, if you had never met me, the girls wouldn't exist, and so on until he felt crushed by the exhaustion of imagining the tragedy of his non-existence. When we were still all about sleeping together, and about the phone calls to arrange the sleeping together, Jorge's non-existence hurt me, so thoroughly had he persuaded me that my life would have no purpose without him by my side. Since then, things had changed, things always changed, regardless of my determination to make sure they remained the same, and on the day of the Euros final the tightness in my chest was not caused by hurt, but by exasperation. I was fed up with Jorge's stories, with seeing him entrenched behind them as if that poor summary of himself was the only thing he had to offer me. I could no longer tell whether my Jorge was still hiding behind the endless iterations of these tiresome stories, or whether he had been devoured by them, but I felt he was increasingly reduced to his tales, a crude and lazy simplification of himself.

Among Jorge's stories, the one I found most irritating was the tale of his fisherman grandfather, because it created an illusion of simplicity, the idea that there was an inescapable destiny, a destiny with the power to bend reality into improbable events to fulfil itself. As his fisherman grandfather was destined to die of old age, reality had been reshaped, making him oversleep that morning so that he missed his appointment with death. As I refused to believe in destiny, I attributed the story's implausibility to its countless repetitions, which would have modified the truth of the original facts with the same casual carelessness with which the wind shaped the dunes on the beach at Guincho, making the past so difficult to unravel that it wasn't hard to see the hand of destiny in it. The day of the Euros final, the story of the fisherman grandfather revealed itself to me in a new way, I started to believe that sometimes reality bent itself so that something might happen, it didn't matter if, to die of old age, the grandfather needed to oversleep in an improbable coincidence, or if Portugal needed to win the European Cup for my betrayals of Jorge to be witnessed.

Grandma nodded as Jorge spoke, adding here and there some personal recollection of what Cascais was like when Senhor Pereira brought her, and I thought I might now be able to answer the doctor's question, Have you noticed any unusual behaviour? Grandma was no longer quite Grandma, even though parts of the past remained intact in her mind. She forgot where she had left things, she shuffled the sequence of simple events, she sometimes said she hadn't eaten even though she just had, she even got lost in the streets of our neighbourhood. I was saddened by her dwindling capabilities, but what unsettled me most was not recognising Grandma in some of the strangers who seemed to take over her body. The stranger who walked out into the street in a nightgown had been joined by the talkative stranger, the singing stranger, the angry stranger, the mistrustful stranger, the spendthrift, the liar and so many other strangers that I wasn't sure if I knew who Grandma was anymore. Sometimes I caught her smiling with a sweetness that did little to soften the severe wrinkles carved into her face, other times I noticed elegant and coquettish gestures that seemed to mock the country bumpkin that she had never stopped being. I wouldn't, however, have had the courage to tell the doctor that, if I had a choice, Grandma would have died, I would have preferred the pain of a dead Grandma to the pain of witnessing the parade of strangers who took over her body, and that the platitudes of all those specialists we had taken her to, Dementia blah blah blah, Alzheimer's blah blah blah, the diseases of people who live long lives blah blah blah, were no good at all, not even to give me some comfort. Grandma's head and body were dying, anyone could see that, except her head was dying faster than her body and, even if this didn't hurt Grandma's body, it hurt mine.

About a week before the day of the Euros final, I was going to bed when, out of a sense of duty, I peeped through the half-open door of Mârcia's bedroom. Grandma, still fully dressed, was sitting at the foot of the bed, her head lowered and her hands folded on her lap. The forced smile she gave me as I came in emphasised the disquiet and sadness in her expression, I'm so tired and my head is so empty, I can't even remember where Senhor Pereira is, she said, lowering her voice. I thought Grandma had forgotten in which cemetery she had buried Senhor Pereira, whether it was at Torre or at São Joaninho. I tried to reassure her, told her not to worry, Senhor Pereira was buried near Father, we could visit them at the cemetery the following day, we would buy them some nice flowers. It didn't occur to me that Grandma's disease had already suppressed Senhor Pereira's death, and that, for Grandma, he was still alive in his study at the end of the corridor, a corridor that became longer every day, so long that Grandma was always getting lost in it. Grandma's memory still clung onto Father's death, her Antoninho, who had died thirty-eight years back, but it had already let go of the death of Senhor Pereira. That's not true, it can't be true, Grandma shouted, putting so much suffering into her widow's sobs that Jorge and Inês looked into Mârcia's bedroom, alarmed. What will become of my life without Senhor Pereira, Grandma asked, how did this happen? At the time of Senhor Pereira's death, twenty-two years earlier, I had witnessed Grandma's pain, and the tragic repetition of her shouts and words startled me. I went looking for the tablets the neurologist had prescribed for emergencies, in case Grandma became agitated or started displaying psychotic behaviours, that's what the doctor called them. The following day, Grandma woke up earlier than usual and I could tell from her restlessness that she was still mulling over Senhor Pereira's absence. Perhaps she was making an effort to remember what had happened the night before, she was screwing up her eyes, as if the trick that allowed her to see further might also allow her memory to see things closer up. It occurred to me, then, to say that Senhor Pereira had called and said that he would be back a few days later. Her worry dissolved immediately into a rapturous smile, He's always worrying about me, she said, but there's no way he can give up his job on the packets. I realised that keeping Senhor Pereira's death from Grandma would be necessary until the day when the disease wiped him forever from her memory, so I raised him from the dead, and whenever Grandma expressed any worry about Senhor Pereira's absence, I reassured her by saying he was working on the packet ships.

I wonder what happened to Senhor Pereira, he likes football so much, Grandma asked on the day of the match, forcing me to repeat the lie that shuffled past and present. Even though the idea of Senhor Pereira serving up drinks and conversation on a packet ship amused me and made me imagine Father, smoking, sitting at a luminous blue bar, behind which Senhor Pereira mixed him a brightly coloured cocktail, even though I liked to imagine that there was a world after this one where all objects emit a soft light, a multi-coloured world where we would find everyone and be happier than we had ever been, even though I liked to think about death as a large ship on which we would all be reunited, it saddened me to know that Grandma was no longer subject to any temporal coherence, that her memory kept a part of the past intact, but it had become impossible to access it without subterfuge, just as it was impossible to prevent its loss. I was trying to convince myself that my little fantasy about Senhor Pereira on the packet ships was harmless, and I even put effort into making it believable by adding details that Grandma certainly didn't need, but the truth is that I didn't know how to bear witness to Grandma's slow death inside the body that imprisoned her, nor did I know how to help her. Just as I didn't know how to help Inês.

That day, Inês hadn't wanted to have breakfast. I'm not hungry, she told us. She had agreed to spend the Sunday with friends on the beach at Abano, the same friends she would later be watching the match with on the giant screen at Terreiro do Paço. She put on and took off countless shorts and blouses, tried on hats, scarves, considered taking platform clogs. Who are those friends, I asked, trying not to sound disapproving, who are those friends that make you try on so many clothes and wear uncomfortable clogs to the beach? She limited herself to giving me one of those smiles that Mother called as fake as a three-escudo coin. I insisted, so she explained that there was no point in me knowing the names of her friends, as I hadn't met any of them. There was more worry than annoyance in her words, and she hurried into the bathroom where, facing the mirror, she drew a dark line around her eyes. And since when do you go to the beach wearing makeup? I asked, no longer worried about my tone, Inês was my daughter and I had a right to know what was happening in her life. Mum, that control-freakery is so old-fashioned. In other circumstances, perhaps the frustration of feeling like such a useless mother would have made me stop asking questions, but I couldn't stop then, so I lashed out, point blank, with the ill-conceived question that I immediately regretted, Your sister's boyfriend, Nuno, is he going too? It had been more than two weeks since the late morning, at Grandma's house, when Inês said she had been out to dinner with Nuno. There had been more than two weeks to ask what was going on between them, and many opportunities to bring it up, in a calm conversation between mother and daughter, but I had avoided it and now I was slapping her with a loaded question. I told myself that I had done so because that calm conversation would never happen, that Inês and I had no way of interacting other than behaving like cats in a sack, as soon as one of us came close the other showed her claws. Before long the reasons I gave myself to calm myself became self-recriminations, making me feel responsible for the distance Inês tried to keep with me. More than once I had tried to grow closer, many nights I found myself outside Inês' bedroom, knuckles poised to knock on the wooden door, but I was never able to do it, to find an excuse to have a conversation about what was happening or to simply ask her if she wanted to talk. I could imagine the answer she would give, Why would I have anything to say to you? I could imagine her haughtiness as she asked me to leave her room, and so I never followed through. So the days had passed and we had arrived at that moment when, unable to control myself, I had ruined everything with that stupid question. If I had stopped to think for a moment, I would have realised that my aggression wouldn't get me an answer, it could only push her further away from me.

Given the similarities that the whims of genetics had foisted on us, I took Inês' behaviour that morning to be a cry for help. Our resemblance allowed me to deduce with some confidence that Inês was being brazen in trying on clothes and putting on makeup so that I would know that she wasn't spending the day at the beach with her friends, but was on her way to a romantic rendezvous and the romantic rendezvous was with her sister's boyfriend, Inês was asking for my help to stop betraying her sister. And what did I do? I pushed her away with stupid remarks and loaded questions, proving yet again that my mothering skills extended only to practical aspects. Any good mother would know how to make a daughter in distress trust her, but I wasn't a good mother so I limited myself to spying on her Instagram account, and my daughter was becoming more of a stranger and more unreachable every day. Once again, the psychologists' platitudes were of no use, conflict between a mother and daughter is natural and even necessary blah, blah, blah, daughters have a right to keep to themselves the most intimate aspects of their lives blah, blah, blah. I recognised myself, with disgust, in Inês' reaction, I had also pretended to be surprised and offended when I was caught lying, I had also played for time, as Inês did that day, pretending to rummage in her makeup case, I had also replied arrogantly just as Inês replied, It's my life, I'll do what I want with it. Grandma was nodding off on the sofa and didn't wake up when Inês left, slamming the door behind her.

I don't know whether, on the day of the match, there was a moment when I thought, Actually, I don't know the people I love the most in my life, but I suspect not, I was hardly ever able to think about what I was I feeling or to match what I felt to what I thought. But, even if I hadn't thought it, I felt surrounded by strangers, Jorge seemed to be no more than a rough sketch of himself, Grandma was no longer present, Inês was becoming increasingly difficult to reach. Time, or tiredness, or who knows what, had turned Jorge into a stranger with Jorge's body, illness had turned Grandma into a stranger with Grandma's body, and Inês, whether it was my fault or not, was determined to become a stranger to me. Despite the different speeds and the paths they had taken towards it, Jorge's slow and distracted, Grandma's abrupt and out of control, Inês' hurried and careless, they had all become strangers and I no longer knew what to think of them or how to relate to them. I was sharing my home and my life with strangers, my loved ones, and the question I should have been asking, the million-euro question like they always have on television shows, should have been: who were those strangers? Or, perhaps, and even more worryingly, a question about myself: if Jorge and Inês had changed to the point of becoming unrecognisable to me, if Grandma's illness had changed her to the point of no longer being the same person, I too might change to the point of not recognising myself. And what if that had already happened? Given the improbability of Grandma, Jorge and Inês having all turned into strangers at the same time, might it be me who had changed?

That was the question darkening my thoughts on the day of the Euros final, a day that started with the promise of celebration, a day made for happiness. I too willed myself to be happy, and for that I needed to unburden myself of that question and of other thoughts that affected my emotions, I had learned already that happiness was selfish and fickle, it slipped away more quickly from those who didn't embrace it in full, I had to stop giving so much of my attention to the strangers I loved or used to love, I had to tune in to the happiness the day had started with, join in with those walking down the street with scarves around their necks and the colours of the flag painted on their faces, with those praying to the saints Grandma so fervently believed in to ensure our boys won the match, with those already armed with a list of excuses in case of defeat or a plethora of boasts to proudly puff up their chests in case of victory, the ones who had rehearsed a thousand times the spiel about beating France to avenge the humiliation by Greece in 2004, I had to ride the echoes of happiness wafting in from the street to tune in to the grand event taking place in a few hours, who cared whether I liked football or not, what mattered was that family, friends, acquaintances, all were preparing for the grand event, millions of people preparing for the grand event that would give them the illusion of being less alone, the same thing happened during wars and catastrophes, but it wasn't a good idea to declare war or to welcome a catastrophe only as a cure for loneliness, and that's why there were these special days when everyone could bond over the same event, New Year's Eve, for instance. I had spent New Year's Eve on my own too many times and perhaps it was my memories of past New Year's Eves that betrayed me that day. My memory of the sadness and the anger of knowing that everyone but me was having fun was pushing me to make sure it wouldn't happen again, but that time the stakes were even higher, Mother had sworn on many New Year's Eves that she would find a better job than the one she had at the bridal shop, but no-one could experience more than once the day when Portugal played in the Euros final for the second time, so it was essential that I tuned in, that I stopped being like the broken dial on the radio Senhor Pereira kept in his study, on the right as you entered.

Can I come and watch the match with you? Milena had asked, by text, earlier that afternoon. If it had been a normal day when I was a bit sad, if the cause of my sadness was not being able to feel the excitement and expectation of all the people around me, people in cafés, at the beach, on the street, all the people on television, if I hadn't felt I was surrounded by people I loved and who had become strangers to me, I would have hesitated to say yes to Milena coming to watch the match with us, because, apart from her love life, Milena was more successful than me in everything, and on the days when I felt sad I found it impossible not to measure Milena's success against my own failures, I couldn't shake off the guilt of having failed when it was apparently so easy to succeed. But that day I was glad to get Milena's message, because I could confirm with her whether I had changed as much as I feared. If Milena could still recognise me and if I could still recognise her, that would surely mean I hadn't changed, that the things that seemed to be new were happening outside of me and, for now, I remained the same. For now. It was impossible to remain the same for long when everything around me was changing. You know you're always welcome, I wrote back to Milena, adding party emojis and of course the special football emoji.

There was still an hour to go before the match when Milena rang the bell. Her cheekbones were suntanned. Her khaki shorts showed off her long and slender legs, which seemed immune to the ravages of time. Jorge had gone to the supermarket and Grandma was keeping me company, seated at the kitchen table. Her relaxed expression suggested that she had stopped worrying about Senhor Pereira or about anything else, that she was with us in the present, and that she was happy to see Milena again. I brought this,

Milena said, showing me a bag filled with delicacies too expensive for my family budget, before walking over to the refrigerator, into which she put two champagne bottles to chill. She walked as if she couldn't help making everything she touched her own.

With the champagne bottles in her hands, Milena was once again the girl who, many years ago, had walked into Mother's flat with a fancy bottle. Moay Shandon, she said, emphasising the French accent, Moay Shandon, we both said, our lips whistling, trying to repeat the name that Milena had heard at the shop where she bought the bottle, the fine food shop in Estoril, the one right above the Hotel Paris. It was the priciest, she said, satisfied, if we're going to celebrate your freedom let's do it properly. At that point, Milena didn't have much money and I never knew how she managed to get that bottle to comfort me after my break-up with Marco. Mother had left at eight in the morning for the bridal shop, making it clear she didn't want anyone coming to the house. She came back on the 18:54 bus, with swollen feet and pretending not to notice that I had disobeyed her. Despite what Mother thought, I rarely brought school friends home. With Milena it was different, Milena was like my sister, so she didn't count. We were used to spending our free time at school together, and to keeping each other company during our dull study sessions. We read photo novels, we painted our nails, we imagined the clothes in which we would break hearts in 2021, while at the same time training to be young ladies who would bake cakes and prepare meals, who would surprise their future in-laws, the exemplary housewives that our mothers and grandmothers had condemned us to be. Amid the strangeness of our bodies growing and filling out there was always the boys, and talking about the boys, the ones who were interested, the ones who weren't, the shy ones, the fun ones, there was always the joy, the disappointment and the sadness that boys gave us. Marco, who instigated my dream of becoming a poet, was often the subject of our conversations, as he was again that day because he had replaced me with Sandra. I wasn't as sad as Milena thought I was, although I'd never confessed to it I was fed up with the oracle cock, which became more demanding and more fickle by the day, and with Marco's dreams, which became more self-centred by the day. What hurt me most was the reason Marco left me. Not that he had given me any reason, in fact, he hadn't even told me he was breaking up with me, he simply took advantage of one of the minor disagreements we often had to start making out with Sandra, in front of me, Milena and other schoolmates on the bus, but I knew that he had left me because I was incapable of having any dreams. Marco and Sandra's heavy petting didn't anger me too much, at least it didn't anger me as much as it angered Milena to see her best friend humiliated. She took my hand and led me off the bus, we crossed the bus station and sat on the wall overlooking Conceição beach. It was a cold night, every now and then we lit a cigarette to stop trembling. We also struck up the lighter and waited for the wind to blow out the flame. Marco is right, I said to Milena, there must be something wrong with me. Marco can go fuck himself, she replied angrily, and the following day she showed up with the bottle of champagne to celebrate the end of my relationship. I've been thinking, I said, helping her put the bottle into Mother's freezer, cluttered with bags of frozen meat and fish, that Marco must need a girl more like you, a girl who has some ambitions. Milena shut the freezer door and replied with unexpected seriousness, I have no ambitions, my parents had ambitions their entire life and they never stopped struggling to make ends meet, ambitions are for those who don't mind waiting. Perhaps Milena was right, I had never thought of it that way, I cried a few more tears of romantic disappointment. Until I fell in love with Jorge, romantic disappointment was part of the learning process that would help me choose my Prince Charming, the man I would spend the rest of my life with, the father of my children, until I fell in love with Jorge romantic disappointment was like a childhood disease that we needed to catch to acquire immunity. He became fed up with me because I had no dreams, I said, everyone has dreams. Milena didn't reply, but I noticed later that she was mulling it over. She took the bottle from the freezer, filled two glasses with the bubbly liquid, So what do you think? she asked, clicking her tongue like a sommelier, it's nicer than the horrible fizzy plonk we drink at New Year's, isn't it? I remembered being a child and telling my mother that the sparkling mineral water she gave me whenever I was feeling nauseous tasted like pins and needles, but I didn't dare tell Milena that her precious liquid tasted like pins and needles. It's much nicer, I replied, even though in reality I could hardly taste the difference between what we were drinking and the fizzy drinks Mother opened to usher in the new year as we made twelve wishes while swallowing twelve grapes, and the dregs of which Mother would use to cook her chicken in a pot. Putting down her glass, Milena said, Marco is a big idiot, he doesn't even know what really matters, dreams are for those who are asleep, what matters is to set objectives, and the only people who completely succeed are those who have a single objective, a goal.

Despite not having heard Milena talk about goals, dreams and ambitions before, I didn't think she had come up with that theory only because she was furious at Marco, surely she must have thought of it before. I want to be rich, very rich, Milena said whenever anyone asked what she wanted to be when she was older. Almost everyone laughed at her, because she didn't possess any of the attributes that would allow her to reach that goal, she had been born to a family of limited means, she didn't stand out for her beauty or her intelligence, she'd never displayed any obvious talents, she was an unremarkable child, even I had more suitors and got better marks than she did. Not that I had ever seen her lose sleep over school marks or over boys, Milena probably knew even then that, if she achieved her goal, she could have all the boys she wanted at her feet, and that our school teachers would retroactively praise the genius they had failed to notice. Like any other athlete determined to win, Milena focused on training to reach her goal. A runner or a swimmer trains to increase their speed or endurance, Milena trained to be rich and her training consisted of learning to behave as if she already were rich, as if she had already won, to learn to be confident, self-assured, unaccountable as the rich are, qualities that were not innate but could be acquired. When she finished university, the word that Milena-Lewinsky used most was investment. The expensive clothes and the jewels she bought with borrowed money were an investment to be able to secure contracts with banks and insurance companies and to appear in court. What client in their right mind would hand over the defence of their interests to someone who can barely take care of their own? What judge would respect the closing arguments of a lawyer who looks broke? Who fears coming up in court against someone who appears to have already given up? Life is a game, you either win or you lose, you can come up with excuses, claim that you didn't know the rules, but life's rules are simple, there is one goal, you only need to know where it is and then run towards it. That is what Milena did. Because she had a single goal, Milena didn't let life knock her down, even when life put challenges in her way, like having to live in an overcrowded annex in Alapraia, taking on loans to pay her loans, having to pay moneylenders whatever interest they demanded, having to defend the interests of developers who had covered the city with tons of concrete, of banks that claimed the possessions of people who didn't know any better, of insurance companies that were trying to wriggle out of any obligation to indemnify victims of misfortune. For years, Milena did nothing other than train for her goal, not caring about losing friends, about shamelessly missing weddings and baptisms, about falling out with boyfriends when they criticised her priorities, she did nothing other than run towards the goal she eventually reached, the new millennium had barely started when she bought, with cash, her spacious luxury apartment, from which she could see the ocean as soon as she woke up. Full sea view, she had said to the estate agent, if it's just to see a sliver of ocean in the distance I'd rather not have any view, why would I settle for just a sliver of what I know I deserve?

I had a quick dip before coming over from the beach, Milena said, I took off my wet bathing suit, but if it's a problem maybe I can borrow some of your clothes. Milena's blouse was see-through, allowing a glimpse of her rounded shoulders and the dark nipples on her small breasts. I told her not to be silly, it's been so long since Jorge looked at my tits that if I catch him peeking at yours I'll kill him, and then you can defend me in court. We laughed again. I didn't know why I always wanted to laugh when Milena was around, but I suspected it was because laughter contained traces of our youth. Even if it wasn't a very efficient way of summoning the past, I found it as comforting as my recollections of Grandma keeping food warm for longer by wrapping her pots with newspaper. In fact, laughter was one of the few things in our body that a lifetime couldn't ruin.

Do you want to see my new sweetheart, Milena asked, pulling out her phone when Grandma went into her room to rest before the game. Another Brazilian Adonis? I asked, knowing Milena's preference for Brazilians. If this country did one thing right it was discovering that remote corner of the world with all its precious woods, Milena laughed, but this particular deity isn't Brazilian, he's African, God bless Diogo Cão who went and discovered Africa. She zoomed in on a photograph, pinching her phone's screen with her thumb and index finger. He must have been some ten years younger than Milena and fit the pattern of her earlier sweethearts with his muscular physique and a profusion of tattoos, Believe In Yourself, said one inked beneath his neck, in English and in gothic font, like a necklace. I see he has a lot to say, I said. And do, Milena said, winking at me, we can't keep our hands off each other. So far nothing new, Milena always said the same thing about each of her sweethearts, in the beginning they couldn't keep their hands off each other, by the end they couldn't stand each other. She showed me more photographs, pointing out her sweetheart's physical attributes and asking rhetorical questions, How could anyone resist those eyes? How can a back be so sexy? or reassuring me about his intentions, He left Tinder the day after we met, he wants to introduce me to his daughter, he's one of those men who remembers the old-fashioned things that us girls like, just look at these roses he sent me when we'd been going out for a week, so sweet.

I think I got it right this time, Milena said, after a pause, he makes me feel so alive, do you get that? Even if I hadn't suddenly remembered Milena, years ago, bursting with happiness after finding blackberries hidden among the brambles, I wouldn't have ruined her happiness by reminding her of the many previous sweethearts who had made her feel so alive. Not that Milena complained about the disaster that was her love life, she had only talked about it once, while confessing her regret for being so rebellious, so wilful, so naive. After all, men are not like dogs who always come back because they don't know any better, she said on the day of her fortieth birthday, she had already polished off a bottle of wine, As it happens, men are scared of a woman who is on her own, especially if that woman isn't sad. She lifted her head, I want them to go fuck themselves, preferably to go fuck each other, she said, and then she never spoke about it again. One sweetheart followed another as though they came fully equipped with a self-destruct button or were ready to launch themselves into space after a couple of months.

Jorge came in carrying some shopping, a crate of beers and snacks for the game, and the conversation moved onto how hot it was outside, and the fan zones with giant screens to watch the match. Grandma came back into the kitchen, she wanted to help with putting away some of Jorge's shopping, but she gave up before long, who knows whether because she was tired or because she couldn't remember where things should go. The game was about to start, and Jorge had said countless times, Whatever happens, just making it to the final is no bad thing. He was winding up Grandma, Who's going to win the game, Dona Lurdes, Portugal or France? Portugal, Grandma replied, Portugal is a great country. Wise words, wise words indeed, Dona Lurdes, said Jorge, putting his arm around her, We are a colossus, and we'll chew them up in no time. We then got caught up in logistical matters, should we eat on trays in front of the television? Should we pull the small table closer to the TV? Might we improvise a little buffet on the kitchen counter? As much as I wanted to be in sync with their excitement and expectation, everything conspired to make me feel excluded from the day's uniqueness, the dinner I still had to cook, the still-warm beer, the lime I needed to make mayonnaise for the king prawns Milena had brought, my surveillance of Inês' Instagram account. Her most recent photo, showing Inês wearing a scarf with the colours of the national team around her neck, had been posted that morning. It had been taken inside a car, and Inês was in the passenger seat.

Do you want to invite your sweetheart to watch the game with us? I'd love to meet this hunk, I said to Milena, and Jorge wolf-whistled, Someone's got a new man! We're still keeping it casual, he's watching the match with friends, Milena replied, trying to hide the awkwardness of her sweetheart having excluded her from his plans. Make the most of phase two, I'm already on phase one hundred: no hair, no patience, and still no money, said Jorge. Knowing how sweet Milena found him, I felt even guiltier for my irritation with almost everything he did and said. I took the opportunity to ask if he knew where Inês was, since they were always sending each other photographs. Jorge shrugged his shoulders, Let the girl be, she must be getting ready to watch the game with her friends somewhere, she must be doing the same things that all kids her age do.

Milena opened one of the champagne bottles as the Portuguese anthem started playing. There were many Portuguese flags in the stands, the whole world seemed to have been strangely painted with small green and red rectangles. On the pitch, a gigantic Portuguese flag quivered, the players were all duly lined up, the trophy shone brighter than an ancient treasure, I noticed Milena had goosebumps, Jorge beat his chest many times while the national anthem played, and Grandma moved her lips as if she were singing to herself. I felt like a spy watching them all, perhaps I could imitate them, perhaps imitating them would induce the kind of rapture I saw in them. Nothing. The more I tried, the further I felt from the blind and inexplicable sense of pride shared by millions of Portuguese people around the world, the further I was from feeling I belonged to whatever it meant to be Portuguese. More than watching the game, I watched how we watched the game.

And then the improbable happened. At the end of the first ninety minutes the score remained nil–nil, the game was nine minutes into extra time when, with Portugal in possession, Moutinho passed to Eder, go Eder, go Eder, go Eder, Eder was going to get through, Eder was through, Eder was going to shoot, goal, it's a goal, it's a goal, it's a goal. Jorge and Milena were jumping around the living room, Grandma was putting her hands together to thank Our Lady, and I burst into tears, happy to be able to cry without knowing why I was crying and with no-one asking why I was crying, not even me. None of us sat down until the end of the game, none of us kept quiet, we're going to win, we're going to win. Watching the exchange of hugs between Grandma, Milena and Jorge, even the hugs they gave me, I thought that happiness had come into my home only to mock me. It was our time to party, we won, we won, we won, Eder, Eder, Eder, the ugly duckling scored, Little Eder, born in Bissau and brought to Portugal aged three, raised in an orphanage in Braga and another in Coimbra, one among the millions of inheritors of the Portuguese world that Senhor Pereira had hanging up on the wall of his study, one among the millions left behind after the dismantling of the grand empire in the history books, the ugly duckling had saved us, Eder, Eder, Eder, we won, we won, we won. There were no more words, there was no talk of anything else at home, on the television, in neighbours' houses, on the street, on Facebook, on Instagram. Inês had still not posted anything. During one of the television repeats of the goal that gave Portugal its victory Jorge kissed the screen. I love you, Eder, he shouted. Africans are always on target, Milena said, winking at me. She texted her sweetheart with the same joke on WhatsApp. I like him too, Grandma said, watching footage of Eder celebrating with his teammates, he took good care of my garden, he always came on Wednesdays. Oh, Grandma, I said, and, teary-eyed once again, I hugged her. I didn't fully understand the reality around me, but Grandma must have felt reality escaping from her suddenly and at speed, so she had started to develop techniques to avoid becoming completely lost from reality, perhaps Grandma had started to tell herself stories that linked her to what was happening, perhaps that was the only way to remain in the present while tethered to the past, But where is Senhor Pereira, such a nice party and who knows where that man is, have you seen Senhor Pereira, Eliete? Grandma was a small boat unmoored from the dock, trying to sail back to the shore, blindly throwing ropes that connected with nothing, the ropes becoming thinner all the time, shorter, now just a few strands, pointless yarns, Grandma now forgetting where the shore was, forgetting how to feel despair. I gave Grandma her emergency anxiety medication. It was the wrong thing to do. Grandma wasn't anxious, all I needed to do was go through the make-believe of bringing Senhor Pereira back to life and Grandma would

155

have stopped asking the same tiresome questions. But I didn't want to ruin the celebrations pretending that a dead man was alive, I wanted to feel as alive as the others were feeling, I wanted to experience the happiness I saw in others.

Grandma fell asleep shortly after, on the sofa. I joined Jorge and Milena's toasts, but I felt more sober as time passed, more alert, instead of dulling me, alcohol sharpened my senses, making me painfully self-conscious. I drank more. If I couldn't manage to feel like the others, to be like the others, then let me fade away, let me stop hearing the excited voices of the commentators, Portugal are the European champions, today history has been made, let me stop seeing Jorge, remote control in hand, playing back the broadcast to watch the goal yet again, let me not hear him saying, Look at the way that Eder dribbled past Koscielny, he's the best, look at his finish, Lloris had no chance, but alcohol wasn't making me fade away and I could still see the footage of happy Portuguese people around the world, millions of Portuguese people feeling avenged for years of humiliation by Little Eder's goal, Grandma was right, Portugal was a great country, it was no longer a small country, there were Portuguese people spread out all over the world, popping up all over the world, as if they had been hiding and now appeared en masse everywhere, Portugal was no longer a small country, just ask the old toothless men with one cheek painted in the green of hope of the Crusaders, and the other cheek painted in the red of the blood spilled in far-away places across the vast world, the braves and the immortals wearing the knock-off Portuguese team shirts because they couldn't afford the official ones, the people getting drunk in Praça do Marquês de Pombal with cheap beer bought at shops run by Indians discovered by Vasco da Gama's fleet, Portugal was no longer a small country, just ask the portresses who for once left their hovels with heads held high, Márcia who lost her voice from screaming about the victory in a café on Piazza della Repubblica in Urbino, Inês who sent Jorge selfies from Terreiro do Paço, just ask those who didn't tire of shouting out their pride in being Portuguese, those continuing the shout first let out by Afonso Henriques, the shout that stuck spears into Africa and carnations into the barrels of machine guns, that killed kings and dictators, that expelled Celts, Visigoths, Romans and Spaniards, that lined churches with gold from Brazil, that burned heretics, that sailed around the Cape of Good Hope, that traded slaves, that signed the Treaty of Tordesillas, that built bridges and monasteries, that gave tea and Bombay to the English and tulips to the Dutch, the shout of the children of Portugal's splendour, just ask me, the one person who couldn't be happy on the day when everyone was happy.

We won, fuck yeah. I don't know how many times Jorge and Milena repeated that, until Milena needed to get an Uber because she was in no state to drive. When we walked her out, I realised Jorge was drunker than I had thought, saying goodbye to Milena as if it were us leaving her house. Later he was circling me, and I no longer knew if I wanted him near me or not, We're the champions, Eliete, fuck yeah. He fell asleep shortly after, face-up on the floor, legs spread, remote control in his hand. I pulled his shoes off, put a pillow under his head, covered him with a thin cotton blanket. I did the same with Grandma, I muted the television. Without the commentators' voices, the images of collective happiness became even more depressing, perhaps because they were now being commentated through the sounds coming from the street. Cars drove down Avenida Engenheiro Amaro da Costa honking their horns, neighbours left their homes in a hubbub to get together and party, they went out in their flip-flops, nothing mattered other than the need to celebrate, in one of the buildings of the old J. Pimenta neighbourhood an old couple danced merengue on a balcony, perhaps among the few still remaining from the wave of returnees who moved into the area in 1975. I was the only one who wasn't part of the celebrations. Milena sent me a photo on WhatsApp to thank me for dinner and the company. On a normal day, Milena would never have taken a selfie in which she was sandwiched between her sweetheart and another man, possibly one of his friends, but on that day everything was allowed. I opened Facebook, my colleague from the competing agency had published a picture in which he and his wife were wrapped in a Euro 2004 scarf, kissing and drinking out of plastic cups, nothing in the photograph was noteworthy but I would have given anything to be like her, I also wanted to be out on the streets with Jorge drinking from plastic cups, to kiss him wrapped up in a Portuguese flag, to think that only we mattered, to pretend we were happy, I would then embrace those who were crying tears of joy, laughing and drinking beer, those singing and drinking wine, those who reeked of sweat and hugged one another, those stopping at the food stalls for grilled pork sandwiches, fried doughnuts and candyfloss, those celebrating and cursing their wretched lives, those who were proud and those who were ashamed of being Portuguese. Knowing that Grandma would sleep until the morning, I tried to wake up Jorge to drag him into town with me, but he wouldn't budge. After a few attempts, he mumbled, Eliete you're the best, and curled up even tighter.

I felt alone, inhumanly alone. It was no longer because I couldn't synchronise with others, we can never know what others are feeling, but because I was alone at home while everyone was celebrating outside, that was the truth. I was objectively alone and no self-help trick could help, we can feel more lonely surrounded by thousands than in a prison cell, blah blah blah, loneliness only exists inside our heads, blah blah blah, it is in solitude that we find our true selves, blah blah blah. I made a mental list of the reasons that justified my loneliness on a day of collective celebration, that justified my being there alone sitting at the table looking at my disjointed family. I didn't like football or get-togethers, I never even went to the fireworks at Cascais Bay, that was no celebration, it was the bread and circus that rulers used to continue mis-ruling over us, it was a sad manipulation of television and social media, it was just drunks, frustrated people needing to seize those moments to pretend they were happy, I made a list of the reasons why there was nothing to celebrate, why there was nothing wrong with staying at home, I deluded myself about my superiority, I wasn't uncultivated or ignorant like others, I didn't need the artifice to feel good about myself, I didn't want to be surrounded by drunks, I had never much liked football, but the more I tried to convince myself the more I sunk into the darkness of the living room.

I sat at the dining table. I didn't know what to do. I wasn't going to cry again. I could cry as much as I wanted, I could wail and shout, after all Jorge and Grandma wouldn't be waking from their deep snoring slumbers, but I didn't want to cry. I thought of things I'd enjoy doing, yes, that was it, I'd watch an episode of one of my favourite series. I realised immediately that I wouldn't be able to concentrate, and besides I didn't want to associate that seemingly infinite sadness with anything I enjoyed doing. Perhaps I might use the time to fold the clothes that had dried on the line, to read the building administrator's annual report, look out for advertisements from the competing agency, always so many things to be done. Impossible. I was left breathless just thinking about it, how could I go about those routine chores, when everyone else was celebrating an exceptional occurrence?

The victory was proof that luck and the right circumstances might be met with talent or skills to make things happen. Portugal had defeated France, Milena had reached her goal, I had no excuse not to achieve what I wanted to achieve, even if I still didn't know what I wanted to achieve. I pictured myself again with Marco on the beach at Azarujinha, with no dreams to speak of. I didn't want the racket of the party going on outside, nor did I want the peace of the indoors solitude, but how could I say to Marco, to the world, to Jorge, to myself, without feeling ridiculous, that I wanted to be loved, how could I say it, to all of us, loud and clear, Yes, yes, I want to be loved, yes, I want a tempest, but a tempest that will protect me from the world, I want to be the eye of the hurricane, the calm around which everything spins, I want to be the cause and the consequence of what happens around me, I don't want to stand still, I want to walk with the uncertain force of a storm, I want the brutality of what is temporary instead of the eternal solid composure of gravitating planets, I don't want to be immersed in the monotonous coming and going of days and tides. Yes, that was it. I wanted, above all, to not have to think about all those crazy things. I wanted to stay sober and not be sad.

I got a message from Inês telling me she was spending the night at a friend's house, but I suspected the friend must be a male friend, and that male friend must be Nuno, and the house must be a garden where they hid, which would explain the dirt stains I'd see on her clothes the following day. I used Google to look up Piazza della Repubblica, where Mârcia had watched the match, on our next Skype call I would ask her what she was doing in Urbino, I looked up Urbino's history, I noted the restaurant recommendations, I saw the arcades and the fountain, I left Urbino and followed links to diets, I found myself reading the blog of an anorexic singer, from the anorexic singer I clicked through to symptoms of the peri-menopause just to make sure that I didn't have any of them yet. I sat at the dining table, pondering my disjointed family, some of it right there in the living room, Grandma's body on the sofa, Jorge's on the floor. I had drunk too much, and the alcohol that up to that point had made me more alert had perhaps also switched me off momentarily. I couldn't say how much time had passed before the phone buzzed with a new notification and gave me a fright. It was from Tinder. Someone had installed Tinder on my phone and that someone could only have been me.

I had been thinking about signing up to one of the dating apps that Milena and my colleagues kept talking about. But I had been thinking about so many other things, about telling my boss to sod off whenever he boasted about the Super Platinum Agent, about getting a butt-lift whenever I saw younger women's bottoms at the beach, about parachute jumping, about robbing a bank and fleeing to Hawaii, about doing a paleo diet to recover the slim waist I had lost the previous century, I had been thinking about so many things, the lives I had stopped having, the ones I could have had, the ones I could still have, and in all my thoughts always the vague regret that it was already too late, the hope that I still had time, the fear of the unknown and the tempting comfort of not having to face any more surprises, and in all my thoughts the tiredness, the persistent tiredness, the fragile laugh with which I was putting off the grand finale, the ceaseless pursuit of anything, of the thing that would happen next.

I didn't know what the word "tinder" meant, my English wasn't very good. Every New Year's Eve I promised myself I would sign up to an English language course that might be useful when it came to selling houses to foreign customers, but I never followed through. According to the online dictionary, tinder is a dry flammable material used for lighting a fire. My hair is tinder and it goes up in flames, I thought. Where had that line come from? It made me laugh.

I wouldn't be putting Jorge or Grandma to bed, we would remain in disarray that night, a night that would be forever different to all other nights.

I became Mónica. In the profile I created for her, Mónica was my age, had a successful husband and two loving children. She was interested only in men, preferably married. She declared herself to be against prejudice and bigotry and described herself as fun, fiery, loyal, passionate. Her work was challenging and motivating, her hobbies were relaxing and rewarding, she enjoyed cooking for friends, swimming, taking long walks, liked a hot chocolate by the fireplace in winter, and appreciated everything life had to offer. Mónica disliked injustice, lying and spelling mistakes, and she didn't post her photographs.

Led by Mónica, I was introduced to a catalogue of men of all ages, blond and dark-haired, tall and short, fat and thin. For every man, a profile, a description and half a dozen photos. I liked some and unliked others, until a notice appeared on my screen, Someone matched with you on Tinder. My first match described himself as fun, loved travelling to discover new cultures, and had a profile name that made my eyes hurt. SeNsUaLmAn72: Hi, Mónica. :-) How are you?

I was no longer alone.

For me, Tinder started as a game. A game not unlike the video games Jorge enjoyed, like Half-Life, where he was Gordon Freeman. In the same way, I had become Mónica. Mónica and Gordon Freeman were characters, but while Jorge had to accept the character he was given, I was able to create mine. The aim of my game was to get as many matches as I could, I could see the male users' profiles, and if I liked anyone who had liked me, or rather, who had liked Mónica's profile, there would be a match. We could, at that point, start chatting. If the chat wasn't interesting, I could undo the match, otherwise I could add him to my list. I had as many as fifty-seven matches. It was an addictive game, probably as addictive as Half-Life had been for Jorge. Not being naturally competitive, I was never interested in gaming, but on Tinder I had no adversaries and winning wasn't an end in itself, but a beginning, every time I got a match I thought it might be the beginning of a new future, even if that future only involved chatting.

Mónica wasn't me, but nor could I say she was my opposite. It gave me great pleasure to create her. Until Mónica came along, my creativity always fell short, the proof was in the words forever missing from my poems, the pathetic reiteration of my usual argument that it takes all sorts, my uninventive use of spices in cooking, my unoriginal choice of clothes, until Mónica came along I had been so uncreative that I believed my body was more creative than my mind, my body had created the girls and that was my greatest and only work. The process of creating Mónica was slow, it was largely the result of the chats with men on Tinder who helped me compose her, giving her everything that I regretted not having had. Perhaps that's why Mónica appeared to be so confident. Even if she didn't talk about it, Mónica could swim front crawl perfectly, she still wore her hair as long as she had in her youth, wore shorts to show off her legs with no cellulite and worked at the European Parliament, she was a senior official, not a dispensable and anonymous official like Guidinha. Guidinha had been my classmate in secondary school, until she failed five subjects in the second semester of ninth grade. Faced with this catastrophe, her parents thought it a good idea to place her in a private school, in which Guidinha always got top marks, so that she might continue without further hitches towards the fate that her family name ought to guarantee. Added to Guidinha's lack of intelligence was her lack of language skills, unless we count as a language the one spoken by the posh kids from the Linha, their affectations, how they let out little cries and swallowed their words. Guidinha was an expert at that language, and wouldn't have needed to use the family name to get one of those plum European posts, or one of those good jobs that Mother so desperately wanted me to have. I crossed paths with the grown-up

Guidinha half a dozen times, neither of us old enough to pretend we didn't recognise one another, and we exchanged polite words and offered an embellished summary of our successful lives, that is one of the uses of classmates who appear unexpectedly in our present lives. During one of those short conversations, Guidinha deigned to reveal the European Parliament's greatest problem, You'll never guess, and me hanging onto her words while in my head I shuffled through all the things I had heard about on television, saving the banks, the common agricultural policy, the single currency, the greenhouse effect, human rights, and Guidinha stretching out the pause so that her revelation would have a greater impact, the big, big European problem, the real intractable problem, was that the Parliament's plenary sessions took place in two cities that are more than four hundred kilometres away from each other, You cannot imagine the work and the stress, we have to carry dossiers and papers from one site to the other, busloads and busloads of documents, you cannot imagine. Since then I have always felt sympathy for Guidinha and all those who, like her, spend their lives shuttling between Brussels and Strasbourg, Strasbourg and Brussels, victims of that most respectable institution. Luckily for them there were the generous wages, the maintenance support, the travel expenses, the big offices with heating and air conditioning, the champagne and canapé receptions, luckily there were all sorts of benefits that allowed them to get over their professional trauma.

Another difference between my little game and Jorge's video games is that his were understood by everyone to be games, whereas only I considered Tinder to be a game, for everyone else it was a dating app. I couldn't, therefore, let anyone know I was also Mónica, which forced me to take certain precautions. No-one would consider Jorge an assassin because he stepped into Gordon Freeman's shoes, but everyone would call me a slut for stepping into Mónica's shoes, even though Mónica wasn't a slut. They were wrong. I wasn't a slut, I wasn't even an adulteress, I had invented a game and I was playing it, nothing more. It's true that Mónica spoke matter-of-factly about sex, but that was because most men on Tinder wanted to talk about sex and, unlike me, Mónica didn't avoid it, she was fearless and shameless. As the chats went on, her language was moulded into the female echo of her interlocutors, which made her very popular. There were few men who didn't feel regret at saying goodbye, or who didn't seek her out again, or didn't grow curious about her, or didn't want to get closer to her. The considerable interest Mónica attracted quickly created a problem due to the lack of photographs. For her first two weeks on Tinder, Mónica had no face, but soon the men's questions about her looks became tiresome, as did the constant requests to see her, the intrusions on her anonymity. Mónica invoked the need for caution because she was married, she promised to show herself when she and the men got to know each other better and knew whether there were any affinities, but they insisted, Send a picture, please, I can't chat with someone faceless, how do I know you're not a man? They either seemed to have no imagination or too much of it.

That was how Mónica acquired the face of an Australian, showing a face was an easy problem to solve, I had millions of faces at my disposal, I could show any one of them as long as it wasn't my own. It wouldn't, however, have been prudent to choose the face of someone who might discover my deception and, who knows, might even sue me, I knew nothing about the law but it seemed obvious to me that I couldn't just pretend to be another person. In the beginning, Tinder felt like a minefield. Despite it being a game I was playing, and despite the fact that I was playing at being Mónica, who existed only on my phone, I felt that at any moment I might find myself in danger of committing a serious transgression. Ironically, I was able to stop worrying when Tinder stopped being only a game and I started taking risks. But I was still afraid when I chose a face from a faraway country for Mónica. Looking at the Facebook profiles of Australian women, I decided that many of them could have passed for Portuguese women, but the choice was complicated further because I wanted Mónica to share some physical attributes with me. I hoped this rule would mitigate my actions, so I chose an Australian who was slightly uglier than me. In this way I found a better way to play the game. When, after a month, there was a match between Mónica and Carlos, Mónica was already a mix between an Australian woman's face and my own body parts. The initial rule of not using photographs had given way to the rule of only using photos I stole from the Australian woman's Facebook feed, a head shot and a full-body shot, but the men liked Mónica's photos, and instead of calming down they demanded more, I want to see you in a swimsuit, send nudes, go topless, show me your tits, your ass, your legs, show me your whole body, from the back, legs spread, on all fours. To convince me to do this, they sent me photos of themselves, even though the cropping of most of the ones in which they were nude left out their heads. I wouldn't have agreed to their demands if a rivalry with the Australian woman hadn't started to insinuate itself. Mónica's chats with the men might not be my chats, but her words came from me and I couldn't remain immune to the men's interest in Mónica's words. Things were different regarding their interest in Mónica's photos, they were nothing to do with me. Once again I rewrote the rules of the game, replacing the rule about Mónica only using photographs of the Australian woman with another that established that Mónica could also use photos of my own body parts, satisfying in this way the men's increasingly insistent demands. Except that, once those demands were met, new ones emerged. When can we meet? When can we have coffee? When can we fuck?

So I began to show my body, even if in a fragmented and non-identifiable way. Whenever I took photos, I was careful not to capture any distinctive detail, the birthmark right above my left breast, the scar near my elbow, the little red spot on my thigh, and that care extended to the photographs' backdrops. The houses I had to sell and the gym I went to became my backdrop of choice, because the tiles in our bathroom and the walls in other rooms in our house would give me away much faster than my breasts, my buttocks or my legs. With all bodies being so similar, only Jorge could identify me. And perhaps not even he might be able to do it, such little attention did he pay to my middle-aged body. I couldn't, though I sometimes tried to, overlook the fact that Jorge spent his days distracted from me, living his own life, on his own laptop, on his own phone, busy with the work he brought home, with his video games or his flirtations with #tableforone or others like her, I couldn't overlook the fact that Jorge hadn't noticed me for a long time.

Whenever we were together, it wasn't unusual for the girls and Jorge to be on their phones, browsing the Internet, on Facebook, on Instagram, sending and receiving messages as I spoke to them. The question I usually asked at first, Who is it? was most often met with the answer, You don't know them, or other expressions of annoyance that told me I was invading their privacy. I learned to remain quiet, and our family time soon included the spectres that each of them were connected to, and with whom they often seemed to get on better, or have more fun, than they did with me. The girls spoke frequently with those spectres, but it wasn't long before Jorge started doing the same, even if, at first, he claimed it was work-related. Of course there had always been thoughts we didn't share, but the brazenness with which his new behaviour made that obvious was hurtful. Over time, I came to accept that the new behaviour was proof that, no matter how much we loved someone, no matter how much they loved us, no matter how intimate the relationship, we would always be inaccessible to others. Even more worrying than not having access to their phones was not having access to what happened in their hearts and souls, but there was no point in getting dramatic now if I had always been able to accept that. Nor would I want things to be different, because if any of them had access to my phone they would surely be scandalised by some of the chats I had, but it would be even worse if they managed to get access to what went on inside my head. None of them would forgive me for the times when I disliked them, or even wished them ill. I comforted myself by thinking that the presence of the new spectres had an honesty about it that I found healthier.

So I began to spend more time on my phone, just as Jorge and the girls did, I exchanged messages with men on Tinder in front of them, showing my skill at managing parallel conversations. Perhaps they noticed the change in me, but, more than suspicion or curiosity about what had happened and who I was communicating with, they must have felt relief. If I was as busy on my phone as they were, there was no reason for them to feel guilty, and no reason for me to feel left out when they, though physically present, went on their virtual escapades. I only left that family togetherness when I had to exchange naughty photographs with strangers on Tinder. Dirty pictures, in the men's words. At those moments, I would lock myself up in the toilet and later rejoin the family, feeling victorious, as if I had finally managed to become a Bond Girl walking out of the sea, a desired woman whom everyone was applauding. To describe to strangers, in great detail, my preferred sexual positions, to confess to them that I liked doing this or that, gave me a thrill similar to the one I felt as a teenager when I imagined that, suddenly and inexplicably, my body would learn to do the front crawl or dive gracefully into the water.

It was around that time, also, that I decided to look after my body. I had grown used to the ravages that the passage of time had caused and I even added a few more, after all only Jorge witnessed them closely. But I now had an obligation to minimise them, it wasn't fair to subject Mónica and the men on Tinder to my neglect. I started a diet and signed up at a gym. For years I had been saying that I needed to eat less and exercise more, but I had never taken steps to make either of those things happen. If one day I looked at myself in the mirror with disgust and pledged to follow a healthy lifestyle by cutting down on chocolates, cakes and crisps, the following day I changed my mind and laconically declared that the secret to happiness lay in accepting things as they were. I didn't specify what things I was referring to, nor did anyone care to ask. Until Mónica came into my life, my idea of physical exercise only went as far as the gym clothes I wore to the supermarket or as I sat on the sofa to enjoy an episode of the television series I was watching, and my greatest dieting effort consisted in drinking Coke Zero. The one time that the girls managed to drag me to a gym, I left terrified at the sinister world of treadmills, rowing machines and stationary bikes that appeared ready to shoot off at any moment, such was the speed at which their users cycled. I couldn't understand the point of most of the other fitness machines, and I was nauseous from the smell of the rooms filled with sweaty, second-rate Rocky Balboas and dedicated followers of Jane Fonda and other gurus of the cult of firm glutes. The withered family men with towels around their necks, looking like they were on the cusp of a heart attack as they worked out, the women in their forties chasing their lost youth in Lycra outfits that mercilessly emphasised their flab, the wannabe gigolos cowboy-walking around as if some invisible rope were pulling back their shoulders, like ridiculous inflatable dolls, the neon pink, orange and green of the girls' gym outfits, the yoga instructors' seemingly catatonic state, the receptionists' overly friendly smiles, it all inspired repugnance and contempt rather than admiration or envy. The only thing that escaped my scorn was the swimming pool. I liked swimming pools. I was happier in a swimming pool than I was swimming in the sea or a lake, I always felt more comfortable with the far-from-perfect small-mindedness and pretentiousness of human creations than I did with the grandeur and the faultless perfection of divine creations. I had a soft spot for the poor, futile and very human attempts to imitate God's initial act of creation, even if they led only to the creation of laughable swimming pools where old people splashed around as if enjoying a second childhood, or proper pools with swimmers going up and down the lanes trying to knock a thousandth of a second off their laps. With Mónica in my life, however, all ideas seemed possible, so I started a diet and signed up at the gym. I also booked myself into thirty lessons to learn front crawl.

Healthy body in a healthy mind. Becoming hooked on Tinder and on being Mónica wasn't a moral weakness, or a betrayal of my family. If there was anything reprehensible about my behaviour it was the lies Mónica told the men as she chatted with them, stoking their fantasies with false promises, despite being a virtual creation that none of them would ever meet. But surely the men lied too, they must have exaggerated the interest they professed to have in Mónica, there must have been more fakery than sincerity in

173

the desire they claimed to feel for our body, mine and hers. If I didn't mind them lying, then surely they couldn't mind me doing so, at least regarding the fact that Mónica was not me. Lying on the Internet wasn't really lying, and even less so on Tinder, it was a form of reinvention, it contained within it the intent to hide or misrepresent relevant information, and the casual matches on Tinder couldn't care less whether I was Mónica or Eliete, as long as they could fuck one of us. And I couldn't care less who they were, I only wanted to feel the desire that, with varying degrees of sincerity, they said I awoke in them.

Because of the lies they told and the kinds of wariness they displayed, it wasn't long before I was able to identify, within half a dozen messages, what Tinder type my interlocutors belonged to. On Tinder, humanity seemed much less complex, its behaviours and desires much less diverse. So, there were the long-suffering men who were there because their ill wives couldn't satisfy them sexually, the men who distinguished between wives, mothers and all other women and who refused to do with their wives or the mothers of their children what they wanted to do with other women, the righteous defenders of traditional families who were unhappy in their marriages but remained married because they believed all the world's problems were caused by broken families, the tormented men who would sooner die than let their wives know that they liked to dress in women's clothes or liked to be pissed on or beaten, the newly divorced men who had moved back in with their parents, the house-proud home owners who believed themselves to be good catches, the desperate, the eternal singletons and the one-night-standers, the insatiable men who fucked at home but wanted to fuck more, the seemingly bold ones whose first message would be Wanna fuck? but who, upon getting a positive reply with a suggested time and place, would immediately undo the match, the ghosts who might spend hours typing out messages but would never post a photograph, the ones who wanted to be best friends from the first hello and believed every match to be an indestructible blood pact, the spiteful ones who didn't hold back on their insults when they didn't get the reply they were expecting, the controlling ones who wanted to know whether I was chatting to other men, whether I had met any of them, the voyeurs and exhibitionists who only wanted to see and be seen on camera, the stand-up comedians who made every message a failed attempt at humour, the unfortunate ones whose personal tragedies made any documentary about the world's greatest catastrophes seem like light entertainment, the bad liars who a couple of messages in confessed that their profile was fake and, to compensate for the falsehood, immediately volunteered their real names, their addresses, and their phone and Citizen Card numbers, the good liars who believed more in their fabrications than in the truth of their own lives, the unemployed with time on their hands and the hope of finding someone who might help, ready to rage against anyone who appeared to have a good life. There were so many men, and so few differences between them, that it was impossible not to think of types, and almost impossible to find an individual.

It didn't take me long to confirm what I had always

suspected about myself, I felt better when I was wearing a mask, when I wasn't being quite myself, when I could be a little bit someone else. The multiple identities allowed by technology seemed much more interesting to me than the multiple identities of that poet I had studied in my Portuguese literature class in year eleven, and which bored me to death. Mónica didn't save me from Grandma's illness, from the tediousness of most of my conjugal and family duties, from my concerns about Inês, from missing Márcia, from Mother's selfishness, from my envy of Natália the Platinum Agent, she didn't save me from the problems, the nuisances and the mishaps that made up my daily life, but she gave me the lightness that allowed me to put them in context and the self-confidence to tackle them.

Had I not had Mónica in my life, I wouldn't have dared suggest to Jorge that we put off our two-week holiday in the Algarve until the low season, citing the unpredictability of Grandma's illness and arguing that it would be both inconvenient and irresponsible to take her with us. It was much more fun to seduce strangers than to try to refresh my marriage by spending an unsatisfactory fortnight making monotonous preparations for the beach and queuing for hours at restaurants. Jorge protested but, when he found out we would get a full refund, agreed that it made sense to wait. He seemed as relieved as I was to be free of the obligation to pretend we were still the passionate couple we had stopped being many years ago.

It was around this time that I became interested in the idea of narrowing the gap I had created in my virtual game by trying to reverse the sort of relationship I had established with Mónica. If I existed in the virtual world, lending Mónica parts of my body, why shouldn't Mónica exist in real life? The game I was addicted to was no longer just a game, or rather, it had become more of a performance than a virtual game. As there can be no performance without a body, the urge to allow Mónica to show herself became greater and more insistent. The men's requests to meet became more tempting, never in my life had I felt so desired, I felt tempted to experience that desire in person. In the long monologues I had in my head I told myself that it would be enough to see the desire in the men's eyes, to feel their proximity, I told myself that they wouldn't touch me, I wouldn't touch them, perhaps a handshake, perhaps a kiss, only that, we would behave like friendly acquaintances. It went without saying that I wouldn't fuck anyone, Mónica wouldn't fuck anyone, she would only bring out into the light of day the conversations that took place on mobile phones. After a cup of coffee or a walk along the seawall, the most pleasant ideas for a first date, the men would almost certainly lose interest in Mónica once they realised they wouldn't be fucking her, perhaps they might even stop talking to her, they might become angry, but Mónica would be skilful and clever in finding excuses so they wouldn't feel rejected, the refugee crisis or Brexit had made the workload at the European Parliament overwhelming, or maybe she had felt too attracted to the man and now she feared risking her marriage, or perhaps one of her daughters or even both had fallen ill, any excuse would do, what mattered was witnessing their desire for Mónica, for me.

Despite it being Mónica who always showed up for the

meetings, I wouldn't let her do any of the things she promised in the chats, the first meeting would always be brief, Let's see if there is any chemistry between us, I made her explain to Carlos, not worrying about elaborating on the fabrication, If there is then we can agree on another meeting, and she'd finish by adding something reticent but suggestive. From the moment I decided that Mónica would come out of my phone, I was willing to meet any of the strangers she chatted with, as long as she stuck to the rule I had for turning an online match into an in-person meeting, the man had to be married, and the more tied up he was in his marriage, the better. The game had to remain a game, I had to choose men who were even keener than I was to separate the actor from the role, to prevent a man who just wanted to fuck a married woman on the quiet from becoming a man who wanted to drag the fling out into the open. That way, Mónica wouldn't put me at risk, we wouldn't do anything we shouldn't, what difference would there be between Mónica having a cup of coffee with a stranger and the Facebook flirtations between my agency colleague and me, or between Jorge and #tableforone? I might even prefer their flirting to happen in the intimacy of a café rather than for everyone to see, on Facebook. Even though Mónica's messages were sexually explicit, they were much more innocent than the chats with the competing agency colleague, in which sex was always implicit, and if I considered its intention, the photograph of my legs taken in the storage unit was more obscene than the one of my buttocks reflected in the gym's bathroom mirror.

It was Carlos whom Mónica finally agreed to meet. He

happened to be one of the most insistent on meeting in person and he fulfilled the rule of being married and wanting to remain married. Besides, he was agreeable and found me agreeable, he was reasonably good-looking and claimed to like my body and my banter. Carlos had other advantages, he belonged to the category of men who fucked at home but wanted to fuck more outside of home, he openly confessed to being stuck in a marriage of convenience with an older and wealthier woman, one of those posh ones from Linha, and, more importantly, he calmly agreed that we wouldn't fuck on our first date. Other married men were usually quick to suggest meetings in motels, they talked coarsely about sexual acts and the places where they might happen. As much as the idea of meeting with them excited me, they were a risk, and so I insisted, Let's see if there's any chemistry between us. They often blocked me soon after, saying things like Piss off, or Go fuck yourself cock teaser, or Do you think I want us to pray together?, or If I wanted to have polite conversation I'd ask my wife.

I agreed with Carlos on a time and place for a meeting so that I didn't have to worry about getting caught. If Jorge or Inês happened to see me there, I would explain that I was talking with a friend or a client and that was all, nothing would happen between Carlos and me that might betray us, no touching, no kissing, Carlos wouldn't pat my buttocks like the man from the Readers' Circle did to Mother, even if I liked the idea of him doing it as if by accident, showing the desire for me that his words had already hinted at, giving me goosebumps, sending a wave of heat coursing through my body.

It was also Carlos who explained to me the difference between a fling and an affair. A fling can be chosen like a hobby, an affair happens and imposes on us another life, there is no urgency in a fling, we can weigh its pros and cons, an affair cannot be delayed or avoided, a fling has an end date but an affair poses a dilemma, a fling is for the cynics, the bored or the cowards, an affair serves the unhappy, the romantics and the dreamers. So what are you after? he asked me. I couldn't reply honestly, I couldn't tell him that I wanted neither of those, I wanted only to feel wanted and for that I needed him and some of the other men I chatted with. A fling, I replied with no hesitation, Intelligence is the greatest aphrodisiac, Carlos wrote, you're making me rock-hard, and then the chat went down other routes. Remembering again the multiple identities of the poet I had studied in year eleven, who wrote about how love letters are ridiculous, it seemed to me that it was really sex messages that are ridiculous. I was unsure about whether to mention the Australian woman, if I confessed that the headshot and the full-body photo were not Mónica's I might scare off Carlos, men could be so easily frightened. I decided to go with the surprise, and as I was more attractive than the Australian hopefully it would be a pleasant surprise.

I had never tried on so many clothes as I did that day searching for the ones that would make the best impression. It was a warm day, not a speck in the blue sky and the cicadas were singing their hearts out, a good day for summer love, and I was elated, wondering whether it would be a good idea to deploy stiletto heels on a first date, whether I should go in for the kill, whether the blouse was too revealing and might suggest that Mónica was up for everything, whether I should be more cautious, because men needed to think they were in charge. I decided to wear a button-up shirt, that way I could show more or less of myself depending on how I was feeling. If the situation called for it, I could undo the third button and appear more daring. I chose the shirt with the green stripes, the one my boss had said gave me a cosmopolitan air. I had lost weight, so the dark-blue skirt looked good on me. I looked at myself in the mirror with satisfaction. Only a few more weeks and I would attain the objective I had set myself and written down on a card the day I joined the gym, To wear a bikini again. I hadn't worn a bikini for more than twenty years, since I had Márcia. I blamed it on the c-section scar, but that wasn't the reason, even more than the scar I was ashamed of the folds of belly flab like an accordion's bellow, the breasts spilling out of the bikini top, the horrendous wobbliness of my thighs. It scared me to think how my middle-aged body might be viewed by a strange man, a man who hadn't witnessed its gradual deterioration, even though I had no reason to worry, Carlos already knew the parts of my body that men paid the most attention to, I had sent him photos that showed them accurately, and he had seemed enthusiastic about what I showed him. Perhaps too enthusiastic, to judge by the selfies he took soon after. In any case, we would only be meeting for coffee, I wouldn't be undressing and Carlos didn't have x-ray vision to see the marks left on my body by pregnancy and by age, the body hair that had escaped depilation, the defects big and small that obsessed me, and obviously nobody expected to find a Victoria's Secret model on Tinder, especially at our age. There is no need for you to be nervous, I reminded myself every five minutes.

I applied my makeup slowly, following the advice given by experts, blush lengthened the face, eyeliner intensified the gaze, highlighter on the lips made them look plumper, how many centuries of female anguish condensed into that advice. Though I was mindful of the old maxim that makeup shouldn't be used to conceal, I tried to make the marks of age disappear, spreading foundation over the squint lines around my eyes and the wrinkles around my lips. I chose a simple handbag, classic pearl earrings, silver rings, and the result was an unhappy mix between a femme fatale, a successful businesswoman and a girl at the shopping mall. Regrettably, I had never had a style of my own.

I took the keys to the car and kissed Grandma goodbye, she was sitting on the sofa, watching the television programmes that kept her so entertained in the afternoons. I had two hours before the meeting with Carlos, but I still had to stop by the house in Adroana to put up the "For sale" placard and take photos for the website. Where are you going?, Grandma asked, I'm off to work, I said, in a hurry. Grandma said nothing, but I could read the question in her eyes, Dressed like that? Although she hadn't asked, I thought I might tell her I had a meeting but I was distracted by an incoming message which turned out not to be from Carlos, so in the end I didn't. At that moment, everything was pushing me to leave the house. Before leaving, I told her Inês was in her bedroom, if she needed anything they could just call me, and I didn't even reply when she said goodbye with her usual, God bless you.

Looking at myself in the car's rear-view mirror, I noticed that, by applying so much foundation around my eyes, I had created a dark paste that made me look older. I was so nervous that I let the car lurch forward. I no longer knew how to do these things, I no longer knew how to go on a date, I no longer knew anything about meeting men. The last time I had gone out on a date, Princess Diana had just got divorced, the cows were all mad, and I truly believed you could die of love. Now no-one cared anymore whether Princess Diana had been murdered, cows were once again sane and succulent, and love was a practical arrangement that included paying the condominium fee, keeping our diabetes in check and a mattress with an indentation on my side.

I had sprayed on so much perfume that my head began to hurt. The A5, A16, Rua das Figas, Rua das Papoilas, no-one knew the roads around Cascais better than I did, I was born there and that is where all the important things in my life had happened. I knew what had happened before me, what would happen after, and what would happen after that. Adroana, an out-of-the-way place, seemed pleasant to me for the first time. The abandoned houses appeared romantic, the small cultivated fields spoke to me of freedom, and I tried my best not to feel too desolate when I saw the children's park boxed in by buildings on the Largo do Amor Perfeito. My stilettos were making it difficult to walk carrying the "For sale" placard with my photo and my phone number, it dragged on the floor and banged on the

183

steps as I climbed them. The house for sale had been shut for years due to a dispute between the owner's heirs and when I opened the windows it filled with light as if waking from a long slumber. My job didn't seem difficult, almost everyone needed a house, but I had to admit that I wasn't a good salesperson. The envy I felt towards Natália and her Platinum Agent trophies wasn't enough to push me to be better, to make an effort to win them myself. When I went on stage at the agency's annual meeting, I mouthed the words to our motivational oath, without really concentrating on what I was saying, distracted as I was with minor worries, whether I had chosen the right dress, whether the piles of plastic cups on the tables were the same height, whether A or M had arrived, whether D was sucking up to Z, I stood on stage next to others, but I was really noticing how the room's decorative mouldings were chipped, how many times the senior managers yawned, I distracted myself with pointless things, until the applause for the president's dull speech tore me away from the torpor. At the end, the president invited the winner of the Platinum Agent award onto the stage. For the past three years we had only heard the name of the competent Natália, who would walk onto the stage like a machine and never missed a word of the speech of thanks she had memorised. She would then smile angelically and shake hands limply in a way that irritated me, and I would applaud the Platinum Agent overzealously, trying to disguise the resentment I could never confess.

I chipped a fingernail as I was trying to twist the wires that secured the placard to the balcony railings and my head was aching more. Was it the universe telling me to forget about the date, I wondered, but I immediately put the bad omen out of my mind. I chose the best angles for a few photographs with a single thought in my head, in an hour's time I would be sitting with Carlos on a bench on the seawall near the Santa Cruz fort, in Estoril, that was the place we had agreed on for our meeting. I imagined how pleased he would be when he saw me, when he realised that I was hotter and more interesting than the Australian woman whose photos I had sent, then I imagined the rest of the date, we would sit at a café table, no, better not, we might find ourselves too tethered to the café table, we would take a stroll along the seawall, engaged in animated conversation, he seemed to be the talking type. I photographed the rooms, avoiding the lighter-coloured rectangles on the wooden floors that showed where beds had once been, the broken mirror in the toilet that meant seven years of bad luck, the dented pots in the kitchen cabinet, people left behind so many things, the bundle of letters tied up with string in a desk drawer, the expired passport on the bookshelf, the photo of a soldier inside a church service book, I photographed the house without taking the time to think about how many parties, how much crying, how many births and deaths had happened there, the house was simply the past encased in a certain smell and a certain light, a mute past, with no narrative.

I looked out a window at the back of the house. Beyond the high wall surrounding the property was a chestnut tree, and closer by a flock of magpies picking away at the ground. I gazed lovingly at the birds. I didn't like birds, but that first Friday in August the world seemed beautiful, despite my chipped fingernail and my aching head, the meeting with Carlos was nothing special, betrayal wasn't a lightning bolt out of the blue, instead it was an idea that had sprouted like the parsley and coriander plants that Grandma grew in clay pots along the kitchen wall, betrayal was nothing special, it merely made my head spin like when I used to go dancing at the 2001 nightclub, head spinning beneath the dancefloor's mirror ball. I would wait for Milena, locked up in my room to avoid having to hear Mother's sermons about delinquent boys spiking girls' drinks and then doing all sorts of things to them, Milena would ring the bell twice and I would fly down the building's staircase, the following day Mother would blame me for her not being able to get a moment's sleep because she was so worried, and she would threaten to throw me out if I ever came back home after the sun had come up, Mother pointing her finger at me, If you fail the year again I swear I'll kick you out, and me, higher than Ozzy Osbourne, singing back to her in my bad English the Ozzy Osbourne song that an old boyfriend had once recorded for me on a mix tape, Mama, I'm coming home. Despite being a better student than Milena, I ended up flunking the year because of poor attendance, Milena never flunked, she didn't like playing truant and, at that point, didn't like drinking, I thought of Milena and me all those years ago catching rides to the 2001 nightclub with our hook-ups, and now there I was, driving to Estoril to meet with a stranger. I parked the car near the Casino Estoril, I crossed through the garden that once had mushroom-shaped lights, the tunnel beneath the railway, only a few more minutes before I was sitting on the bench nearest to the Santa Cruz fort, the bench where Carlos would be waiting for me.

Through nervousness and a sense of anticipation I had arrived twenty minutes early. Five o'clock, on the bench nearest to the fort, he had suggested, the bench furthest from the beach. The bench was taken by a family, mother, father and two small children, who had sat down to brush sand off their feet. I missed the time when the girls were young, brushing sand off their feet, having them asleep on my lap, their sweat mixing with mine, knowing I was theirs and knowing they were mine. My stilettos and the shirt with the cosmopolitan air seemed out of place amid the summer visitors, I could feel my makeup melting, it wasn't hard to picture my oily skin, shiny like the custard dough-nuts being loudly advertised by a beach vendor, not to mention the bags under my eyes becoming smudged with foundation. I thought it might be a good idea to sit at the nearest café. I would touch up my makeup, take some paracetamol and calm myself. It's only a meeting over coffee, I kept saying to myself.

Minutes after I sat down at the café, the family left the bench and in its place sat a man who looked nothing like the photograph Carlos had sent, the man was much more handsome than the photograph he had sent me. He did the same thing I did, I thought with the enthusiasm of a girl on her first date, not only did he choose another man's photograph but he chose a less attractive man so that I would be favourably surprised, he and I are soulmates, I thought, letting loose a string of nonsensical reveries. The jetty where young boys used to jump into the water, and from which I once managed to jump myself, was full of people walking from side to side, the café was full of people talking, many of them tourists, people sheltering from the sun under the thatched huts that had replaced the striped fabric parasols, the shoreline was full of people walking from side to side, wherever I looked I could only see people, people, people, I felt at peace with all those people, the stranger I had been chatting with for weeks was a handsome man and was waiting for me on the bench. I took a deep breath, straightened my back, paid the waitress for the coffee and water so I could get up as soon as Carlos replied to the message I had just sent, confirming that he was the cute guy I was watching. Are you there? I texted him. I tried to busy myself reading the file for the house at Adroana to settle the nerves that made my hands shake. At the next table, a child was throwing a tantrum about ice cream, and the father threatened with some punishment I couldn't make out. A woman vaguely resembling #tableforone was rubbing sun cream into the tip of her nose and saying to her friend, If I don't do this I look like a drunk. It occurred to me that she was so ugly that it made no difference whether she looked like a drunk, and that her friend must be thinking the same thing, and that they must both be thinking something similar about me, that it was a blessing not to know other people's thoughts.

The sea shone in emerald tones, some children ran towards the surf to dive in, further away were the sailboats and speedboats. It wouldn't be long before I could swim out to the boats, before the swimming lessons finally rescued me from the shame of my past, it was too late for me to come out of the water looking like I was on the catwalk, but I would still be achieving the great accomplishment of swimming front crawl out to the boats. The shirt with the cosmopolitan air was sticking to my back, and I noticed with alarm that patches of sweat were now appearing in the armpits. Looking at my feet, I was reminded of Grandma's bread dough leavening, because that's what was happening to my feet inside the stiletto shoes, it looked like my feet wouldn't stop swelling.

Carlos' message didn't take long to arrive, You're not on the bench. A choir of angels singing Hallelujah wouldn't have been too much for the happiness I was feeling, he was the handsome man sitting on the bench and now he was asking to see me. On my way, I wrote. I got up. The sun in my face made my head throb in sync with the beating of my heart, it felt like a thin nail was being hammered into my head with every pulse. I was going towards the bench when I saw the handsome man stand up and meet a woman who had just arrived. She was younger and prettier than me, she was wearing a strappy cotton dress and leather sandals that emphasised the wrongness of my shirt with the cosmopolitan air and my stiletto-heeled shoes. They greeted one another with a brief kiss on the lips. I felt helpless standing between the café and the bench, not knowing what to do, whether to turn back, whether to move ahead. Of course it couldn't possibly have been him, I thought, how could I have believed that the handsome man was waiting for me? But I soon got over my disappointment, better if he wasn't handsome, I'd be biting off more than I could chew, as Mother liked to say, more important than me liking him was him liking me. That was why I had agreed to meet him, that was why I signed up to Tinder, I wanted to feel that people might like me in a more definitive way, I was well aware that Facebook likes were easy and inconsequential, but to be chosen as a Tinder match, to chat for hours, to exchange photos and then agree to meet by the seaside was different. I looked around, so confident that I would see a man looking for me, that I found it hard to believe that there was no-one looking for me. I got another message, You can sit down now, the bench is free. He must have been nearby, otherwise how would he know that the handsome man had left. With the most confident steps that my leavened feet could muster, I walked towards the bench to sit down. A young man was busy on his phone, but looked too young to be Carlos. Another man put into his shirt pocket something that might have been a phone, but he looked nothing like the photographs Carlos had sent. Of course his photographs could be false, I reminded myself, if mine were his could be too. I looked at my phone again, surely in no time I'd get a message explaining what was happening, a few more minutes and everything would be resolved.

I sat on the bench, phone on my lap, my head like a periscope scanning left and right. I'm here, where are you? I wrote. What if he was that young man who, a moment ago, had been busy on his phone, what if he was hiding to see how I would respond? My shoes felt increasingly tight on my feet, the veins in my temples throbbed, the nail was opening a path of pain in my head, the sea and the sky blurred into each other, I remained seated on the bench, it excited me to feel I was being watched and controlled by him, to think that he was guiding me, he guided me when I seemed lost and surely would appear soon. I can see you, nice shoes, you made an effort, he wrote. I smiled, satisfied, his compliment for my shoes was his way of saying that he liked me, the woman sitting there instead of the Australian. I uncrossed my legs and crossed them again, now the right one over the left, pausing briefly halfway through the motions like Sharon Stone in *Basic Instinct*. Like what you see? I wrote, aiming for ambiguity. Just as I was about to send my message I got one from him, a kiss emoji, the one with the heart coming out of the lips, and then . . . then it disappeared. Poof. I couldn't even tell if my message had been sent because, just like that, poof, he disappeared from my phone, just like playing cards, handkerchiefs and bunnies disappeared inside the top hat of a magician I had seen at the circus once, poof, the sunset he used as his profile was replaced by a white circle with a man's empty silhouette.

It took me some time to realise that this wasn't some technical malfunction, that there hadn't been a problem with my phone or with my network. I didn't know what to make of it. I'd been blocked by, and had myself blocked, many men, but never in these circumstances. I couldn't tell which feeling was stronger, shock and anger and humiliation were mixed in equal parts, making me hostage to a despair and impotence that made me want to cry in front of everyone. One question after another came to mind and I couldn't properly answer any of them. Who was he, what had just happened, why did he do it? He could have been anyone, the young man with the phone, a boy curious about women, a shy and cowardly boy, it might have been a neighbour from the building next door, it might be someone abnormal, someone crazy, it might even be Jorge, I came up with one hypothesis after another to avoid facing the most obvious and terrible one, he didn't like the look of me and so he left. I felt everyone was staring at me as I sat there, lost, I tried not to look but it was impossible to avoid seeing the people around me. Even if it appeared like they were not seeing me, like they were only there to enjoy the summer afternoon, it was obvious that they were looking at me, that they were witnessing my humiliation and trying to hide their pity.

The walk back to the car felt a hundred times longer than the walk to meet him. As I went through the tunnel under the railway I cursed the men who urinated there, impregnating the ground with that nauseating smell. I took off my shoes as I approached the car and walked barefoot without caring that I looked like a madwoman. I remembered the chats I'd had with Carlos, trying to uncover any warning signs for my humiliation, but could think of nothing. He had come to the meeting, otherwise he couldn't have known if I was, or wasn't, on the bench, he had been close to me, unless he had been at a lookout and used binoculars, but who would be crazy enough to do something like that? No, he had come to the meeting and he hadn't liked me or my dating outfit that pretended not to be a dating outfit, he hadn't liked my awkward walk, which gave away the fact that I only wore stilettos for weddings, christenings and corporate conventions, that was why he had sent that mocking message, nice shoes, you made an effort. And I had smiled, I had crossed and uncrossed my legs, I had asked him, Like what you see?, I was trying hard to believe that he hadn't received my message, that my humiliation hadn't been so complete, that I had somehow managed to escape total ridicule, but then I'd change my mind and think, he can go fuck himself, the stupid man I had set up a meeting with was a coward, a parasite surely on the hunt for other women to live off, that older wife he was taking money from was probably not coming through for him.

In the car, with my head on the steering wheel, I cursed Tinder, Mónica, Eder's goal, Milena's sweethearts, Grandma's illness, Jorge and the girls. I don't know how long I was like that, concentrating on my headache, feeling Mother's index finger poking the centre of my forehead, Nothing happens to us if it doesn't happen here first. I had never experienced a failure when I didn't feel Mother's index finger poking the centre of my forehead, sometimes strongly, sometimes faintly, but I always felt it, Mother's index finger poking my forehead was the deserved punishment for having had the wishful thought of creating the intelligent and seductive Mónica, now laughable and humiliated, now mortally wounded.

Despite my fears, no-one had witnessed my humiliation. There were people all around, on that first Friday of August there were so many people on the beach that it was hard to see the sand, but no-one knew of my humiliation, even if some people had seen me, had seen my pathetic dating outfit, but seeing was never enough to know what was happening to someone, it always left out the mysteries of the mind, and now it also left out the phone, the phone that before too long would be part of our body, another mind, another chest of secrets. I was increasingly inaccessible, increasingly in thrall to what was happening in my mind and in my phone, that is why even if someone had seen me they wouldn't have known what was happening, no-one could help me. I kept my head on the car's steering wheel, the pain continued to radiate as if it knew the path to other pains, becoming stronger so it could defeat me implacably.

The phone rang. For a moment, I thought that it might be Carlos, that he had miraculously found my personal number and called to say, Don't be silly, you can't get rid of me so easily. Instead of Carlos, it was Inês, her voice trembling, Grandma swallowed the pillow stuffing, I called 112, you have to get here fast. At first I didn't understand what Inês was talking about, the tone of her voice frightened me. Pillow stuffing? How could someone swallow the pillow stuffing, are you sure? I asked. Yes, I've already called 112.

If reality weren't so determined to ruin our lives, no grandmother would swallow a pillow's stuffing and no-one would be left abandoned by the seawall on a first date, much less would the two things happen to the same person on the same day. If reality weren't so determined to ruin our lives, I would at that moment have been drinking coffee with Carlos or walking along the seawall, letting our hands touch. But reality always ruined our lives.

Or perhaps the two things weren't separate, they were

linked, one had led to the other and in this case it was all my fault, had I not been in a hurry to meet a stranger by the seawall, had I taken the time to reassure Grandma, telling her I was going to work but would be back soon, Grandma wouldn't have swallowed the pillow stuffing, perhaps she had done it on purpose as payback for my hasty exit, if I knew how to do things properly Grandma would be well and I wouldn't be in tears on my way to the hospital. I was solely responsible for my situation.

Grandma was fine in the end. The amount of pillow stuffing she had swallowed wasn't significant and it was all no more than a fright. Her incomprehensible appetite for pillow stuffing was only one of the aftershocks that followed her fall in the souvenir shop, or the episode, as the doctor referred to it, the earthquake that shook all our lives beyond repair. We could have overlooked Grandma swallowing the pillow stuffing with the same compassion with which we had overlooked her moments of forgetfulness, of confusion, her obsessions, the interrupted conversations, we could have put Grandma's absurd appetite for pillow stuffing down to the disease, like the neurologist did so ably in his clinic with the bucolic water-colours of ducks on the walls. The neurologist divided Grandma's illness into phases and warned me that, in the final phase, Grandma wouldn't know who she was, who we were, she would stop talking, walking, eating, would lose control over her bladder and bowels, and, meanwhile, Grandma's fingernails and hair would continue to grow in the body fed by a catheter, blood would continue to run through her veins and her joints would continue to stiffen, in the final phase Grandma's brain would be dead inside her still warm and well-fed body, Grandma's body would outlive Grandma as if it were a scene from a bad horror film. But that wouldn't happen until the final phase, and there was no point in jumping ahead, Grandma was still in the intermediate phase, the phase in which she was noticeably losing her memory and cognitive ability, in which her verbal dexterity was deteriorating, the content and variation of her conversation diminishing, she was suffering significant alterations to her personality, she was becoming spatially disorientated, the phase in which she would resuscitate Senhor Pereira and swallow pillow stuffing, we could have overlooked Grandma's absurd appetite for pillow stuffing with the same compassion with which we had overlooked Grandma's other absurd behaviours, if Jorge hadn't used the pillow stuffing as an excuse to say to me, when I came back from the hospital, Your grandmother cannot continue living with us.

Let's be grown up about it, he said, after Inês had said goodnight and shut her bedroom door. He kept his voice low like a priest in a confessional, Your grandmother only came for a few weeks and now we have to be grown up and recognise that she has become a threat to herself and to others, can you imagine if she sets something on fire, if she jumps out a window, you have to be grown up, it's not a good idea to have her with us, we don't know how to take care of her, if Inês hadn't made the connection between the ripped pillows and your grandmother being sick there could have been a tragedy, how would you have felt if . . . think about it, you don't have the time to look after her, especially now that you have more work because of all the foreign buyers, your grandmother isn't just some little old lady in need of company, your grandmother is ill and needs specialised care, people with know-how, let's be grown up about it and admit that, in the current circumstances, the best solution is to put her in a home.

We were sitting at the dining table and we were being grown up. I was still wearing my sad dating outfit, I had put the Adroana house file on the table beside me. I was sure that the idea of putting Grandma in a home hadn't just occurred to Jorge that day because of the pillow stuffing, he must have spent a long time preparing the list of reasons he gave me to send her away, otherwise he wouldn't have immediately argued that in a care home Grandma would be looked after night and day by professionals, that she would be in a safer environment because they would know how to prevent domestic accidents, that she would have people her own age to interact with, she would be among her equals, so many advantages that the only thing Jorge appeared to leave out was telling me that Grandma would live happily ever after in a home. Once he had given me the list of benefits, Jorge played his trump card, You have to sort this out, because Márcia is coming back soon, and how's that going to work, I don't think the girls can share a room, especially after Márcia has been away for so long, you know how it is, they come back more independent, we can't sacrifice the girls. We couldn't sacrifice the girls, so I would have to sacrifice Grandma. Putting aside the kind words, he concluded arrogantly, Your grandmother can afford a good care home, you have to sort this out, it isn't the girls' fault. And is it my fault, or Grandma's fault? I asked. Focus, Eliete, this is no time to get side-tracked.

It wasn't the time for me to get side-tracked or deviate, but that's what I did, launching into preposterous suggestions, If it's about space we can sell this flat and Grandma's house and buy a bigger place, a house, we always wanted a house, a proper family home, in no time the girls will be married, we'll have grandchildren, Mother might also need some help, we can buy a house where we can all spend Christmases together, a proper family home. Do you realise what you're saying, Eliete? Jorge said, irritated, Have you ever heard me saying that I want a big family home? And even if you could sell your grandmother's house, have you thought about how long it will take to make all those arrangements? She needs to be sorted out now, we need to sort things out now.

Instead of calming me, Jorge's words infuriated me further and made me feel as though I was at the edge of an abyss, an unexpected breaking point. Instead of overwhelming me, everything that had happened that day was now coursing through me like a strong drug, it wasn't the paracetamol I had taken, it was those other things I had done which suddenly felt like an adrenaline shot that made me seem like a madwoman, to judge from the way Jorge was staring at me.

I stood up, striding over-confidently, looking around at the space, I made wide gestures taking in the whole living room. In the meantime we can remodel this flat, remodelling can be done quickly, Inês is getting on so well with Grandma, I'm sure she wouldn't mind moving into our bedroom with her, there is enough room for both of them, we can split it up with a folding screen to give them both some privacy, we can move into Inês' room and Márcia can move into hers, the girls are always complaining about how ancient the furniture is and they're right, we can seize the moment and throw out this old thing. I felt increasingly confident, possessed by a strange strength and agility that allowed me to hop onto the sideboard in a single motion and pat the top firmly as I perched on it. Do you remember us when we bought this? I felt a great tenderness for Jorge, who was staring at me open-mouthed, and I said with a smile, Sorry, darling, not knowing quite what I was apologising for. I leaned forward, my hands holding up the weight of my body, open legs dangling, my skirt pulled up, Come here. Jorge seemed annoyed, You have to calm down, and he got up to leave. Please, come here, but he was already walking towards the hall and wasn't looking back, The best thing would be for your grandmother to be in a care home nearby so we can visit, he said before disappearing. I remembered the day Jorge and I bought the sideboard, Márcia was only a few months old, Jorge and I were happy, we bought it in instalments as part of the sales campaign to mark World Expo and the new millennium. In the past people used to pull out teeth with no painkillers, the shop owner said, and now everything is done with anaesthesia, with shopping it's the same thing, it doesn't hurt as much when you don't have to put down all the money at once but with or without anaesthesia you end up toothless, that's right, my friend, I don't know what the future holds, but I know we'll be paying for it in credit, the shop owner didn't shut up, I too had no idea what the future held, but I knew it had to be good. When the sideboard was delivered, we realised immediately that it was too large for the living room, but why should it matter that the sideboard was too big? Inês wasn't even a twinkle in Jorge's eye, Márcia was so young, we saw her grow from day to day with that same ingenious determination with which plants push skywards towards the sun that will scorch them. At that moment, everything was about the body, the soul, about blood and sweat, everything was declared, exposed, affirmed, a girl was a girl, a sideboard was a sideboard, love was love, nothing was clouded by wariness or doubt, nothing existed outside the realm of perception. Only when things started existing imperceptibly did it become tedious to discover them. And then we gave up on them.

But at that point nothing existed imperceptibly yet. The turn of the millennium was fast approaching and there was so much money going around that the land once occupied by shipping containers, slaughterhouses and shut-down factories was now filled with fountains, cable cars and the world's largest concrete canopy, the times of plenty had arrived, that is what everyone was saying on television and in newspapers. Meanwhile those of us born after the Carnation Revolution were spoiled and had grown up not experiencing poverty, the Colonial War, the Berlin Wall, we were ingrates for failing to thank the previous generations for their achievements, we drove new cars on freshly tarmacked motorways, and even then we complained about everything, never did a whole generation have so much, and we, utterly spoiled, a generation subsidised by European

Community funds, moaning about everything while we fell into debt to buy oversized sideboards, the World Expo was opening in a few days and fifteen million visitors were expected, the whole world was coming to Lisbon, the fifth empire was rising, we, the spoiled generation, had new motorways, the Expo, the 2004 Euros, credit to buy houses, cars, sideboards, honeymoons in Cuba, Cancun and the Dominican Republic, we had everything until the future arrived and shut down the furniture store, *Bankers are murderers*, *Fuck the crisis*, someone wrote in red spray-paint on the shop's pulled-down shutters, the future dried up the fountains, killed the olive trees on the Avenida dos Oceanos, and turned the world's largest concrete canopy into a urinal for louts and hoodlums, we had everything until the future arrived and found me sitting at the dining room table, where Jorge was trying to patiently tell me that my problem was always getting side-tracked when I should be trying to focus, as if he could see what was going on inside my head, When will you start doing things properly? he asked, as if he knew I was indirectly responsible for Grandma having swallowed the pillow stuffing.

The Good Shepherd, Home of Good Rest, Our Lady of Mercy. I wanted to swallow the care home leaflets like Grandma swallowed the pillow stuffing, no, not swallow them, stuff them in my mouth, chew them up and spit them into the faces of those who gave me the guided tours, but I would fold the leaflets carefully and say to myself, This is no country for old men. When I gave up being a tour guide to become an estate agent, I found a job in a small family firm whose owner, a man in his late seventies, would say whenever there was a problem, This is no country for old men. Although the phrase came from the depths of the owner's soul and was loaded with bitterness, the other newly arrived interns, young whippersnappers who walked backwards out of his office to show their deference, would often laugh as if he had just told a joke. This is no laughing matter, the boss would say, his voice gravelly and cavernous from tobacco smoke, his shoulders shaking and his hunched back protruding, I don't know whether you're all stupid or insolent, he growled, nostrils flaring, lips tensed and, waving brusquely as if swatting a fly, shut down the conversation. Anyone who dared to say anything at that point was on their own and would have to put up with all the insults and abuse the boss could muster. The interns would learn quickly and, the next time, would replace their laughs with a reverential lowering of the eyes. They couldn't have known that subservience would do them no good, that they would be sent away as soon as the generous contribution the state gave to the boss, in an effort to make local economies more dynamic, ran out, it was a well-greased system, the old man was always taking on new interns to justify the subsidies for the creation of new jobs that would never be created. People used to say that the HR manager, a dandy who hardly ever stepped foot in our office, was working for some twenty small businesses and earning a good part of the subsidies he managed to get them, but people used to say so many things. The country may not have been for old men, but it was a country for shyster businessmen so, as long as the money kept flowing from the European Economic Community the boss could continue to be the boss and enrich himself until the pot ran dry. But the pot would never run dry, the EEC money would never run out, it seemed impossible that the EEC money would ever run out, we were happy, we had finally discovered the thing that many centuries ago had made us take to the sea in ships, the fountain of eternal wealth. And even if there were no kings to maintain, no clergy or nobility to enrich, no fools to feed on the crumbs that fell from other people's tables, there were still their descendants, the ignorant and greedy governing class and an ignorant and submissive people.

It took me many years and a sleepless night to discover that the phrase *no country for old men* hadn't even been coined by the boss, he had stolen it from a famous writer I saw being interviewed by Oprah on one of the many cable channels that, late at night, alternated between repetitions of Oprah and Dr Phil. However, when I visited care homes to choose the one where I would send Grandma, I had forgotten the famous writer on Oprah, but I did remember the old boss living off the subsidies meant to modernise and enrich our country. It was no country for old men or women, as I confirmed with every guided visit, irrespective of whether people referred to the care homes as support service units, geriatric houses of rest, assisted living bungalows, death's waiting rooms, these were places that ruined the word "home" because words, too, could be ruined. Home no longer meant family, or the place where the heart is, but a place where the old are made to sit in lounges with posters of cars they can no longer drive and of journeys they can no longer make, places where the old are made to

sit in u-shaped formation on plastic chairs, because accidents always happen even despite the diapers, and are made
to play ball games, without the carers realising that the
old don't become children again, however much they were
instructed to treat everyone like children, It's your turn
young lady, and the old woman's gnarled hands unable to
summon the strength to throw the ball, Now it's your turn
young lad, the carers tried hard, but the young lads and
ladies in their charge were gripped by the stupor of those
who were waiting for the grand finale, the managers talked
about medical teams, nurses, occupational therapists and
who knows how many other services including dieticians,
manicures and pedicures, as if they were not seeing the
same thing I saw, absent old people smiling with dentures
that no longer fit their gums, old people whose skin was a
collection of scars and eczema, Your turn young lady, as if
the old people weren't groggy with the tablets they gave
them, no country for old people, no times for old people,
Grandma had the bad luck of reaching old age at a time
when the old were wanted for the money they could spend
on medical appointments, on medicines, on vitamin supple-
ments, on physiotherapy, on eyeglasses for short-sightedness
and long-sightedness, on hearing aids, on diapers, no times
for old people, at least not for the unremarkable old people,
with almost identical histories, like Grandma, useless, the
old with their heads filled with out-of-date knowledge,
who wants to know about the old or about what they
have learned in their lives when Google gives us thousands
of up-to-date answers about anything in seconds, above all
who wants to know about a single individual's experience

when we can access the experiences of millions of people?

I'll speak to my grandmother, I would say at the end of the guided visits, with the same matter-of-fact tone I used for more mundane matters, as if I had forgotten how Grandma had looked after me, the birthday cakes she baked for me, always slightly burnt and with a hint of lemon, how she warmed my pyjamas by the fireplace on winter nights, as if I had forgotten the digital watch she gave me the day I started primary school, almost a year after Father had died. That day Grandma walked all the way to school with me for the first time to protect me from the stormy gales and other dangers. We arrived at the shiny metal gates, Grandma kneeled to be level with me and pulled out of her handbag a thin rectangle wrapped with gift paper and a pink ribbon. I opened it and took out the watch that Grandma attached to my wrist. I went proudly into the classroom, my Timex gleaming. I had been visiting care homes as if I had forgotten that I kept the watch in its original box, it was broken and rusty but as long as I still had it nothing bad could happen to me. The Timex had stopped, but beyond it time continued ticking away, indifferent.

I had lost track of how many care homes I had visited before I arrived at the one where I met Duarte. House of Rest. And below, in smaller letters, Azevedo e Silva. I was told by Duarte's mother, a woman of elegant gestures, whose body kept the memory of the care it had received throughout its life, that the small estate, now turned into the House of Rest, was built by her father, back in the early nineteen fifties. Her father, Azevedo e Silva, was a successful civil engineer who built bridges all over the world while nurturing the dream of raising a large family. Once he was back in the home country, he commissioned a developer to build a property with ten rooms and at least one hectare of grounds. Duarte's mother explained that her father had brought bad luck upon himself by putting the carriage before the ox, because his dream of a large family had amounted only to her, other pregnancies had ended in miscarriages after a few weeks, except for the stillbirth, the greatest heartbreak her parents ever knew. Following in the family tradition, she too had only had one child, Duarte, who would be arriving in a few minutes to show me around the property. I took a liking to Duarte's mother, despite recognising in her the mannerisms of a privileged upbringing and being a bit bored by her account of the lives of her parents and the history of the care home.

Having witnessed so much sadness and abandonment in the care homes I had visited before, the simple sight of old people, in the garden, stretched out on deckchairs, soaking up the sun, filled me with happiness. I didn't know whether Grandma still liked sunbathing, or if her love of trees and flowers remained strong, but it seemed to me that she might feel at ease there. It was September, the summer was flying away with the swallows and the sun shone on the oleander hedges that grew against the garden walls. When Duarte joined us, I saw in him a clumsiness that I would stop noticing over time. I'm sure that your grandmother will enjoy staying with us, Duarte's mother said as she left us. I suddenly broke down in tears, these days I cried about everything and anything. It wasn't quite everything and anything, but things happened to me that made me cry or perhaps it was me who made them happen, or I simply didn't know how to avoid them. In any case, I didn't like crying in front of strangers.

I had spent the whole visit with a lump in my throat, but when I heard Duarte's mother say, Your grandmother will enjoy staying with us, I couldn't hold back the tears. Duarte and his mother comforted me with kind words that seemed to be genuinely felt, but I couldn't stop crying. Because I was about to put Grandma in a care home, because my life had lost its footing, because I was now anchored in doubt. I calmed down, reminding myself that Grandma's internment would be temporary, I had promised myself that I would soon find a carer I could trust to stay in Grandma's house. Duarte took me round the care home's facilities. Unlike his mother, he didn't seem to be one of the posh people from the Linha, even if he had some of the mannerisms of those born into privilege, the cocksure voice and the casual walk, chest thrust forward, with no fear of what might happen. His slicked-back hair made his forehead seem higher. I found his angular features off-putting, the way they made him appear distant, and the uncertain colour of his eyes, somewhere between light brown and green. You can't trust someone who doesn't have a well-defined eye colour, I thought. He seemed to be older than me, but I was wrong, we were only a few months apart. When he walked ahead of me to open the door leading to the main hall, I noticed that his thinness and height made him more gangly than elegant, but that his smile was pleasant and kind.

That was undoubtedly the best care home I had visited.

It didn't smell of fried food or oily soup, the walls were painted in bright and luminous colours, the furniture was sober and elegant, the spaces had been redesigned to combine functionality and aesthetics. As I made my way towards the left side of the main hall, and a solid staircase of reddish wood leading to the top floor, Duarte drew my attention to a lift, further down a narrow corridor. We encourage our residents to go up and down the stairs, though, it's good for the heart. It's good for the heart, I repeated as if I hadn't understood what he was saying. I was constantly apologising to Duarte, for not immediately understanding something he said, for walking ahead of him, for walking in the opposite direction to the one he was showing me, sorry, sorry, sorry, as if I were apologising to Grandma. Duarte, who couldn't have known about my all-consuming guilt, would have attributed my behaviour to the embarrassment of having cried earlier. Arriving on the top floor, Duarte signalled for me to walk ahead, this time towards the meeting room and the two corridors leading to the bedrooms. The closeness of our bodies gave me goosebumps, Pathetic, I don't even find him attractive, I thought, while trying to make sense of the feelings I was having because I was about to put Grandma into a care home.

Perhaps because he could sense I was fragile, Duarte remained close to me. When we entered the room that would become Grandma's bedroom I mumbled something confusing about the furniture being in good taste, about the room being large and well ventilated, about adjustable beds being very practical, and about the two cotton-sheet covered armchairs being so comfortable. Duarte led me to the window overlooking the garden where we had been only minutes ago. From above, the sight of the old people taking in the last of the day's sun in the garden seemed even more extraordinary. Everything that I found sad and sometimes repugnant about the bodies of the old seemed beautiful in that light, distance made everything prettier. Ugliness was only visible close up. So, too, was suffering. They like to catch a bit of sun before dinner, or to wander around our greenhouse, Duarte explained, pointing at the glass and green ironwork structure at the back of the garden, topped with an attractive dome.

Duarte had held back a little, was now walking slightly behind me, but so close that if I had moved slightly I would have touched him. I could only hear his voice, I wanted to be a botanist, imagine that. In the glasshouse's jumble of green I was able to identify, alongside the begonias, ferns and bracken, a climber like the one on Grandma's balcony, the same balcony where Grandma put her trays of quince jam out to dry, the climber curled and twisted and Grandma would say, That blasted . . . I need to pour salt onto the ground so it dries up. What's that vine called? I asked. Honeysuckle, Duarte said. I told him that Grandma had one on her balcony and that I had been desperate to eat its berries which seemed to me like cherries, that Grandma warned me about the danger of eating berries, but that I disobeyed her, I couldn't accept that such beautiful berries would do me any harm. The honeysuckle is tangled up with the jasmine, Duarte said and, pointing his index finger, began naming the plants and trees we could see, dahlias, hydrangeas, purslane, gladioli, anthuriums, I followed Duarte's voice and index finger as if they were the voice and the pendulum of a hypnotist, roses, calla lilies, snapdragons, Duarte's voice more and more like an incantation, suddenly it was no longer his finger pointing at the plants, but his tongue clicking against his teeth, the veins bulging on his neck, his body lean and bony. When the grandfather clock in the hall struck five o'clock, and I regained some self-control, I found that my lips were stuck to the lips of Duarte, son of the care home's owners.

We let go of each other, embarrassed. I wanted to say something, anything, but I could only think that Jorge was right, my problem was getting side-tracked when I should be trying to focus, I had just kissed the son of the owners of the best care home I had seen, I needed to start to do things properly, to behave like the grown woman I had been for quite some time, I had to fight the urge to run away, I had to listen to everything Duarte had to say, then I would say goodbye and tell him that I would think about it, that I would take into consideration the warmth with which I had been welcomed, I had to concentrate to avoid ruining everything. Duarte led me to the gate. He put his hand out to say goodbye, It was a pleasure to meet you, I hope to see you again. I took Duarte's words to be the words a gentleman would use with a woman who was out of control, or the words of a professional who wanted to cause a good impression with a client. I had almost reached my car when I turned back. Duarte was still by the gate. Will you look after my grandmother well? I asked. You can count on it, he said.

The following day, I told Grandma that I would be taking her to a clinic run by friends. Your stomach still needs sorting out, and they'll be able to treat it. Grandma said nothing and allowed herself to be taken away.

The first time I cheated on Jorge, or rather, the first time I fucked another man who wasn't just a fantasy, was in the Venus suite, the cheapest in the motel on the IC19, the cost of which I split with the man in question. When we were done, the man – Manuel, he said his name was Manuel – claimed there was some work meeting at which his presence was absolutely required and apologised for having to hurry off. Grateful for his work meeting, or for him lying to me about it, I pretended to be sad. It would have been a form of punishment to have to make small talk with a stranger I had just fucked, but it would have been indelicate to seem too relieved about his departure. The man, a simple and vulgar man, said, If it weren't for the meeting we'd go a third round, and, as he awkwardly climbed off the side of the round bed to take a shower, he pinched one of my nipples. It hurt, but I didn't complain, I knew that he hadn't meant to do me harm, that for him being manly meant behaving as if my body was his. My interactions with other people were hardly ever satisfactory, which led me to accept and be unusually tolerant of all that was awkward and inconvenient about them. Before entering the shower, the man said, My wife is worse than a hound dog, she can smell other women miles away, but today is one of my gym days, so . . . he thought himself to be the most creative of adulterers for substituting his visits to the gym with quick shags in sleazy motels on the IC19. He might as well have added, We had a good workout, anyway.

I allowed myself to stay in bed. Although my body was recovering slowly, and my senses were still in disarray, I was able to identify the feeling that was coming over me. Not guilt, not regret, not anything. Peace, a growing sense of peace. The peace that followed a crash, the peace of not being able to go any further. I knew that the trigger had been pulled a long time ago, that betrayal, real betrayal, had heavy machinery but a sensitive trigger. Once it was in motion, nothing and no-one could stop it. Because its machinery was heavy, there had been a delay between the moment the trigger was pulled and the moment its effects became apparent, the moment of impact. That slowness had made me hopeful at first, it had given me the illusion that everything could be stopped, and it had been easy to delude myself, sometimes it seemed as if everything had indeed stopped, that was it. That was it and there would be no damage. But, as I would later understand, that wasn't it, things continued to move forward slowly, but persistent and unstoppable. Until the moment of impact, nothing could stop the heavy machinery, and the slowness was agonising. Now came the moment of impact. Finally.

That simple and vulgar man never knew that he had just been in bed with a woman who had been fucking the same man for more than twenty years, and no longer knew how to do things properly. Easy, he said when, my knees digging into the old mattress' springs, I took his penis into my mouth. He was afraid, perhaps he thought I was going to bite it off, there are so many crazy women out there. Slower, he said again when I mounted him. Looking at the mirrors covering the Venus suite's walls and ceiling, I felt I was watching a wild horse, an out-of-control locomotive, something out of sync with itself. Earlier, there had already been the awkward moment when I had struggled to put on the condom. Are you fucking around without protection? he asked, mistrustful, my mouth and my vagina probably beginning to seem like a Petri dish culture of bacteria and virus that might damage his thingie. I'm just not very experienced, I said, I was never very good at manual work, but you can trust me, I'm cleaner than a virgin. Even if I managed to reassure him about my clean bill of health, the damage was done and I had to suck him off once more to get him hard again. *Back to business*, he said, in English, as I slipped on the condom. *Oh yeah*, I replied, also in English. It seemed the best reply in that context.

While it lasted, I kept thinking that it wasn't really happening, even if a stranger was panting over me and asking me every two minutes, Who's the daddy? It seemed unreal, and the sense of unreality was seeping into the things that I had left behind, Mónica, Tinder, me at the seawall waiting for a coward who didn't show up, me perched on the sideboard waiting for Jorge who refused to come closer, Grandma at the care home, Grandma in our flat, Grandma falling, Inês and Márcia so far away from me, Mother always so close, all of it going round in my mind, and the relief after the big pain, peace, an unreal peace. Perhaps unreal because I had been there before, this was the suite I had visited online so many times, and now nothing seemed too different from my fantasy with the doctor who discussed Grandma's episode or with other men. The criminal returning to the scene of her crime. That simple and vulgar man had seen me naked, had his pleasure with me and, to ensure our orgasms were equally matched, had pretended to have his pleasure once again, all with copious moaning and shouting and swearing, but the doctor had seen into my soul, he had seen how fragile I became in wanting him and had left me exposed, and all with silence and smiles and courteous words. It was obvious to me that, if any of the situations might be considered obscene, it would be the latter more than the former.

Except now it was happening for real, everything was carefully planned and thought through, and it had happened more or less as I always imagined it would. It hadn't been done on a whim, it wasn't a quickie in a public toilet or on some stairwell, I hadn't fallen hopelessly in love, such betrayals were not a heavy machine, the trigger was too easily pulled, too many drinks, love at first sight and the consequences were soon obvious. No, it hadn't been any of that. It could have been that man or any other, but I had taken my time agreeing to the rendezvous, I had exchanged many messages, had pondered the advantages of the motel on the IC19, had shared my sexual preferences and other intimacies.

Since Grandma had moved to the care home I had started using Tinder as it was meant to be used, as a dating app. I started doing it on the very same day I kissed Duarte.

215

When I got back from the home, I went to Grandma's place to find some warmer clothes. I opened the wardrobe and sat on her bed looking at her clothes. On the left the finer black clothes for going to church, on the right the black clothes she wore around the house. It wasn't true what people said, that life burns quicker than a match, most of the time life was horribly long, decades seemed to be compressed between one clothes hanger and another. Using the hanging clothes, I tried to join the dots of the always inaccessible constellation that is the past, but I ended up hastily pulling out half a dozen comfortable items and slamming the door of the wardrobe shut. I selected a few of the framed photographs in the living room so that, once in the home, Grandma wouldn't miss Father, Senhor Pereira, the girls. I also took the wooden box in which Grandma kept her sentimentally valuable objects, two small potted plants, two of the smaller saints and a few other trinkets that would help her feel more at home. Bardino disappeared again. The food I left out for him kept disappearing, but I couldn't be sure it was Bardino eating it, there were other stray cats in the neighbourhood, but still I wanted to believe that Bardino would be guarding the house while Grandma was away. I sat at the dining room table in the place that always belonged to Grandma. In the middle of the table, inside the bowl that many years ago held a little red fish with a long tail, were half a dozen walnuts. I took out my phone and sent Jorge a message, I found a care home that seems OK, but . . . He replied immediately with a smile emoji and I felt a lump in my throat. I remained there for some time feeling abandoned, an abandonment that had no witnesses and was therefore less shameful than when I sat alone on a bench near the seawall or when I perched on the sideboard. The phone buzzed on the table, I was hopeful that it might be Jorge calling to say, Let's get on with remodelling our home, let's get on with moving house, let's get on with reclaiming our lives, but no, it was a message from one of the Tinder contacts, Wanna talk? Since the day of the meeting on the seawall I hadn't been reading the messages sent by various men on Tinder and WhatsApp. If Grandma hadn't swallowed pillow stuffing, if I hadn't been left alone perching on the sideboard, if I hadn't just packed the suitcase I would bring when I dropped Grandma off at the care home the following day, perhaps I would have taken refuge in the little life I had lived until recently. But things had happened the way they had, and so, as I deleted Mónica's profile, I whispered, Bye bye. I felt I had killed something, that something had died within me. I waited a minute, maybe two. Then, strangely calm, I created a new profile that I also called Mónica. The new Mónica wouldn't hide behind the Australian woman or any other person. For the profile photo I chose a picture of the palm of my hand, showing the line that represented my destiny. Neither my hand nor my destiny were identifiable. If men wanted to see more of my pictures, I would show them some of the ones on Facebook. I would be me. If someone did recognise me from Tinder, I could say that my Facebook photos had been stolen, it was plausible, after all I had stolen the Australian woman's photos. Some days later it dawned on me that I would end up having sex with one of those men. And that there was no reason to hold back.

I was lying on the bed of the Venus suite, listening to a man singing to himself in the shower, a man I wouldn't have looked at twice if I had crossed paths with him on the street, a man even less interesting than Jorge, who fucked worse than Jorge, though he wanted to fuck me more, a man who sang worse than Jorge and who would probably lose out to Jorge in almost every way. And yet that man, who took care to trim his pubic hair and to freshen his breath, was saving me from the judgemental gaze of the doctor who asked me about Grandma's episode, from the idiot who left me waiting by the seawall, was saving me from all those times I felt rejected or was rejected, saved me from Jorge himself. Amid the peace that was coming over my body and my mind, another feeling was taking hold, gratitude. I was grateful to that man for showing me I was wrong. After so many years of marriage, I was convinced that men no longer looked at me with interest because I had given up on the art of seduction, I had unlearned its basic principles and no longer knew how to play in the ways they wanted. If that were not the reason, I would have to accept that the only appeal I had ever possessed was the appeal of youth, and once that was gone there was nothing left within me that might interest men. What man would want to be with me, then, when there were so many other younger women? Women who still had ovaries bursting with good little eggs, who still had shiny hair and hard fingernails, women without foreheads like old treasure maps, without turkey necks, without barcode lips or Fu Manchu moustaches across their faces, women who could wave goodbye without trembling bat wings, to hell with ageing and with whoever invented these names. But that simple and vulgar man had chosen me, he had shared the cost of the Venus suite to fuck me and had been courteous enough to express his regrets that a work meeting forced him to leave in such a hurry. Lying on the ridiculous round bed I could hear him singing in the shower, satisfied, and an immense gratitude took hold of me.

I didn't feel guilty. Nor would I blame Jorge, it hadn't been his aloofness that made me put on cheap lingerie, that took me to the Venus suite, that opened the door and pushed me in, even though both of us knew well enough what was happening in our marriage. I was fucked poorly. Not that Jorge was a bad lover, but in what other way could one describe a woman who was only fucked on specifically agreed days? It's easier that way, Jorge would explain. He said the same thing when he stuck onto the fridge a rota for domestic chores, It's easier that way. Inês still complained about the chores she was given, Márcia didn't even bother to complain because she knew that she would never carry them out anyway, that the list was no more than a vain attempt to idealise our domestic life. It's easier that way, Jorge said, as if sex were a chore as boring as cleaning the kitchen after dinner. And if I got playful when we went to bed he would push me away, Tomorrow, he said. Except that Jorge's tomorrow was like the dawn of freedom in workers' anthems, it never arrived. The following day he would be sleepy, the next he had an aching back, and so we got through to Friday. I don't think he ever knew how annoyed I was by his calm sleep. There were sleepless nights when Jorge, fast asleep, became monstrous to me and I had to get out of bed and watch television in the living room, but then morning arrived with the reasons that made everything continue as usual, reasons that might be summarised as, Jorge was the father of my daughters and no-one should discard a relationship of more than twenty years. So, my mild unhappiness became my little happiness. I wasn't happy enough to stop feeling neglected, but nor was I unhappy enough to want to leave Jorge.

I didn't blame him and didn't blame myself, because there was nothing to blame anyone for. Not at that moment. Betrayal, true betrayal, that heavy machinery with a sensitive trigger, had happened long before, a moment I hadn't registered, possibly the moment when I started fantasising about other men, colleagues, neighbours, strangers, a sensitive trigger, anything would have pulled it, any little thing, and the machinery became unstoppable. What was happening with my body was less important than what had happened with my soul, the body was unimportant, what mattered was the soul, Father Raul never stopped saying that in his endless sermons. And in the Venus suite it had been only my body together with that man's body, long after my soul had started to entangle itself with others. Which is why, that day, I was no more adulterous than the day before, or the one before that one, or the week before, the month before, the year before, for how many years had I been an adulteress without being judged? Now I could be judged and that was what mattered most about that afternoon at the Venus suite.

I switched on the suite's fairy lights. I had no interest in seeing them lit up, but I wanted to appear relaxed, I turned the music up, that way we wouldn't have to talk when the man came back into the room. I had nothing to say to him, I wasn't looking for friends, I didn't even do small talk with the women in my aqua-gym lessons who were so sympathetic about my inability to do front crawl. Nor would the man have anything to say to me, other than appreciate the nightclub ambiance I had created. He came back into the room naked, trying out some vigorous dance steps, and offered me an amusing reverse strip-tease as I swayed along on the bed. I took his goodbye kiss as a gesture of thanks for having spared him the need to have a conversation.

The betrayal was consummated, that man had witnessed it, others might witness it, know about it, others might now accuse me, judge me, condemn me. I no longer needed to do it myself. I recognised then what it was that, for years, had cluttered my days and left me so exhausted. I had been alone, lost inside myself, searching my mind and my body to find evidence, proof, alibis for a crime I knew I had committed, a perfect crime. But I wanted an imperfect crime, I wanted to be a hostage to the biggest crime I had ever committed in my whole life, the crime of no longer loving, for that, too, I wanted to be in the hands of others. What had been happening inside me was finally exposed, my body had fucked that man's body and I could finally be at ease.

I knew that I wouldn't escape the condemnation, that I would be called a whore, but I was innocent. Yes, other women had husbands who were less attentive than Jorge, yes, other families were sadder than mine, yes, other people, all people, pulled the trigger of betrayal, if only once, but few of them ended up on the round bed of a motel on the IC19. All of that was true and it was also true that I hadn't deliberately assembled the machinery of betrayal, in the days after I left Grandma at the care home, to legitimise what I had just done, but only a body that was soft and dense could have slowed and stopped the advance of the heavy machinery. And mine was almost ethereal, almost lighter than air, a body as fragile and tenuous as the soap bubbles I used to blow out of a straw, on sunny mornings, sitting on the cement island, in the garden of Grandma's house, water, white and blue soap, the air blown out of my lungs and thousands of brightly coloured reflections. Everything pierced me, everything undid me, nothing held me, I was unable to hold anything, how could I have stopped the betrayal?

I remained nude in the middle of the round bed, lying on top of an uncomfortable synthetic silk blanket that made me itchy and hot. My body, showered in the tiny colourful lights that twinkled round the room, was reflected in the countless mirrors decorated with images of couples in daring positions out of the Kama Sutra, which due to their designer's lack of talent appeared to be the victims of some catastrophe that had left them in strange poses. Although there were still two hours remaining of the three we had been asked to pay for upfront, we had barely made use of any of the things that the Venus suite had to offer, the love swing, the pole-dancing pole, the jacuzzi, the massager. One of my hook-ups would later tell me about motels in other countries that charged by the minute, Everyone knows you don't spend a lot of time on these things, he said. He was right and yet he wasn't, indeed people didn't spend much time having sex, ten minutes, twenty, thirty, an hour, the amount of time it took me to drive into Cascais from the Ring Road at rush hour, the time I spent at the gym, people didn't spend much time having sex but you could spend a lifetime analysing, judging, condemning or excusing matters of betrayal.

I, Jorge, take you, Eliete, as my wife, and promise to be faithful, to love and respect you, in happiness and in sadness, in sickness and in health, every day of our lives. Jorge hadn't wanted to say those words, he found the whole thing unnecessary and trite, so the vows were neither said nor written and signed. My bridal dress would forever remain on the mannequin in the window at the shop in Parede, no *Amour et Bonheur* and no dates to celebrate, no anniversaries revealing the deterioration of the thing being commemorated, life was to be lived as a continuum, without disruptive events beyond those that mark the beginning and the end. Jorge and me with no vows, but together, joined in practice, even if later disjoined, in practice, later, years later, how many years?

There had been no vows, but there was an understanding, an implicit understanding, undeclared, that silence had reshaped over the years, I believe you love me, had become, I trust that you're not cheating on me, and then, I trust that you know what you're doing. I trusted that Jorge knew what he was doing, even if I didn't know what he was doing. Perhaps at that very moment he was in the neighbouring suite with #tableforone. The shower of colourful lights, or the idea that Jorge was doing the same thing I had just done, made me slightly queasy. The room started spinning as if I had just been twirling around the pole-dancing pole. I felt sick, as I had the night before.

Having returned just over a week earlier, Márcia had bought some special ingredients at a gourmet food shop to cook one of the recipes she had learned in Italy, a pumpkin pasta she called, with impeccable pronunciation, *ravioli alla zucca e amaretti*. Inês had set the table with the flowered linen tablecloth and had taken out the finest dinner plates. When I asked her what the reason was she replied, Do we need to have a reason? She wasn't trying to be aggressive, she was merely trying to say that she didn't agree with the idea of using the finest dinner plates only on special days, or even with the idea of special days. I sat at my usual place at the table, even though my mind was far away, still thinking about the messages I was exchanging with Manuel and other strangers on Tinder.

Márcia's time in Italy had made Jorge and the girls rediscover the importance of family, at least that's what seemed to be happening. The only one not sharing in the spirit of recent reunion was me, but I was trying not to show it. I had also been the only one resisting the end of family rituals, lamenting that we had started eating on trays in front of the TV or in the bedroom or sitting at the computer, Come on, Eliete, no-one sits down at the table, maybe just for Christmas, what you see in films isn't what happens in real life, Jorge said whenever I complained. I had been alone when they had all needed the space to feel like individuals, and I remained alone now as, nostalgic for some sense of community, they wanted to revive the family meal, suddenly happy and willing diners.

At the start of dinner, Jorge and the girls took great pleasure in recounting their recent adventures, but soon they were deep in discussion of complex and current issues like global warming and the harms of plastic, Syria, Palestine, Hillary, Trump and Putin. I complimented the food with sincerity, but I had lost my appetite, I was nervous and everything made me nauseous. Nuno is lucky, Jorge joked, serving himself a second helping. I glanced at Inês, but didn't detect any signs of upset. When was she acting, I wondered, was it when she seemed to want to come clean at Grandma's house and on the day of the Euros final, or was it at that moment? Was she faking her unhappiness before, while in reality she was OK, or was she not faking it before but faking it now? Was Inês better at faking unhappiness or at faking happiness? I preferred to know that she was faking unhappiness, and that my girl would always be happy. That was the problem with the theatre of life, when the stage wasn't clearly identified I couldn't tell what was authentic and what was acting, I couldn't tell to what extent someone talking to me was a character or an actor, to what extent I too had to be an actor or a character. For as long as I hid behind Mónica, I didn't have that problem, the stages on which Mónica acted were well defined, whether it was a phone, a hotel suite, a car parked at the side of a deserted road, or the vacant houses I was arranging to sell.

Besides not having an appetite, I found the conversations tiresome. I had heard a thousand descriptions of

Márcia's daily life in Italy, I was irritated by Inês' questions about the handsomeness of Italian men, as if she hadn't visited her sister and seen with her own eyes what there was to see, and by Jorge's loud interventions and unfunny jokes. I was taken aback by the ease with which they seemed to be moved by the plight of refugees, by the beached whale with a stomach full of plastic, and by the woman murdered by her husband, I disliked the fact that they seemed to increasingly resemble their Facebook profiles, that their digital personalities appeared to be encroaching on their real personalities, if that was the right way to describe it. My lack of interest in their conversations was inversely proportional to the curiosity I felt about my conversations with men on Tinder and the time I spent mulling them over. All of that prevented me from enjoying the rediscovery of family harmony that should strengthen us as human beings and catapult us into happiness.

By the time Márcia returned, I had stopped thinking of Tinder as a game, and I was affirmed in my conviction that seeing the betrayal through wouldn't affect our family. It had all been easier when the family was disjointed, when Márcia was far away and during that short period of time when Grandma was living with us. Back then I thought to myself, if our family could so easily disperse, if it could unravel, or at least change, then whatever phase I was going through must surely be part of that. Everything had been significantly altered with Márcia's return, as if the return of a family member had served to tighten the knots that had been unravelling. I remained the loose end, unable to enjoy the reattachment, but also incapable of disturbing it.

May I serve you, Márcia asked, bringing the dessert to the dining table, tiramisu topped with a raspberry, two mint leaves and thick drizzles of liquid chocolate. Wow, Jorge said, satisfied, I demand one of these dinners every day, and Inês joked with her sister, shamelessly displaying her envy, And still you're not putting on weight, you lucky cow. They laughed, and so did I. Since her arrival, Jorge and Inês had amused themselves pointing out the changes Márcia had undergone during her time away, she was thinner, she had stopped biting her nails, she was smoking less, her taste had become more refined, she had changed her hairstyle, even if it was only in the way she held it up, she was now cycling into town, whereas before she used to drive even to the local supermarket, and yet no-one seemed to have noticed the change that to me seemed most important, Márcia had acquired the self-confidence of those who can take care of themselves and now appeared ready to take care of others. It might have been unconscious, but the process was already in motion. When Márcia asked if she could serve us, it was no longer teenage Márcia pretending to be grown up, or even the newly grown-up Márcia trying to please others, but the new Márcia who had confided in me some days earlier her wish to move in with Nuno, to start a family and become a mother, the new Márcia from whom, obviously, I would keep my suspicions about what her boyfriend was doing. All families, the happy and the unhappy ones, had secrets, all families knew that the truth was something to be avoided like all those other inconvenient details that belittle our lives.

Because they were all so busy with the newly returned

Márcia and with recovering the family spirit, no-one noticed me, how I too was different. In the beginning, I felt proud of being able to exist beyond them and hide my situation, but it wasn't long before I started to feel irreparably and miserably alone, because loneliness was the obligatory consequence of lying. None of them commented on how I was making an effort with my clothes these days, or dressing more provocatively, or that I had signed up to the gym, or the self-confidence I now displayed, none of them noticed that I was undergoing a more substantial change than Márcia, that I had taken leave of my usual place and that, unlike Márcia, I couldn't return unscathed because no-one could return unscathed when they spent an entire family meal thinking about messaging a stranger to arrange a rendezvous at the Venus suite, thinking that I had to pay cash for the room, wear understated clothes and sunglasses and take a change of underwear, no-one returned to their family unscathed when they lied as shamelessly as I did that night before I fucked a stranger for the first time, no-one could return unscathed to their family when their heart skipped a beat and their breath was made shallow by the confirmation, received there in front of everyone else, of tomorrow's meeting.

No-one paid me any attention at that moment, no-one wanted to hold me. When I talked about my swimming lessons, they limited themselves to the pitying smiles with which they generally welcomed my ideas or my topics of conversation, I've already shed two kilos, I added, and the general silence made it clear that I had never been, had never wanted to or had never known how to be at the centre of a conversation, much less the topic of a conversation. They had hardly ever taken notice of me and, if they did, it was mostly to say unkind things, like when they concluded that I had reached the age at which I should stop wearing my hair long. I stopped wanting them to notice me, scrutinise me, I didn't want to hear them making comments that would make me feel ashamed of certain things, and that I needed to ditch them, like when they talked about cellulite while referring to the fact that I still wore hot pants in the summer. And they didn't only comment on my body, they also let me know that I needed to be more proactive at work, kinder to Mother, more pleasant to shop attendants. So that they would stop noticing me, I pulled away from them and, if I felt compelled to take part in any conversation, I kept my defences up by uttering the usual, It takes all sorts. It takes all sorts. And that was true. It took all sorts and the proof was right there, in the phone buzzing in my trouser pocket, bringing a message from a stranger. The simple and vulgar man saying he had just made himself come thinking about me, and me, making the most of a trip to drop off dirty plates in the kitchen, replying that I had just done the same and adding that I was dying for him to fuck me.

I took half a Zolpidem to make sure I'd be asleep by the time Jorge came to bed. But I was so anxious that the tablet had no effect on me and I was still wide awake when Jorge joined me. It's going to rain tomorrow, make sure you take an umbrella, he said. I almost burst into tears. How could I have a fling with a stranger in the Venus suite when Jorge was worrying about me getting soaked by the rain? For a few minutes I thought about calling it all off, deleting my Tinder profile and asking Jorge to take me on a honeymoon trip. It would only take a small effort on his part and I would become a bit less ethereal, I might absorb the impact better, perhaps I might still be able to stop the machinery of betrayal. But Jorge said goodnight, turned his back on me and fell asleep. I didn't feel alone when I started to hear his heavy breathing because, the following day, I would be pulling into the car park of the motel on the IC19 at the agreed time, my body awakening as it did when I first saw the boys from Torre shirtless on their bicycles. Come here, Eliete. Anything could happen and everything did.

A message on my phone let me know that my time would be running out in fifteen minutes, and asked if I wanted to extend it. Like the man who had left more than two hours ago, I hummed a ditty in the shower and lathered myself in a soap with a sickly smell of peach. It was raining as I pulled out of the motel's car park, just as Jorge had predicted the night before, and I looked ridiculous in my dark glasses. I remembered that we had run out of coffee, I stopped to buy some, I patiently listened to the saleswoman's explanation about coffee-producing countries, fruity and floral aromas, allergenics, she was a good saleswoman, sweet-natured, proudly wearing a ring on her left ring-finger. That night, I sat down to watch television with Jorge. Every now and then he exchanged messages on his phone, I kept mine on silent. I was experiencing the blessed peace of not being afraid of discovering I was someone different, of knowing that I remained the same as ever, that I couldn't go any further. For almost two months I told myself that I was right, that I couldn't go any further, that the heavy machinery of betrayal had reached its destination and that, from thereon in, everything would be a variation on that same action.

But the rigorous understanding of what I felt that day, of the trajectory leading to that day and beyond that day, only came later. It would take a few more strangers in motel suites, in cars parked at the side of deserted roads, in the vacant houses I was trying to sell, before I was able to find the words to reflect what I was feeling, before the unmediated desire, fear, pleasure and peace I was feeling could be translated into words and be shaped by them. Only then did I feel myself to be more solid, more substantial, emotions are volatile, they have little or no weight, like air, but words can have weight, they could weigh down my feelings. That was the illusion I had, as words emerged to explain everything and make me feel powerful.

Meanwhile, fucking other men, actually fucking them and not just doing it in my mind, required actually lying. What I did and where I went might now actually be witnessed by others, it wasn't only happening in my mind or on my phone. I turned out to be surprisingly effective at satisfying this new requirement. I discovered, early on, that the best lie isn't the one that pretends to be the truth, but the one that creates the impression of truth. I'm sure Grandma's neurologist would have been able to explain how my brain acquired such an outstanding capacity to come up with excuses and lies. If someone took a magnetic resonance image, they might detect alterations in my brain, like they detected white spots on Grandma's MRI scans, and the neurologist would talk about a new paradigm, as he did in Grandma's case. My brain was no longer interested in what was commonly understood to be the truth, it had stopped distinguishing between invented and actual stories, it equated the stories made up by me with the stories made up by God, destiny, astral charts, whatever we wanted to call it. I'm certain that the neurologist who charged one hundred euros per appointment would have spoken of the cortex or the hypothalamus, words and more words that Grandma, trying to make sense of them, condensed into a question, So what you are trying to tell me doctor is that I am going crazy, and which I would condense into my own question, So what you are trying to tell me doctor is that I am becoming a whore? And if there were a second appointment perhaps I might ask, for an additional one hundred euros, So what you are trying to tell me doctor is that I cannot reinvent myself, that I am condemned to remain the same poem, even if I delete it a thousand times to keep its sense and its purpose, the same poem in search of the missing word to make it eternal.

A whore, I would be a whore. Even if the MRI scan showed nothing, even if Jorge didn't exist, those who knew I was fucking strangers would still call me a whore. They would condemn me for being a woman and behaving as if I enjoyed sex. It hardly mattered that this wasn't the main reason I fucked with strangers. A woman who liked fucking was a whore. I would be a whore, like Milena was when she became a successful lawyer. Decent women didn't like sex, decent women didn't succeed in roles meant for men, women were not biologically programmed to succeed in roles meant for men so the power some women attained came from having sacrificed themselves sexually, women weren't biologically programmed to enjoy sex. As soon as she started having power, Milena became Lewinsky to her colleagues, she became a whore, They and their little wagging tongues can fuck off, she would say, voice rising above the clamour, like the fireworks at the Festas do Mar. I remained insecure, tethered to the ground, in the shadow of family life, making every effort to comply with what was expected of me, at the service of others, in fear of a God I didn't believe in, respectful of traditions that often made no sense, that often seemed so cruel, and in the end . . .

I didn't have to lie much, during those almost two months, even without employing the trick I learned from another of the Jorges who wasn't my Jorge, nothing would have given me away. That other Jorge was one of my least remarkable flings, but I learned a trick from him, which was to name all partners after one's spouse, Two birds with one stone, you avoid getting the name wrong and then you're not really cheating, it's as if we were screwing the people who are waiting for us at the end of the day. Everything about him irritated me, his haste, his odour, his perspiration, the spit that gathered in the corners of his mouth as he spoke, the swagger, the birds and the stone, the cowardice of pretending he was screwing the wife who was waiting at home for him, but after him all the men became Jorge and I became Ana, Isabel, Paula, Cláudia.

Jorge, my Jorge, and the girls had noticed that I spent less time at home, but my absence was justified by my visits to Grandma and the sessions at the gym and, of course, by work, those foreigners wouldn't stop buying up houses, everyone and their mother seemed to want to move to Portugal. I hinted that, after having Grandma living with us, everything at home now reminded me that I had put her in a care home and that upset me. They would have concluded that was the main reason for me joining the gym and they avoided the topic, they knew Grandma was, for me, a painful subject that it was best to leave untouched, none of them wanted to turn back. Nor did I. Silence was, now, and for different reasons, the best solution for everyone.

Grandma seemed to be doing well in the care home, or at least didn't seem to be unhappy. She complained every now and then, but she was easily cheered by the lies I told her, that her time at the care home was almost over, that Senhor Pereira would be back soon, that the following day we'd go for a little drive along the Guincho road. Visiting her was less awkward than I had feared. It was partly due to Duarte's efforts to seduce me. Perhaps he had misunderstood our kiss, since he was always pursuing me. I had to agree with Márcia when she remarked that men are simple creatures. At least Duarte seemed to be, as he had failed to understand that the kiss wasn't born of irresistible attraction and wasn't a case of love at first sight. Weeks later, he could have been in no doubt that it was merely a little transgression, like running a red light, shoplifting a chocolate bar at the supermarket, emptying the vacuum cleaner's bag over the clothes my goody two-shoes neighbour had just hung up on the line, little transgressions I indulged in to avoid a big transgression, driving the car off a cliff, holding up a bank, disfiguring my goody two-shoes neighbour and so many other horrors I imagined, not because I had a bad life, not because I actually wanted to do any of that, but merely to entertain the possibility. Duarte might rightly suppose I was no longer in love with Jorge, but he couldn't suspect, with any certainty, that I had many other Jorges to sharpen and satisfy my desires.

Men don't have the courage to engage with the essence of things, Márcia had said some years ago, after a fight with an ex-boyfriend. I didn't know whether Márcia remembered ever saying that or if she even still believed it. Grandma's illness taught me how important it was that we remained boringly predictable so that others might continue to love us, but it hadn't taught me how much we might change without becoming total strangers. Duarte needn't have engaged with the essence of things, he only needed to have been a bit smarter to realise that I was flattered by his interest in me, that the adolescent cat-and-mouse game between us diminished the anguish of facing the deterioration of Grandma's mind, but that I wanted nothing to do with him.

Besides spending less time at home, some of the other changes Jorge and the girls may have noticed about me might have been more interesting. I looked after myself better and was, overall, kinder and more attentive. They understood this to be a hidden personality trait that had emerged in the face of strong pain, the pain of Grandma losing her mind and me putting her into care, I had been able to transform that painful experience into an engine for changes that increased everyone's well-being. I could sense that they were grateful and proud of me, as they hadn't been in a long time. The girls started asking me for advice on all sorts of things and Jorge once again got into the habit of putting his arm around my shoulders as we walked to the café. We seemed to be riding a wave of enthusiasm, the country was being reborn after the humiliations of austerity imposed by international organisations, I was being reborn with the country, we all seemed to be well, we were enjoying the moment, no-one needed to know the real state of affairs.

And since everything seemed to revolve around them, why would they have noticed that I now had others revolving around me? Márcia, just returned, was catching up with friends and boyfriend, Inês, busy with rehearsals, performances and shows, had fallen in love with theatre, Jorge, stuck to his phone, wandered out of the house in search of Pokémon. That was the summer when we discovered that we were surrounded by colourful creatures that only our phone cameras could reveal. Inside our house, on the street, in shops, in gardens, on public transport, in the car, invisible to the naked eye the Pokémon could be spotted if we interposed a phone screen between reality and our eyes. All around the world, crowds gathered, armed with phones, to hunt Pokémon. In the end, technology not only condemned us to live in the isolation of a virtual world, it also allowed us to be closer to one another. Body to body. Jorge went out hunting for Pokémon and I went out hunting for men.

Even if unconsciously, I made the changes needed for everything to continue, for everything I loved to remain. The hope that my girls would attain the things they longed for stopped being tainted by the intimate and shameful envy that came from knowing I was falling behind. I no longer saw myself as some abandoned tea-towel when they made plans that didn't include me, like going interrailing the following summer. I no longer found their bodies, in the splendour of youth, hurtful because they reminded me of the tragic ageing of my own. Inês was raising the possibility of a gap year abroad and Márcia wanted to share a flat with Nuno, and I no longer beat myself up thinking that they would abandon me after I had given them my life. I wanted them to be happy in their choices, regardless of the role I played in them. I also stopped comparing Jorge to the successful men who asked to buy spacious homes in good neighbourhoods because their families deserved only the best, or with my boss who worked fourteen hours a day because his beach house, his wife's car and his children's riding lessons weren't going to pay for themselves, or with Nuno who was always talking about the start-ups that would make him rich, or with my colleagues who envied Bill Gates, Zuckerberg and Cristiano Ronaldo. Accepting Jorge's placid listlessness and his eternal deferment of everything, I once again took pleasure in small things, buying flowers to put into a vase, cooking a Sunday lunch, inviting the girls for a walk along the seawall, retelling Senhor Pereira's old tales about the time when Estoril had some glamour, tales of secrets, of Nazi spies and fugitive Jews during the Second World War, tales of exiled kings, of film stars addicted to gambling, of Arab princes.

The day I first cheated on Jorge was eighty-eight days before I found myself by the gate of the Vimeiro cemetery.

But just imagine if Salazar really was your grandfather. Duarte was descending the staircase when he turned back and said, But just imagine if Salazar really was your grandfather. I was standing outside Grandma's room, I had said goodbye to him with a formal nod, I had draped my jacket over my arm and was rapidly opening and closing my fist. Though I knew that gesture didn't calm me down or help me confront Grandma's illness, I always did it before I turned the doorknob to her room. Most of my gestures and my words, like most of other people's gestures and words, were of no use and that was probably for the best.

I took Duarte's comment about Salazar to be no more than a jibe, Duarte was always teasing me. That day, I saw him as soon as I parked, he must have been waiting for me, I hadn't even stepped out of the car and already he was heading in my direction, with his jaunty walk, a determined and proud air, Look what your grandmother did to me, he said, pointing at his forehead, without even waiting for me to pass through the heavy gate to the care home. At a distance I was unable to make out the light scratches on his forehead, I had no idea the women in your family were so dangerous, he joked. His mischievous smile made him seem more handsome.

If, before the fall that landed her in the hospital, someone had complained about Grandma scratching them I would have laughed. Grandma wasn't one for a scrap and even less for hitting and scratching. The few spankings she had meted out were meant to protect me from insolence and a poor education, which she thought were greater dangers than the minor pain she was inflicting. But, now, one of the strangers that had possessed Grandma liked to insult and hit others for no apparent reason, and the nurses that helped her with washing, eating and other daily necessities had complained, many times, about her irascibility, even if they immediately brushed it off, as it wasn't uncommon in those circumstances. Since Grandma had become detached from us and reality, everything had become normal, the greatest aberrations were also a part of her condition, just as it had become normal for me to foolishly hope that some revolutionary treatment might appear to liberate us from that suffering, that everything would end well, that Grandma's final heartbeat would happen in her own house, beneath a warm spring sun, with Bardino by her side.

Your grandmother scratched me this morning when I delivered her morning tea, Duarte explained. Grandma was no more hostile to Duarte than to any other member of staff, even if she sometimes accused him of keeping her imprisoned and called him her jailer, her aggression towards him was no different to the one she had displayed towards other people. Who can be sure that I'm not at risk being so close to you, Duarte said as I came in and put out my hand to greet him. His hand lingered on mine, but I pulled away. My flirtations with Duarte since I had left Grandma in the care home were very different from the body-to-body encounters during my flings with the various Jorges, they were more like flirting over Facebook, but in person.

I apologise for my grandmother's behaviour, I said, and walked on, Life would be very dull if we didn't take some risks, he replied, allowing me to move towards the staircase that led to Grandma's room. Determination and persistence seemed to be Duarte's primary character traits. Realising that he wouldn't easily let go of the subject of the scratches, I asked him what had happened, Your grandmother must have thought I was making fun of her because I laughed, he said. I thought I knew what had happened, Grandma never liked people laughing, Too many smiles not many wiles, she used to say.

The conversation, banal in every way, might have ended there if Duarte hadn't had a plan for me. The kiss we had shared had created a misunderstanding that Duarte seemed not to want to clarify. I couldn't understand his interest in me, but I was gratified to notice the efforts he made to be near me, leading to such innocent gestures as offering me a beautiful bunch of gladioli from his greenhouse, claiming that he needed to make space for other plants, or crossing the sitting room to offer me a glass of wine on the day of a resident's birthday, taking Grandma to her physio sessions himself and walking her out into the garden, displaying his sympathy for my concern at seeing her in that state, helping me make appointments to deal with paperwork, remaining excessively present. Our brief interactions were not unpleasant, but they didn't make me want anything more. Are all the women in your family so fiery? he asked. One of the nurses was walking a couple of old men to their rooms so we hurried up the stairs to let them pass. The strong smell of disinfectant on the landing calmed me, as if it were reassuring me that the world was in order. Duarte, no doubt thinking himself very witty, continued the conversation, Fine, but I must now raise with you the matter of reparations I am entitled to. We had reached the entrance to Grandma's room, the grandfather clock was striking three o'clock, Surely Eliete must agree that after what her grandmother did to me I have a right to expect reparations, and so I demand that Eliete has dinner with me tonight, he said, with mock solemnity.

I smiled, perhaps showing that I was pleased, although I understood the invitation to be one of Duarte's many flirtations. What man in his right mind would ask a woman he barely knows out to dinner, on the very same day, and on the eve of a public holiday? It seems like a fair demand, I replied, making a joke of it. I thought Duarte might laugh and then say his farewells like a boy caught doing something naughty. I admired the clever way he had introduced the idea of a dinner for the two of us. In matters of love and the end of love, as in life more generally, the hardest thing was to have an idea and put it out into the world so that it landed on fertile ground to germinate and grow. Instead of laughing as I expected him to, Duarte pulled his phone out of his trousers' back pocket, he started tapping on it and, seconds later, I received two new messages from an unidentified number. The first message had the location of a restaurant in Guincho, the second message said, See you at 20:30. When, after reading the messages, I raised my eyes again, Duarte, still standing in front of me, was no longer an awkward and uninteresting man and had become instead a matinée idol like the ones in Mother's photo novels, a man who might be described as possessing an iron will, a man who knew what he wanted and how to get it.

I thanked him, but politely declined the invitation, deliberately distant, and trying not to show how much it stoked my vanity. I was unsure about offering an excuse for my refusal, perhaps I could mention my agency's Halloween party, but I chose not to, there was no reason for him to know about my plans for the evening. Duarte remained serious, still playing his role, expressing his disappointment at my refusal, Tell me something, who is Antoninho? he asked. My father, I said, why? Duarte said then that, when he had entered Grandma's room with her morning tea, he found her staring intently at the TV and that Grandma had refused her tea and biscuits, a most unusual behaviour for her, she always had a healthy appetite, the illness had made her almost ravenous. Grandma was inexplicably absorbed by a TV documentary on Salazar, and Duarte couldn't decide whether her behaviour was caused by an unexpected interest in what she was watching or whether she was more absent than usual. He asked her, So, Dona Lurdes, do you know who that man is? He asked again, since Grandma didn't appear to have heard. He is my Antoninho's father, she replied a moment later, annoyed that Duarte was distracting her from her TV viewing. Duarte must have smiled,

I could easily imagine him smiling with kindness, I had seen him do it with other old residents when they had said crazy things. But Grandma didn't like it. Perhaps in her illness Grandma was too aware of reactions that might seem to be mockery, perhaps Grandma's fragility alerted her to those parts of other people's behaviour that rebuked her for that fragility. For one reason or another, Grandma thought Duarte's smile disrespectful. It was also possible that Duarte's scratches might have been caused by one of Grandma's many inexplicable reactions, triggered by the darkness that her illness dragged her towards. Duarte was halfway down the staircase when he turned back and said, But just imagine if Salazar was really your grandfather. I remembered Grandma on the day of the Euros Cup final and thought to myself, Sure, Salazar is my grandfather and Eder is the gardener at home.

When I opened the door to the room, Grandma beckoned to me from the small armchair where she sat with the checked blanket over her legs. Her docile and calm expression made it even harder to believe that she had clawed at Duarte like a cat earlier that morning and that she would do it again if she felt like it. *De mentis*, from the Latin, empty mind, if we think about the etymology we'll understand the disease, said the second neurologist we consulted. Instead of bucolic watercolour paintings of ducklings, the second neurologist had a print of Leonardo da Vinci's *Vitruvian Man* and prints of the morphology of the human brain, to which he pointed every now and then as if they might validate his words, We are our memory, he said, memory determines what we feel, what we know, what we imagine, what we sense, we are our memory and when we lose access to it we find ourselves diving into an unimaginable emptiness, with no access to memory we have no moral values to guide us, we know nothing of our loves and our fears, our ambitions, our mistakes and failures, we become as unpredictable and mysterious as any newborn, but while a newborn lacks any memory and is programmed to create a memory, to become an autonomous and independent grown-up, our un-memoried people are prevented from making and retaining memories, they are prevented from once again becoming, they are *de mentis*, from the Latin, empty mind, it would be no exaggeration to say that we are witnessing the construction of nothingness, do you understand?

I sat on Grandma's bed. I greeted her with two kisses, and fixed the hair on her nape where it had come loose from the hairpins. When I saw her hands, I thought that they were becoming less like human hands, so deformed were her joints, and then I remembered Mother's hand formed into the shape of scissors. I looked at my own hands, now bonier and mottled, so different to the smooth hands of my adolescence and youth. I asked Grandma the usual questions, had she had a good night's sleep, had she eaten well, had she enjoyed her walk in the garden, to which Grandma replied in monosyllables. I then gave my full attention to the daily inspection, Grandma was neither losing weight nor putting it on, the small sores on her feet were healing, there were no finger smudges on her glasses, her ears were clean, her nose hairs clipped. No matter how much care I put into the task it never took more than ten minutes, I was then free to go, Grandma wouldn't care, she could no longer keep track of time, she wouldn't thank me for staying any longer, she wouldn't hold it against me if I didn't. I always ended up staying about an hour. Not out of the love I felt for Grandma or a deep sense of duty, but out of guilt. Guilt for not having loved and treated Grandma as I should, the guilt I would feel when Grandma died, when I could do no more for her, past guilt, which I was too late to do anything about, and future guilt, which I couldn't avoid. Guilt, always guilt, the black root that clung to my heart.

Even though I spent an hour with Grandma every day, the darkness in which she was losing herself became increasingly mysterious. Sometimes I wondered whether Grandma was aware that she was in a care home, but then she started asking when she would be discharged, and complained about missing home. But home was frequently not the home where Bardino was waiting for her, but the home where she grew up, the one in Vimeiro. In those moments, her silent companion was one Alzira with whom she had to go to the baker, or a Fernanda with whom she had to put the goats out to pasture. When her current house did make an appearance in the swamp into which she was sinking, Grandma asked me to go and find Senhor Pereira, who was reading the newspaper on the balcony, or told me to make an appointment with Dona Rosália, the hairdresser at the salon in Birre where Grandma liked to have her hair done. But, even when I went along with the fiction of the resuscitated Senhor Pereira, all of Grandma's memories were now intermittent and Senhor Pereira would once again disappear and in his place were the boys from Vimeiro with whom Grandma carried out her daily rural chores. Even though Grandma's unreachability hurt me so much, I couldn't bring myself to adopt the behaviour of other residents' family members, who spoke to their old people as if they were children, as if they were accompanying them in a painful return to childhood. I asked Grandma why she had become angry with Duarte, and for a moment she seemed to understand what I was saying, but then she switched off. I helped her out of her chair to take her into the garden. In the lift, Grandma took a deep breath and said, Cedar oil. The fact that Grandma could still identify the smell of the cedar oil used to polish the wood in the lift made me want to cry, perhaps because I desperately felt my impotence regarding her illness. The cedar oil and many other things were still inside her head and it hurt me that my love for her wasn't enough of a key to open the locked chest of her mind.

As we walked through the sitting room I noticed the light shining on the polished wooden floorboards on which Grandma took small steps, the robust wooden chests and wardrobes, the dark wooden slats on the ceiling. I didn't think that the house had witnessed many happy days, but it had undoubtedly been a family home. A home for a family that was friendly, honest, respectable. Grandma called out to me and I realised that it wasn't the house I was assessing, but Duarte himself, and that his dinner invitation had moved me to the point that I was now seeking traces of him in the house.

I took Grandma back to her bedroom as soon as she

said she was tired. I often insisted that we should walk a bit longer, but that day it was I who felt impatient. I couldn't remember when a man had last asked me to have dinner with him. Married men on Tinder, even the ones I met more than once, were no good for dining out, they were simply bodies that gave me pleasure and that I gave pleasure to. I didn't begrudge them hiding their daily lives, or telling me in advance what they wanted me to do and what they wanted to do to me, I did the same, no, I didn't begrudge us existing only as bodies with no imagination and no surprise, digital ghosts materialising for every rendezvous. Duarte was different, he was not like heavenandhell, solitary_man27, doall4u, fundude71, ferdy69nando, Mr.Right. As I walked to the car I saw him enter the greenhouse wearing a blue plastic rain cape and black gardening galoshes. Dressed like that, his tall and thin frame acquired a tormented and brooding air that I found attractive.

On the way to the hairdresser I didn't curse the traffic on Avenida D. Carlos I, which brought me to a standstill for at least fifteen minutes in front of Igreja Matriz. I was driving towards the white houses clustering, shell-like, by the sea. To the left, the massive cubes built in place of the old Hotel Estoril Sol had not brought to the town the modernity to which everyone apparently aspired, but accentuated its condition as a suburb of the capital, a decadent suburb, with D. Carlos I's palaces standing out like museum pieces in the land of kings that Senhor Pereira liked to talk about. It was a long time since Cascais had been the land of kings, today it wasn't even the land of fishermen or the bricklayers who had put up the modest two- and three-storey buildings along Avenida 25 de Abril, of the provincials who had helped build the neighbourhoods in the centre of town while they waited for their lives to improve, Cascais, if it was anything today, was the crowning achievement of unscrupulous developers who coveted the names of nobility, who married their children in country estates with private chapels and took holidays in resorts where they gave their consciences and their psoriasis-afflicted feet a good soak.

I'm going to a Halloween dinner with my husband, I said to Julieta, who had just dried my feet before giving me a pedicure. She was a woman of a certain age, as Mother would say, and appeared not to have another life beyond the one she put on display at the beauty salon, skilfully perched on her foot-stool, low down to offer her clients the comfort of not having to raise their legs too much. Wonderful, Julieta said, so let's paint those toenails in a special colour. Looking at Julieta, her face washed out and long like an old horse's, her nails short and chipped, I felt bad for giving in to the impulse of shoving my conjugal happiness into other people's faces. As I had never known how to handle that fragile and frightened animal people called happiness, I limited myself to displaying it, I let it die of hunger and thirst but continued to exhibit its corpse, hoping that everyone would pretend they hadn't noticed the bad smell.

I didn't even know if Jorge wanted to go to the dinner, and, if I had to make a bet, I would say no. I had told him about the dinner weeks before, I had let him know, using many words, how important it was for me to be there, I had even lied to him, saying that my boss was easily annoyed, and that I might be punished if I didn't go, it was the first dinner he organised in the events room of the fancy new building he had recently moved to, a great opportunity to draw his attention to the good work I had done with the Gandarinha flats. After my long explanation I put on my little girl voice to complain about how we rarely went out, It's like we don't know how to have fun anymore, I whined. Let's see, he replied. I was irritated by the *let's see* with which Jorge replied to almost everything. If he didn't want to or couldn't agree to my requests, he could at least have the courage to say no straight away, instead of hoping that the passing of time might make his refusal less hurtful. It's not let's see, it's we're going, I'm going to confirm our attendance, I said. Do whatever you want, it's not my boss's party. Of course I didn't confirm. I didn't want to be embarrassed and it was one of those bring-your-own food and drinks party, so there would always be room for one more, as long as you brought something to eat and drink. But the day of the event arrived and I was up for it, the girls had gone out, Duarte had asked me out for dinner and I not only wanted to go to the Halloween party but also felt that Jorge should want to go or at least pretend he wanted to. I had turned down Duarte, so now Jorge owed me, even if he had no way of knowing about the debt I was claiming.

I realised, as soon as I got home with my fingernails painted exuberantly in Halloween purple, that we weren't going anywhere. Jorge was already in his dressing gown, the fleece one with rockets that Mother had given him the previous Christmas, and, as I peeked into the kitchen, I saw on the counter a roast chicken, packets of crisps and what appeared to be a box of cakes from the Garrett bakery in Estoril. Ready for the party? I asked, pretending to be unaware of the clear signs that we weren't going out, or of the sad fact that he had gone to the bakery to compensate me for his selfishness. Jorge grinned. At times like these his grin irritated me even more than his laconic reply, Let's see. He was incapable of taking into account my wishes or considering how much his inattentiveness hurt me, and yet he grinned as if everything was fine. Let's stay in and watch some films, he said. If he had at least pretended that we might have an alternative to the party, which in my mind was essential, if he had at least pretended to be sorry not to be able to join me, if he had at least not grinned, everything would have been different. I couldn't ignore the fact that Jorge no longer took me seriously when it came to what he called my daily whims, but Jorge had once acted as if he took me seriously, allowing me to react as if I were taken seriously, and the result satisfied us both because love didn't require the truth, or even its simulation. Lately, however, Jorge didn't even bother to simulate, or to apologise, he stuck to single-word sentences so that I might reply with single-word sentences and we could both pretend that we weren't irreparably lonely.

I didn't know how to react at first. I wanted to put on an ugly scene like the ones I remembered Mother putting on for Father, and that Mother claimed were figments of my imagination. For once in my life it made sense to be like her, to sweep the kitchen counter with my arm, dropping the roast chicken, the crisps, the cakes and other food onto the floor, the immaculate floor I had cleaned before visiting

Grandma. I don't feel like being around people in fancy dress, he said at last, by way of excuse, following my long silence, it's not really one of our traditions. He was right, Halloween wasn't our tradition, but by using that argument to avoid happy people in costumes Jorge made me even sadder, undermining any expectations I had developed around this date in my childhood, when traditions were still intact, when we had only All Souls day and our visits to the cemetery and I would go to Father's grave. If traditions were still alive, if Mother and I still lived in Grandma's house, if I were still a little girl, the following morning we would go to the Torre cemetery, Grandma would give me a disorderly bunch of calla lilies and chrysanthemums picked from her garden, so large that I couldn't put my two hands or even both my arms around it, to lay it down ceremoniously on Father's grave. Those days were so sad. There were always flowers standing in buckets of water at the cemetery entrance, the flower sellers with cracked and sore-riddled lips, black silhouettes moving between the tree-lined paths like worldly ghosts, there were always grey clouds crashing into the cypresses, the light draining away from the headstones with their evocations and declarations of eternal love, crosses and angels, marble of all colours, golden candles, plastic flowers, there were always so many things happening in a cemetery that it was difficult to maintain pure sadness. Arms tired from carrying the bunch of flowers, I walked between Grandma, Senhor Pereira and Mother until we arrived at Father's grave, where the sense of being orphaned hit me harder than anywhere else. Looking at the photograph of Father stuck to the headstone, encased in its little golden oval frame, I realised with shock that the Father from the cemetery was different to the Father of the Blue Lagoon, from the vividly imagined Father who died twice, the Father of the threads of memory. Father from the cemetery wore a three-piece suit, had a side-parting and seemed to have always been a dead man, so deeply did he appear to be committed to that state. I hardly used the word "dead" when referring to Father but, at school, filling out identification forms, when asked about my father's job I would write, Deceased, just as I'd been taught. Mother's job, Seamstress, Father's job, Deceased. It was a full-time job and much more demanding than Mother's.

When Jorge talked about traditions I started worrying about Father's grave, and what state it would be in now that Grandma could no longer keep it tidy and make it look pretty. Mother didn't like cemeteries, so one of the first decisions she made when we moved out of Grandma's house was to stop visiting Father's grave. I'd prefer to remember him alive, Mother said by way of excuse, and I started saying the same thing, even if I had little to remember Father by. Besides being convenient to my laziness, Mother's excuse spared me the distress I felt whenever I saw my name on Father's headstone. I never knew whose idea it was to chisel onto the grey headstone, Here lies António Cardoso, eternal love from his mother, his wife and his daughter Eliete, though I suspected it was Mother, who else could have done such a foolish thing, who else would not have known that headstones in cemeteries belong to the dead and not the living?

And you've only just realised that Halloween isn't one of our traditions, I thought, enraged, but said nothing. There was no point in complaining, the result would always be the same, I hadn't even opened my mouth and I could already hear him telling me to calm down, as if he were dealing with a crazy woman. I hadn't made a scene, I remained silent, the chicken, crisps and cakes were still intact beneath the kitchen counter's fluorescent lamp, but Jorge pushed his luck, If you don't want to be with me, you can go. Even if he had said it only to brush off my disappointment, who did he think he was to tell me what I could and couldn't do?

Despite the hot rage and the sadness, and despite feeling my stomach churn as if shot through by a strange electrical current, the same electrical current stiffening my neck, I hadn't planned to leave the house without Jorge, but the aloofness and condescension with which Jorge said, You can go, made me reply, I will, as I stomped off to the bedroom. It was meant as a threat, I knew I would spend some time in the bedroom and would then appear in the living room in my fleece robe, the one with stars that Mother had given me the same Christmas when she gave Jorge the one with the rockets, and without saying a word I would go to the kitchen and start setting the table for dinner, it was meant as a threat that would be forgotten when Jorge, wanting to appear attentive, would help me set the table and unwrap the chicken, it was meant to be a threat that would be resolved when, wrapped in rockets and stars, we sat silently in the living room, side by side, eating chicken that was already cold and éclairs that were already soggy. It was always so. I'm certain that Jorge was sure it would also be the same that evening. I was sure. Despite the fact that Jorge had recently given up on pretending we were happy, he continued to know what was on my mind, he knew that, hiding away in the bedroom, I would be wondering what I might do alone at the party, and whether I wanted to be the only poor thing whose husband hadn't bothered to come along, and whether I wanted my boss and my colleagues to know that my marriage wasn't the bed of roses that I pretended it was on Facebook. Jorge was calm and had every reason to be, it was obvious that I wouldn't go to the party alone. Except that he didn't know I had an invitation from Duarte. Nor did I know when I went to the bedroom that I would pick up my phone and, after various draft messages, would write, Is the invitation still standing?

Less than two minutes later came Duarte's answer, For you always, with a smiley emoji and an eye-wink emoji. I wouldn't spend that evening at home. I chose the tight black dress and the high-heeled boots, even though I didn't know what I was preparing for. The meetings with the other Jorges had become so routine that I had developed my own systems, I chose unremarkable clothes that I compensated for with daring lingerie, despite the fact that it made no difference whether the clothes or the lingerie were unremarkable or daring, since the meetings with the other Jorges were all about satisfying our restless flesh. But the dinner with Duarte would be a different sort of rendezvous. Even so, I overdid the lipstick and the eyeliner. I regretted not having new underwear, something more chic, instead of the sad imitation of sensuality with black and red lace that I used for wedding anniversaries and for motels on the IC19. I had no intention of fucking Duarte, I didn't think of him as I thought about the other Jorges on Tinder, but I still checked whether I was properly waxed. When I finished applying my makeup in the bathroom mirror and then saw my whole body, I was surprised to see an attractive woman. The marks left by more than forty years of life didn't seem tragic, I admired the full hair, despite the whitening roots, and I liked the wrinkles that brought some mystery to my ordinary brown eyes. I slowly moved my index finger around the contour of my face, beginning to lose definition but finally gaining in character. Like someone who glimpses an old acquaintance in the distance, I made out my young woman's features. The young woman who was like millions of young women of average beauty had made way for a woman with her own history, and my history set me apart from all others. Even the crooked tooth that I fretted about now appeared unique among the too-certain and too-white smiles from the Spanish dental clinics. I hadn't quite buried the hatchet, but I had agreed to the truces that my ageing body now offered, if we couldn't part ways we could at least find ways of being at peace, and the closer we were the more invincible we would become.

I noticed with surprise that it took me less time to get dressed for dinner with Duarte than the full hour it would have taken for my rage to evaporate, the hour that Jorge, out of habit, would have thought enough for me to get over what he considered to be a strop. I walked to the living room, taking pleasure in listening to the clacking of the boot heels on the corridor's floorboards, a bad imitation of oak wood. So, you're going, Jorge couldn't have been more surprised. It wasn't Mother's expression of surprise, the raising of eyebrows or the face shaped like an egg, it wasn't Grandma's squint as she tried to focus, or whenever life caught her off-guard, nor was it the nervous smiles with which the girls faced the unknown, it was the surprise of someone who saw another person flap her arms and fly away, yet who instinctively thinks, I will pretend I haven't seen anything, that everything is the same. Yes, I'm going, I replied, and bent over to kiss him goodbye on the forehead. That was when he said, looking at my clothes, Isn't that a bit over the top? I wanted to reply, Do you know what's over the top? Your indifference, your lack of interest, your lack of effort to make this work, but instead I smiled and said, It's Halloween, no-one will mind.

I drove to the restaurant. Outside, everyone hurried to get out of the cold. Only the tourists, who a few years ago would have been rare in the autumn chill, seemed to be taking their time. The sea breeze blew the mist onto the land, creating enormous luminous halos around every streetlamp. I tried to remember how long it had been since Jorge and I had done anything together, our last romantic dinner. I had to go back many years, and by then the hurt wiped the shine off anything he and I had done right. The only memory I managed to salvage from my anger was the one from the pizzeria in Carcavelos, from the day I found out I was pregnant with Inês. Jorge asked Grandma to look after Márcia so the two of us could go out on our own, he bought a beautiful bouquet of red roses, he took the trouble to burn all my favourite songs onto a CD that he awkwardly presented to me, Jorge was never good at romantic gestures. It wasn't his gifts that I remembered from that dinner, but the moment when Jorge carried me in his arms so I wouldn't muddy my feet in a puddle left from that morning's rain. It was after the dinner, we were heading back to the car, which was parked some blocks away from the pizzeria, it would have been easy for me to walk around the little puddle, but Jorge wanted to carry me in his arms and kiss me and tell me he couldn't live without me. It was the only time he said it. We have to concentrate on what is essential, Eliete, he said every day, as if he were talking about a truth as inevitable and as vital as breathing or eating. I always admired Jorge's ability to regard his opinions, tastes, inclinations and even his disinterests as general and almost universal laws.

From within the restaurant, it was impossible to hear the sound of mallets pounding the drum strapped across the chest of a man dressed as a mummy. The restaurant windows muted what was happening outside, turning the parade of people in fancy dress walking towards a large bonfire by the sea into an unlikely silent animation. As the man dressed as a mummy beat the right side of the drum with his left arm, the man dressed as a skeleton, silver bones shining in the dark, ran towards the bonfire, and everyone else followed. The revellers forming into an unruly mob, gesturing wildly, didn't detract from the beauty of the spectacle against the dark of night.

The restaurant tables had elegant candelabra and

wilting rose centrepieces, and were draped with proper tablecloths. The cutlery was heavy and glinted with the flicker of candles. We hadn't been seated for more than fifteen minutes, but, if someone were watching us, they would have thought that we were hours into our conversation. As soon as we sat down, I noticed Duarte's body, the thin arms of someone who has been stuck to an office desk, the back curved to compensate for the body's height, the legs as scrawny as pencils, and I once again confirmed that I didn't feel attracted to him, he just wasn't my type of man. And yet, any reticence I felt about Duarte's body was soon overcome by the unexpected and disarming frankness with which he presented himself. Everything about him was an invitation to intimacy, to the hearty and rewarding closeness of true friends. His politeness and affability extended to the restaurant staff, with whom he exchanged thoughts about the daily specials I had to try, which impressed me, so rare was it that the children of the wealthy, when they grew up, would be considerate towards those they considered to be lower class. Can we call each other by our first names? he asked, shyly, a few minutes after we sat down. I was moved by how gratified he looked when I said yes to this question, which might have otherwise sounded contrived. He wasn't faking it, but I found his transparency difficult to understand. If, on the one hand, he appeared sure of himself and certain about what to say and do, on the other he seemed to hanker after my approval for even the smallest things. If, on the one hand it was obvious that he had spent much time preparing his words, on the other he opened up with the sincerity of a child or the naivety of a fool.

Outside, the bonfire's flames were fanned by the wind, jumping like the waves that clawed into the sand as if finding their way to the centre of the Earth. Revellers who were not in full fancy dress were wearing brightly coloured wigs, oversized eyeglass frames, Zorro masks and other cheap accessories sold in the Chinese gift shops. Silhouettes appeared when the wind fanned the fire, only to disappear when the flames died down. I remarked on the elegance of a wiry girl with a lilac-coloured wig, walking alongside a pair of cartwheeling ghosts. The sight of that girl offered Duarte an excuse to confess his life's greatest regret, he had been naive in matters of the heart, he hadn't been up to the challenge of the love he had been offered, he had wasted it hopping from one bed to another.

Sitting there talking about love with Duarte, my Tinder hook-ups seemed pathetic and degrading, the shared motel bills, the faux silk bed sheets, faking a non-existent desire, bad actors imagining ourselves to be on Pornhub. The few conversations I had with the other Jorges on Tinder were inevitably about sex, neither they nor I were there to get to know one another or to discover affinities that might lead to a meaningful friendship, they were conversations that didn't prepare me in any way for my meeting with Duarte.

I always believed in love at first sight, Duarte said, I always believed in miracles. Because it is a miracle, he continued, something no-one can control. I suspected that he was referring to our kiss on the day we met, that his talk about miracles could only be about us. That's difficult to believe, I said awkwardly, taken aback by the certainty of his statements, On the contrary, it's easy, very easy, it just happens, you don't have to make an effort.

Having dealt with love, we moved onto careers. Despite us talking with the light breeziness of two old friends, I once again had the feeling that the topic had been carefully selected to impress me. It had been his idea to transform the house inherited from his grandparents into a care home, he said. What sounded at first like a boast was quickly rephrased, giving his parents most of the credit for managing the project. I knew he was being modest, I hardly ever paid Grandma a visit without witnessing the opposite of what he was saying, his parents asking him for advice and help, it was hard to imagine that they had ever done anything he didn't approve of. Even if he wasn't formally the care home manager, the staff and the residents' relatives treated him as such and always sought him out when there was a serious problem to be sorted. I had four jobs before I started working with my parents, he told me, four jobs and four sackings, looks like my parents are the only bosses I can work for, he laughed. He talked, finally, about the building of the greenhouse and about the small studio where he lived, at the back of the property. I built it all myself, he said, there isn't a single nail that I didn't hammer into place, I built it with my own hands. His childlike, unbridled pride awakened in me a feeling I might have described as maternal, were it not for the sudden urge I felt to kiss him.

I remained quieter than usual and, when prompted by Duarte to speak, was more succinct than I normally was, married for over twenty years, two grown-up girls, an estate agent, father Antoninho dead when I was five, a woman with frequent blackouts. It was unusual of me to speak about the blackouts, and I couldn't remember having ever talked about them with a stranger, but the truth was that I felt I was in the presence of a friend, at no point of the dinner did we treat one another with the cautious reserve we maintain with strangers. It couldn't have been described as a dinner between old friends, but nor did it look like a date in which each one of us was trying desperately to impress and seduce the other. It was an unusual dinner, in which two strangers appeared to be picking up on conversations that were interrupted many years or many lives ago. Despite forcing myself to drink less than I would have wanted, I felt giddy when at the end of dinner Duarte offered me his arm as we left. The restaurant walls were a liquid mass that swayed and twisted as I turned my head. Clinging to Duarte for support, I was reckless enough to cross the restaurant locking arms with a man who wasn't my husband.

As we made our way to the car park, two more cars arrived bringing more masked revellers. Most of them were about the age of the girls, they waved at others waiting for them on the beach, and greeted us as they walked past. The wind was blowing colder, sand hitting my legs and face, Duarte took off his jacket to put it over my shoulders. I felt protected by him, by the smell of his jacket. It occurred to me that some of the costumed revellers might be friends of the girls, but I couldn't pull away from Duarte, I preferred running the risk of being recognised to prising myself away from the tender embrace in which he held me. Come, come with us, the masked revellers shouted at us, and Duarte allowed himself to be pulled away by them and I was pulled away by Duarte, and suddenly we found ourselves amid the youthful happiness. I took off my boots, the cold and the wind woke me up from the wine's torpor. One of the revellers offered us beer and Duarte put the bottle to my lips. He did nothing that night that wasn't kind, attentive, considerate. The revellers' drums, the shouts, the clapping mixed with the crashing of the waves, and I felt that everything was violently good, the sea breeze on my skin, the drumbeats resounding in my chest, Duarte's smell on his jacket, the revellers' happiness, Duarte's hand on my back, me on the beach at that time of night, shoeless, free, my own mistress. Just as one of the revellers in a skeleton costume was saying, We, the bones that live within thee, salute you, I felt the phone vibrating in my handbag. I walked away from the group and answered Jorge's call. Duarte followed me and we walked towards the car park. The slice of moon appeared and disappeared behind the shadows, the revellers and the bonfire faded as we walked away. Jorge wanted to know if everything was OK, and then told me that the remote control batteries were dead, did I know where the new batteries were, he needed to change them. I wanted to believe that Jorge had called because he missed me, that the batteries were just an excuse he was using to do it. It could have been a way for him to keep tabs on me, or he might have actually needed the batteries, but I wanted to believe he had called because he missed me. Duarte fell back some ten paces, giving me some privacy for which I thanked him when I finished the call. When we arrived at the car park, I wasn't sure what to do.

It was then that Duarte, guiding us towards his car, asked, Would you like to come back with me? I can't, I replied, looking at the phone and putting it inside my coat pocket. I'm not in a hurry, he said gently. He walked me to my car and repeated, I'm not in a hurry, we have our whole lives ahead, but then he pulled me towards him and kissed me. And what if it was like in Mother's photo novels, what if Duarte promised that *never would the young smile disappear from my fair face?* What if *Our lips sought each other in the darkness, and in that kiss a world opened its doors wide.* What if life was like in Mother's photo novels that I read on the balcony of Grandma's house and, years later, on the blue sofa in Mother's house? The sky was glittery with stars and didn't disappear when I shut my eyes, I felt connected to everything around me, I was part of the sea, the wind, the cold, the sand, the fire, the happiness of each of the revellers, the drum skins, the magnificence of God that Father Raul talked about at mass.

By the time I got home, Jorge was already in bed. He was slightly startled, when he saw me enter the bedroom, because he was engrossed in a game on his phone, It's very cool, the point is to colonise planets without the natives killing you, when you colonise more than five planets you can have your own empire, and fight against other empires and form a constellation. If he noticed my hair ruffled by the sea breeze and my eyes reddened by the cold and the wind, he said nothing. How was the party? he asked. OK, I said, laconically, we went to the beach, there was a nice Halloween bonfire and people in costumes were dancing around it, I must smell of smoke.

The girls had gone out and the house's unusual silence took hold of everything. That was how it would be when the girls left home again. The problem wouldn't be the silence, or the girls having grown up and not needing me anymore, to be honest I had spent the last twenty years waiting for the day when the girls wouldn't need me to look after them, when no-one would need me to look after them. No, it was a different sort of problem, a more disturbing sort. How could I be sure that without the girls, without the daily noises and chores, I could continue to live without an answer to the question that I had kept within me for more than two decades? That night, unwittingly, the three syllables finally sputtered out of my mouth, Are you mine? It was a simple question, Jorge didn't need to drone on about how worrying about ownership was a sign of insecurity, to repeat the old argument that no-one belongs to anyone else, when what I really needed to hear was, Yes, my love, I am yours and will always be yours. Jorge's answer was wrong, despite it being indisputably true. No-one could belong to anyone, but it would do no harm to pretend that they could. Having asked him if he was mine, all he had to say was yes. There was no science or theological mystery to it, what could be simple should be simple. If he had spent the night pretending to colonise planets on his phone, he could also pretend he was mine. Or was it much more difficult to pretend he was mine than to pretend he was a planetary overlord? That night, I needed Jorge to pretend, I needed him to lie. Lies were the best glue for any relationship, the best matrimonial appeaser I knew of, and whoever had any moral qualms about that deserved to be alone forever.

I went into the bathroom. I said, I'm going to wash the smell of smoke out of my hair, but Jorge was already back to colonising planets. Everything that happened that night, the long conversation with Duarte, the moment on the beach with the costumed revellers, the kiss in the car park, would have frightened me, if it hadn't all been leading to what I longed for, even if I didn't know it yet. I was rarely able to pinpoint what was missing in my life, or what it had in excess. Standing in the shower, every muscle tightened, I pressed the nozzle against my head, hoping that the hot water would calm my body and help put my ideas in order, *Feim aim gonnaliv forevar*, I'd forgotten about the eternal future in the song, but hadn't forgotten about the future Duarte had just promised me. I couldn't get his answer out of my head. I wasn't sure if he'd said, We have our whole lives ahead, or We have our whole future ahead. It's most likely that he had said, We have our whole lives ahead, and that I had heard we have our whole futures because of the boys from Torre, the boys from Torre who had wide smiles filled with happy futures. A message arrived on my phone. I can't stop thinking about you. I can't stop thinking about you. I can't stop thinking about you. To know that Duarte was awake and thinking about me filled me with happiness and made me forget the loneliness into which Jorge and his planets had plunged me.

Duarte and I fucked two days later.

I told myself that the reason I didn't talk to Milena about what I was doing with strangers on Tinder was to spare her the moral dilemma, it would be unfair to make her choose between her friendship with me and her idea of what was right, which would make her side with Jorge. My secretiveness and my continued silliness led me to avoid difficult discussions between us, protecting our long friendship, which was considerably more important than my meaningless infidelities with the other Jorges on Tinder or my need to talk about them. I told myself all of that but, no matter how often I reminded myself of the reasons for my secretiveness, they were never true. I knew, deep inside, that I was keeping the stories of the Tinder strangers from Milena because I didn't want her to stop envying my family life. If Milena knew what was happening, she would stop saying at our quarterly dinners with school classmates, I may have a good house, a good job, good clothes, good people around me, good sex, I may have all of that, but Eliete has a happy family and there is no bigger achievement. If I told her I too was lurking on Tinder, if I told her about the motels on the IC19, I would lose the only edge I had over Milena the fighter and winner. I couldn't allow that. Not being better than her in at least one thing would mean I had failed at everything.

Now it was different, now there was Duarte, and the other Jorges on Tinder might as well have not existed, I simply had to keep quiet about them. I had been with Duarte for almost a month and, no matter how hard I tried, I didn't know what to make of him, how to think about him. The difference between a fling and an affair that I learned from the coward who failed to show up at the seawall was of no use regarding Duarte. He was neither one nor the other. He wasn't like my flings and hook-ups on Tinder, but nor was he a full-blown affair, the promise of another life, perhaps because I didn't want another life. I was trying to refurbish my own, just like, every few years, we refurbish our homes, I wanted to add beauty and comfort to make my life more inhabitable.

To better understand what was happening between Duarte and me, I childishly drew up lists of the pros and cons of having him in my life. The list of pros included, alongside some more trivial points, reasons such as, More convenient and safer than having sex with the other Jorges on Tinder, Better lover than most of them, He likes me. The list of cons was much shorter but included, Too many talks about the future, Son of the owners of the care home where Grandma is so well looked after. But despite the exhaustive lists I still didn't know what to make of Duarte. I didn't know what to think about him, I didn't know how to feel towards him, or better, how to feel about him. And even if I could be clear about what I thought, which was unlikely, it was impossible to be clear about how I felt, otherwise my feelings wouldn't be feelings, reasoning was different from feeling.

Besides causing me anxiety, not knowing what to think or feel about Duarte raised all sorts of conceptual problems, I couldn't even give a name to what I did with Duarte when our bodies were nude, next to each other, when our bodies gave in to one another. It wasn't Making Love. In fact, it had been a long time since I thought of sex as Making Love. It hadn't been Tinder or even my Tinder hook-ups that had made me change my mind. Although I couldn't pinpoint the precise moment when, in my mind, I replaced Making Love with Fucking, I knew the moment had taken place around the time when I started fantasising about other men. When I thought about them and about what I wanted to do with them I called it Fucking and, soon after, I started thinking the same about Jorge, I started fucking with Jorge too. Fucking. Although I never said it out loud, that was how I thought about what I did with strangers from Tinder, that was also what I thought about what I did with Jorge, on Fridays. But what I did with Duarte seemed different and I couldn't call it Fucking. I began thinking about it as Being With Him. Not because there was any less brutality or any more shame, on the contrary, I gave more of myself, I felt more invaded, there was greater arousal in Being With Him than in Fucking. Being With Him was Being in the moment, and Being in the moment created the conditions and the calm that were necessary to Being, more generally, and nothing was more vitally important than Being. The fact that Duarte and I met at Grandma's house may have also contributed to me thinking about it as Being

268

With Him. It was Duarte's idea that we use Grandma's house. I worried that I would feel uncomfortable doing it there, but being with Duarte in Grandma's house worked out unexpectedly well. Unlike the other Jorges on Tinder, who I could get rid of at any point, my feelings for Duarte, even if I couldn't quite say what they were, had condemned me to pull him close, the better to make it possible later, if that was how I felt, to push him away with no remorse. Duarte was now mine. I couldn't identify what linked me to him, but he was now mine.

I had stopped trying to find new Jorges on Tinder and chatting with the ones I'd already met on WhatsApp. I had no time and no appetite to spare for them, Duarte was always making claims on my time and I liked that sense of urgency, even if I wasn't able to reciprocate. For the first month, until the day of the storm, I must have had sex only twice with other Jorges from Tinder. And even then, if I was honest with myself, I would have to admit that I would have preferred to be with Duarte than to fuck them, but I thought I ought to, if only to be sure that I could resist giving up on Duarte.

Not knowing what I thought or what I felt about Duarte meant I didn't know how to feel about Jorge either. The machinery of betrayal seemed to be in motion again, it no longer seemed to be only variations on the same act. I felt that I had pulled some other trigger, I had no more certainty of my own innocence.

On the eve of my meeting with Milena, Jorge had agreed with friends to go hunting for Pokémon before dinner. I got home shortly before he was due to leave. I greeted him with a fleeting kiss on the lips. My phone buzzed, notifying me of an incoming message. I love you. I had already turned my back on Jorge, and was walking towards the kitchen. Duarte's message must have been echoing within me. I love you. I must have said it out loud. I love you. I must have said something for Jorge to reply, Don't worry, I won't be long, as if I were somehow trying to hold him back. Jorge left wearing his lettuce-green jersey, the trainers with orange laces that the girls had given him on his birthday, and the earphones he was inseparable from. He left me with the I love you message written on the screen of the phone, with no hearts, no lucky clovers, no teddy bears with hearts for eyes. I love you. Chasing away the pale imitations of love, letting the word impose itself in all its power, a catapult tearing me away from the uncomfortable present and flinging me with hope into a happier future. How many times had anyone said to me, I love you? Few, painfully few. The boys I had gone out with before Jorge were not old enough or sensitive enough to say it, Jorge hid behind his usual Luv U, and the other Jorges from Tinder were not really there to say things like that. But Duarte said I love you, the words in Mother's photo novels, the words used by maids and sailors, the words hardly uttered because it was too soon to say them or it was too late, the words that sounded so unusual because love wasn't a very Portuguese thing unlike *saudade*, Duarte had written I love you and the words pinned our bodies together, I love you, there was nothing as powerful as the sweet prison of love that, by tethering us to another, makes us another, even if we are only faking it. Not knowing what to reply, and remembering Jorge's non-committal form of honesty, I wrote, I do too. Duarte replied immediately, Your love is twenty-six minutes out of sync with mine, no problem, we'll align them soon. I was moved by the fact that Duarte had counted the minutes between his message and my reply.

Jorge came back with Inês, they had run into each other by accident at the café that makes the hot chocolate they liked. Márcia arrived soon after, just in time to catch part of the heated discussion about the American election and to help me set the table for dinner. It's the beginning of the end of everything, Inês said emphatically, speaking over the television pundit determined to demonstrate that what we were witnessing was in fact impossible, that Trump's victory couldn't have just happened. Other news channels offered their own hypotheses as they tried to explain the blow that reality had just landed on us, hypotheses that Jorge and the girls met with incredulity, outrage, insults. Perhaps it was true, perhaps Inês was right and the world as we knew it was coming to an end, perhaps my life had for once aligned with what surrounded me, the world was starting to end and my own world was also starting to end. Looking at Jorge and the girls discussing an apocalyptic future that so many seemed to expect and that reality seemed to avoid, I was comforted by the thought that it was less terrifying to die together than it was to die alone.

I hadn't given Milena a specific reason for the catch-up, but she immediately made herself available and suggested that I meet her at the law court. I couldn't say over the phone that I needed someone to hear me speak out loud about Duarte to try to figure out what I thought about him, how I thought about him. Perhaps I was moved by vanity, too, it was difficult to resist wanting to let her know that I, banal and uninteresting as I was, had a man like Duarte saying I love you, I had Jorge and Duarte and poor spectacular Milena always ended up with no-one, there was no sweetheart that lasted, regardless of whether they jumped or they were pushed. Duarte might not be as muscular as Milena's sweethearts, but his wiry frame was attractive enough to have the care home's administrators and nurses always buzzing around him. Yes, perhaps there was an element of vanity, perhaps I felt some pride in telling Milena about Duarte, in telling her, as if I were not hurting her, It isn't hard to find someone who takes an interest in us, someone who likes us, the hard thing is finding someone who won't give up on us.

I'd been sitting for more than twenty minutes on the bench across from the courtroom suggested by Milena. I distracted myself by watching people parade down the corridor lit by a skylight, the pair of judges whose gowns, like the wings of a bat, fluttered around them as they hurried along, the clerk running with a bundle of files, a lawyer offering explanations to a couple of unhappy clients, inscrutable lone figures, colleagues talking about the storm that was coming and about a child's duvet that they'd left hanging out to dry and would now get soaked. I hadn't often been in that grand and modern building that could hardly be compared to the old dingy palace by the seaside where the law courts had been located for so many years.

The most challenging part of Lewinsky's battles had taken place in the old law courts where she did her internship, carrying the hopes of those children with the wrong family names, the kids from the valleys and the suburbs where people were already born on the losing side. This will be one of the good cases, just you wait, Milena used to say, and I would watch with excitement and pride those people standing at the front who, whether defending or prosecuting, tried to shape justice with the skills of a potter shaping slippery clay, I sat on the wooden benches, listening to the quarrels among defendants' relatives, the teary-eyed mothers of small-time and big-time crooks, the girlfriends of loving murderers, I would listen with excitement and pride to Milena's statements, as one by one she crushed everyone who had underestimated her because her name didn't suggest she was born with a silver spoon.

Looking now at the long marbled corridors and at everyone walking down them with their expensive brand jackets, warm waterproof boots, phones, real leather folders, it seemed impossible to think that the makeshift law courts by the seaside where rain used to drip into courtrooms through the stuccoed ceilings had ever existed, just like the childhood poverty that Mother always talked about now seemed impossible, the poverty of having to divide a sardine and a slice of bread by seven, of big-bellied hungry children, it seemed impossible that almost all of us had once been so poor. The clerk opened the courtroom door and out came a group of visibly upset people, making their way towards the lifts at the end of the corridor. Milena walked out with a couple that appeared to be immensely grateful. You saved our lives, madam counsellor, the man said, bidding farewell to Milena with an emotional handshake.

So, my friend? She greeted me affectionately, her gown already folded across her arm, like some sophisticated and insolent waitress who had replaced her white waiter's cloth with the black fabric. Now Milena only kissed once, like the posh people from the Linha. I noticed her impeccably coiffed hair, the natural pearls in her earrings, much more beautiful than the cultured pearls in the earrings Jorge gave me for my thirty-ninth birthday.

I brought us a snack, I said, self-satisfied, handing over a Caffè Mocha from Starbucks and a blueberry muffin. Do you remember when we used to pretend we were in an American film? I asked, picking up the Caffè Latte I'd left on the bench. She thanked me for the thoughtfulness, but didn't follow up on my childish talk about pretending we were in a film. I couldn't blame her, Milena had already been to America so many times, she didn't need to remember any films to create memories, she had the time and money to create her own memories of America, which in any case was no longer America, or at least not the America we once dreamed of.

The courthouse had emptied out and our voices sounded more loudly than we wanted, and when we lowered them the surrounding marble whispered every syllable back to us with the deferential tone people once used at church. What's up? she asked, picking at the blueberry muffin with her manicured nails and sipping from her coffee. I wanted to talk about Duarte, to explain that I didn't love him, but that I was acting as if I did, that I felt giddy when I read Duarte's I love you, like the heroines in Mother's photo novels. They always claimed to feel giddy when they got declarations of love. Never ecstatic, enraptured, elated, there were so many words to describe the same thing, you just had to pick up a dictionary to know that, but the heroines in Mother's photo novels had taught me that the more one insisted on a word the more the word's meaning became the same for everyone who thought about it, heard it or read it, the greater the importance of what we wanted to say, the more irreplaceable words became. If instead of saying hunger we said ravenousness, famishment, starvation, malnutrition, how could we know with certainty and accuracy what hunger meant or what a hungry person was feeling. The heroines in Mother's photo novels taught me that if we insist on using the same words there would be fewer linguistic misunderstandings, fewer mistakes and distractions, and we would all know what to think, hear and read when confronted with a particular word because most words wouldn't fall into the category of irreplaceable words like death, mother or I love you. Death was different to demise, passing, life's end, mother was different to matriarch or female parent, I love you was different from I like you, I need you, Luv u. And Duarte had said I love you. I wanted to say all of that to Milena, but surrounded by all that marble I realised I couldn't shake off the role I had always played. Our roles had been set many years ago and were unalterable, we were connected by the past, if we changed what was established in the past we would lose everything. I also realised, as if struck by a lightning bolt of clarity, that to have a husband and a lover was no great triumph, not even a perk, that was what everyone had, the real triumph would be to have a happy, long-lasting and self-contained marriage, the sort of marriages we knew from books and films.

I've missed you, I said to her, trying to hide my distaste at the excessive cinnamon I had put into my Caffè Latte. Milena waited, in silence, for me to open up about the situation I had put myself into. No matter how experienced I was at lying, Milena made her living by sniffing out and building up liars, if there was anyone who could read the pauses and silences in a conversation it was she, so I was certain that, while she pursed her lips to sip on her Caffè Mocha, she was thinking, I'm glad you haven't worked up the courage to tell me what you were going to tell me, I'm glad you're not telling me the real reason why you went on a diet, changed your clothes, got it into your head that you'd learn to do front crawl. It would have taken no more than two or three questions for Milena to have me on the ropes, Tell me, Eliete, what's behind the big change, Milena would have me on the ropes faster than the blueberry muffin was disappearing out of her hands, but I couldn't. When I was around other people I was never truly myself no matter how hard I tried, when I was around other people I was playing a role I had tacitly agreed with them, and when other people were around me they too were not quite themselves, they were performing a role they had tacitly agreed with me, and once the roles were set relationships were paint-by-number, it was like that with Jorge, with Milena and with everyone else.

The sky was angry and covered in dark clouds by the time I left the courthouse. There were warnings of a storm the following day, the day that Grandma, for the first time ever, didn't say goodbye to me with the words she had always used, God bless you. When I was in primary school it embarrassed me when Grandma said goodbye like that, it was because of the students repeating the fourth year, God bless you, the fattest one parroted, as soon as Grandma had disappeared over the hill on her way back home, and then the other children, God bless you, God bless you. Their teasing hurt me and made me determined to ask Grandma, the following day, to stop saying goodbye like that, but I never did. Perhaps I intuited, without yet knowing what intuition was, that Grandma's words were like a charm, that if Grandma didn't use them I would be as defenceless as the blind and featherless chicks that fell out of their nests every year and died on the ground of the garden. That was if Bardino didn't maul them or Grandma didn't shovel them up. Grandma's garden, the garden with the wasps buzzing among the ripe figs, with the orange tree shedding its flowers, with the flowerbeds filled with birds of paradise looking like birds in courtship, was also the garden of the calla lilies picked for the day of the dead, of the chicks falling out of nests, so we never could walk out into Grandma's garden along the same path, nor did we ever return unchanged.

On the day of the storm, when I entered Grandma's room, I found her sitting on the edge of the bed with her legs dangling. She was lost in thought and had on her lap the box of trinkets with sentimental value, its contents scattered on the bed. I took her hands, trying to bring her back from the far-away place she seemed to have gone to, but she pushed me away brusquely.

277

I took the wooden box and picked up the objects scattered on the bed, pieces of Grandma's life, the little box with my milk teeth, the photograph from Father's primary school ID card, a piece of black lace, some escudo coins, two old prayer books, a keyring with a wooden fob that said Graziela, a rusting box of talcum powder, hair clips, two packs of tulip seeds, silver bracelets, postcards sent by Senhor Pereira from around the world, objects that proved how a life can be made up of the most unexpected pieces. As I got up to put away the box of trinkets I saw Duarte through the window, covering the glasshouse panels with boards for protection, the coming storm was the only thing people talked about those days. Seeing him nail the boards into place with his blue rain cape, black galoshes and wind-ruffled hair I recognised again my Duarte, the tormented romantic capable of taking decisive and competent action. Earlier that day he had met me at the gate wearing his oversized rain hat and, before we entered, had said, I'll see you at six.

As I left, already wearing my raincoat, I bent over Grandma to kiss her goodbye, hoping to hear the words she always offered me, God bless you. But, for the first time ever, Grandma didn't say them, which upset me greatly. Grandma had stopped saying and doing many things, but that was different, those words were her protective charm, I would remain unprotected, from thereon in I would be going into the world alone and in danger. Standing in front of Grandma, trying to rescue myself, trying to rescue a time that I had long known to have passed, I heard myself say, God bless you. I took my time pulling away, hoping that Grandma would come back from wherever she was, to say goodbye as she always had, God bless you. Instead, Grandma said, Take care of the Sacred Heart. Take care of what? I asked, but Grandma said nothing else.

The announcement of the storm had scared people off so there were hardly any cars on the road. The California palms were bending in the watery light, a musty cold bore into my bones. I considered stopping somewhere for a cup of tea, it was just past five in the afternoon, but I carried on driving, before I knew it I was in front of the gate of Grandma's house, Dona Maria do Céu, with whom Grandma exchanged fruit and vegetables from her garden, was gesturing from the side of the road, waving at me to come over. For a moment I thought she might have seen us, Duarte and me, going into Grandma's house, or perhaps had even seen other things, and I was frightened. Take this basket of persimmons for your daughters, she said when I came closer, putting out her hands, dark and callused from the earth. Why was I worrying so much, Duarte and I were always careful in our encounters, we arrived separately, he left his car far away, waited until there were no neighbours around, we were careful with the windows, no-one could have seen anything. Recovered from my fright, I noticed how Dona Maria do Céu's humble peasant appearance seemed so out-of-place amid the new homes with their digital alarms, how her house and Grandma's seemed so out-of-place in the street where another new building was going up, their place had remained largely unaltered for centuries and now it was becoming unrecognisable.

I could have made myself a cup of tea at Grandma's

house, I still knew where the teapot was, but I chose instead to go into the pantry to find one of the bottles of wine that Duarte had brought for one of our earlier encounters. I filled a glass and clinked the bottle before sitting in the armchair. It was in that living room that I realised how happy the sound of a glass clinking against another glass could make me. I remembered a birthday party, Grandma and Senhor Pereira toasting with the heavy, opaque wine glasses, I was just tall enough for my head to reach the tabletop, the grown-ups all seemed to be far up in the distance. I didn't remember Father being at that party. Perhaps he was out and about painting sickles and hammers on walls. He must have been alive, because there never were any more toasts in that living room after he died, Father's death robbed the house of any happiness. When it started getting dark I turned on the lights in the house, including the one on the balcony. To block out the noise made by the windblown rain on the windows, and the shadows of tree branches bending and stretching across walls, I turned on the television and logged on to Facebook.

I had a fright when Bardino, coming out of who knows where, brushed against my legs and curled up on the sofa across from me, on top of the embroidered Arraiolos pillow that Grandma liked so much. Grandma would be annoyed if she knew that Bardino was indoors, but I didn't have the will to shoo him off, after all, Grandma would probably not mind these little things. I didn't like being alone in Grandma's house, I felt I was in the company of ghosts, I didn't need to close my eyes to see myself at that birthday party or to picture a much younger Mother sitting there watching television, I didn't need to cup my ear to hear Mother and Father arguing, or Grandma wailing the day Father's comrades came to give her the news, I didn't need to drink too much to hear Senhor Pereira's tales about the once vast Portuguese empire, I didn't like being alone in Grandma's house because it was too easy to return to a world of good and miracles on the one hand, and of evil and enemies on the other, and between them there was only the dignity of work, the nourishment of food and the respite of sleep.

I sent Duarte a message letting him know I was at Grandma's, not mentioning the sadness I felt. The phone rang almost immediately, Duarte was chiding me for not letting him know sooner, he'd be on his way.

Where are you, Eliete, he asked when he called moments later. He was in the car, on his way to see me. So, put on the speakerphone and sit down on the sofa, I need your hands free. Duarte was far away, but I spoke to him without my body being tethered to him, like when telephones had cords, it was almost as if he were there, even when he wasn't. Lick the tip of your index finger, Eliete, I want your finger wet. Duarte's orders had a power that compelled me from within and left me no option but to obey. Slide your hand into your knickers, Eliete. My insides reacted with no shame to the authority he wanted to claim over me, and Duarte's whispered orders made me lose my concentration and focus on my body. I let my gaze wander around the living room, never imagining that it would fix on a small statue of a saint, standing on a table at the far end of the room, next to some framed photographs. Duarte's orders were superseded, suddenly and clearly, by Grandma's voice, Take care of the Sacred Heart. I tried to focus on Duarte's orders, but Grandma's voice was causing as much interference between us as the voices on crossed phone lines, back in the day. Sorry, I'll call you back, I had to say to Duarte.

I went into Grandma's bedroom, to the little altar where the saints were lined up. When I was a child I was scared of those saints who wore their hearts outside their chests, the nails in Christ's hands and feet, the crown of thorns, I was even scared of St Francis' little lambs. I picked up the Sacred Heart of Jesus. It was made of wood, small, almost weightless. I had never been able to pray, not even at times of great worry. I felt compelled to kiss the saint as I had seen Grandma do so many times, to repeat the gestures that Grandma had probably forgotten already. I put the saint back where it was. As I did so, I noticed it was made of two parts, and had a base into which the sculpted body was screwed. I unscrewed the base. The figure of the Sacred Heart of Jesus was hollow, and out fell a piece of paper, folded like a letter. I opened it, and saw that its back and front were covered in handwriting, a man's handwriting, tilting slightly to the right. The letter was worn by time and by handling, it had creases from being folded in different ways, a sign that it had been read many times. The paper was sturdy, perhaps someone had wanted to make sure the letter would last for long. I ran my finger along the lines. It wasn't easy to decipher the handwriting, so I read slowly:

Fort of Santo António, 7 August 1968

Dear and beloved son.

I always took good care of you, even if you never knew about me. The links that unite us are deep and [illegible word] and I feel great pride in them. We never sat at the same table, never walked together down [two illegible words] paths, but I made every effort to ensure you would never lack your daily bread and would live in peace. You can be proud of having the most dedicated father a child could hope for. No matter that simple spirits only recognise love in expressions of [two illegible words]. A tree bears its branches, leaves, fruits and flowers, but it is the unseen root that sustains its firm growth and, quietly but tirelessly, nurtures it.

When you read this letter, I will no longer be living in this cruel world, but you will have inherited the blood and, above all, the spirit that will transmit to future generations my views, my feelings, my words. These I inherited from others, whom I love. To you, whom I love, I now pass them on, my dear [two illegible words].

From your father,
António de Oliveira Salazar
[illegible signature]

You're not fading away now, are you, Eliete?